To Angie, Zee and our beloved sister, Jane.

PROLOGUE

This awful place was not what Irina had expected.

They'd promised her a well-paid job, a flat which she would only have to share with one other woman, also from Ukraine. They said she'd have health care, benefits when she wasn't working. They'd painted a picture of a life she could never aspire to at home, where she was tied to cooking and cleaning for her four older brothers, her mother dead and her father abusive.

It had taken her many months and a lot of lies to save the money they'd asked for. She'd had to do some things she desperately wanted to forget. But she'd finally managed it. The man had been charming, but when they got to Cardiff, he'd handed her over to a bullish, tattooed man. She'd been scared of him. And then she'd arrived in this dirty back street, together with several other women. Her passport had been taken, and she'd been forced to work sixteen hours a day for a cleaning company. Always watched.

Always supervised. Sometimes beaten by that terrifying Russian woman.

Irina had almost lost hope of escaping.

CHAPTER 1

Fabia Havard didn't make a habit of eavesdropping on private conversations, although doing so had sometimes come in useful in her past life as a Superintendent of Police in the Gwent force. On this occasion, however, she was rather trapped. Should she come out from behind the set she was painting to reveal herself or stay quietly at the back of the Little Theatre stage until they went away? What to do?

She'd taken too long to decide. There was no way she could pop out now like some wild, red-haired jack-in-the-box and say, "Whoops! What are you two doing here?" She could answer that question herself.

The voices, one male, one female, murmured on.

"What do I do if he finds out?" There was panic in the female voice. "Oh my God, he'd go completely berserk if he did. I don't know which of us he'd kill first, you or me. No. We have to stop meeting, we have to."

"Don't be silly, my darling." The male voice was quietly reassuring. "I don't think he's got any idea at all. He was fine yesterday when we went for a drink after rehearsal. I'm sure I would have picked up on his mood if he had suspicions. Anyway, he's far too arrogant to think you'd ever look at another man."

"No, he's not. He's jealous if I so much as mention anyone, let alone look at them."

"Sweetheart, he's got absolutely no idea."

"Do you really think so?"

"Yes, I do. Now come here."

There was a gasp, then a low laugh, then some wordless murmuring. Fabia stood there cringing. Listening to other people's lovemaking was not her first choice of activity on a cold November morning. On any morning, for that matter.

But she didn't have time to reveal herself. A moment later there was the sound of feet coming down the ladder from the gantry to the stage and a loud, blustering voice did the interrupting for her.

"Hallo, hallo, and what have we here? Private rehearsal, is it?"

Bugger, thought Fabia, that's torn it. How long had he been up there? No longer trying to hide her presence, she put her paint pot down with a clatter and came out from behind the scenery. "Hallo, Ivor," she said, addressing the newcomer. "Have you got the keys to the store? I need to put my paints away."

Ivor Gladwin's grin faded, and he turned from the couple standing beside him to Fabia, his round, pudding-like face losing its triumphant look. "No, Fabia, why should I have them?"

"I just thought you might," Fabia said. "Sally? Luke? Do you have them by any chance?"

Sally Cadogan and Luke Melville were now standing two feet apart. She was looking a little dishevelled and very pink in the face, but Luke was as calm and smooth as always, his greying hair unruffled, his usual smile in place. "No, I'm afraid not, Fabia. What about you, Sal?"

"Sorry. I think Ellis locked it up last night," she said, referring to her husband. "Would you like me to ask him?" She rummaged in her pocket for her mobile.

"Oh no, don't bother him," said Fabia. "Ivor, you can give me a hand putting the paint pots out by the store and I'll put them away later."

She turned back to the scenery and, after some disgruntled muttering, Ivor did as she asked. As they gathered up the pots, she heard the other two making their way off the stage and out through the auditorium.

"Think I interrupted a little tryst, there," Ivor said slyly.

"Do you? I don't think so, Ivor. I've been here for a couple of hours now and I heard nothing of the kind," Fabia lied.

"Maybe they didn't know you were hiding behind the flats."

"Hiding, Ivor? Not me. That's more your sort of thing, isn't it?" she said, looking down at him from her superior height. Eyes cool and eyebrows raised, she noticed with satisfaction that his face reddened.

"Don't know what you mean," he said, glaring up at her.

But Fabia just gave him a cool smile and made her way to the storeroom at the back of the theatre. Ivor followed her and, once they'd stacked the pots and brushes on the floor, scurried off muttering that he was late for a game of golf and he couldn't hang around nattering all morning.

Fabia watched him go and sighed. She knew from experience that he wouldn't forget seeing Sally and Luke together. She didn't think he'd actually tell Sally's husband, Ellis, what he'd walked in on, he was too much of a coward for that, but she was pretty sure he'd drop hints. He was a nasty little stirrer and loved to wind people up and watch them squirm.

Ivor had made the mistake of trying these tactics on Fabia in the past, asking why she'd had to leave the police force, making remarks like, "What did you do, Fabia? Seduce some hunky young constable?" Since he knew that Fabia's partner, Matt Lambert, was a Chief Inspector in the Gwent force and, what's more, was younger than her, this was more barbed than it might have seemed. He also knew that she had been given early retirement while under investigation for corruption. The fact that she'd been completely exonerated didn't stop him making oblique references to it, such as, "Ah, Fabia, taking kickbacks again?" This had been prompted by the gift of a case of wine from a friend to whom she'd given one of her watercolours of the Brecon Beacons.

On that occasion Fabia had said, "You know what, Ivor, that sharp tongue of yours is going to get you into serious trouble one of these days. Take my advice, watch your step." She had no idea at the time how prophetic those words would turn out to be.

* * *

Matt Lambert packed the last box of books into the back of his car and slammed the door. He pushed his dark hair from his forehead and stretched his long

6

body. That was it. His flat, where he'd lived since he joined the Gwent force, was now cleared. Some months ago, he'd moved in to live with Fabia in her Georgian house in the market town of Pontygwyn, north of Newport. But due to a mixture of procrastination and a heavy workload, it wasn't until now that he'd finally cleared the flat of his remaining possessions. The imminent arrival of the new owners had forced him to pack up these final few boxes.

The drive from Newport to Pontygwyn only took him half an hour as the late Saturday morning traffic wasn't heavy. It was nearly lunch time when he slowed to cross over the ancient drovers' bridge, which spanned the river Gwyn, and turned into Parc Road. To his right a group of rugby players were running around the muddy playing field in Gwyddon Park. Rather them than me, thought Matt, too bloody cold. A moment later he turned left into Morwydden Lane and drew up outside Fabia's house. He smiled to himself. He still wasn't entirely used to the fact that this was where he lived now.

The white-painted, double-fronted villa had been left to Fabia by her Auntie Meg and, when Matt and Fabia had finally admitted they wanted to be together, they'd decided this would be their home. Far better than a flat in a modern block in Newport, slap opposite a noisy pub. Matt leant his arms on the steering wheel for a moment or two, just relishing the quiet and looking forward, as he always did, to seeing Fabia.

He got out of the car, opened the boot and picked up the first box. As he pushed the gate open, someone called out from over the fence. "Hi, Matt, want a hand with those boxes?"

It was Tony Vaughan, their next-door neighbour – definitely not Matt's favourite person. As far as Matt was concerned, Tony showed far too keen an interest in Fabia. But it would have been churlish to refuse his help, so Matt said, "Thanks, that'd be great." And the two of them carried in the boxes and stacked them in the hall.

"Fabia not in?" asked Tony.

"No," Matt said. "She planned to spend the morning working on the scenery for the pantomime. Why?"

"Just wondered," Tony said. "She said she'd pop in to have a look at some of Rosie's work." For some time, Fabia had been giving Tony's twelve-year-old daughter painting lessons, something Matt could hardly object to.

"She'll be back for lunch, I'll remind her," Matt said, and tried to give the man a friendly smile as he stood by the front door, waiting for him to leave. "But we're off up north later, just for a couple of days, so it might be when we get back."

"That'll be fine. Thanks, mate," Tony said, and walked off down the path.

I'm an idiot, Matt told himself. He's just a friendly bloke.

* * *

By the time Fabia got back from the theatre, paint-streaked and hair all over the place, Matt had got a carton of broccoli and stilton soup from the freezer, heated it through, and put out a granary loaf and some cheese.

"You're looking a bit wild and woolly," he said as he gave her a hug.

"I know," she said. She gathered up her curling hair and tried to force it into a knot. "It doesn't matter what I do, my hair always escapes, and I never manage to avoid splattering paint all over, like some kid."

"Talking of kids, Tony asked if you'd pop in and have a look at Rosie's latest artwork."

Fabia glanced at him. She knew that tone of voice. "I'll go over when we get back," she said casually, playing it down. "Did you tell him we were going away?"

"I did."

Fabia nodded. "But now I just want my lunch. We won't have time to unpack those boxes of yours this afternoon. Is that the lot?"

"Yup. All cleared, ready for completion next week."

"Good. About time," she said and grinned at him.

"Shut up you," he said. "Do you want a glass of wine?"

"Better not with all that driving. Let's just have coffee."

Matt switched on the kettle and got out mugs as Fabia sat down at the table.

"I jolly well need this," she said. "It's been a bit of a morning."

"Oh? In what way?"

"Well, first of all Sally and Luke came in while I was busy painting at the back of the stage. They obviously didn't realise I was there because it got rather steamy."

Matt's eyebrows crept up, but he didn't comment as he placed the mugs on the table.

"I thought they were getting quite friendly," Fabia told him, "and Ellis has been pretty disagreeable towards Luke at times, but then he always is with any man that comes within her orbit. But this was far more than I'd suspected, they're definitely having an affair."

"And they're going to be seeing a lot of each other over the next few weeks of rehearsal. She's playing the female lead, isn't she?"

"Yes, Princess Jasmine, and Luke's doing all the stage management and helping to build the sets. Ellis is even jealous of Jason, who's playing Aladdin, in spite of the fact he's gay. It makes for some pretty tense rehearsals, Cath says."

Cath Temple, who was the vicar of St Cybi's church and a close friend of Fabia and Matt's, always acted as prompt for the Players' productions.

"Did they realise you were there?"

"No. But the worst of it was that bloody Ivor Gladwin walked in on them. You know what a dreadful gossip he is, and he loves winding people up. He may make a very good dame, but he's a poisonous little rat. I can't stand the man. Anyway, I tried to retrieve it, popped out from behind the flats and then lied through my teeth to Ivor when he suggested to me that they were up to no good. I told him I hadn't noticed a thing. But if he hints to Ellis about this, the shit could really hit the fan."

"But there's nothing you can do about it, Fabia," Matt said firmly. "You've had your own problems with Ivor. Don't ask for trouble."

"I suppose, but I'm not going to sit back and watch Sally have even more to cope with. She's a lovely girl, but she used to struggle hard with the drinking."

"Drinking?"

"Yes, Cath was saying she had a bit of a problem in that area but that she seems to have got control of it now, maybe because of her relationship with Luke. I have to say, if I was married to Ellis I might take to the bottle. He suffers from serious small man syndrome, makes up for his size by bullying his poor wife. Being married to him is enough punishment for any woman."

"And what about Luke Melville?"

Fabia grimaced and didn't respond immediately. Luke was a newcomer to Pontygwyn and no-one, not even Fabia, with her keen awareness of everything that was going on in the town, knew much about him. Fabia had told Matt that he was friendly but rather hard to get to know. Although it occurred to her now that Sally had succeeded in doing so.

"I just haven't been able to find out any more about him," Fabia said, making her frustration clear.

"What? Not even you?" Matt teased.

"Not even me." Fabia grinned. "But I'll keep trying, particularly as I'm very fond of Sally. I don't want her hurt."

"Any more than she already is by that husband of hers?"

Fabia gave him a straight look. "Yes, that's about it. She's got enough on her plate."

"Just so long as you don't get too involved," Matt warned.

"I'll be good," promised Fabia, but she felt like crossing her fingers. Best to change the subject. "How long do you think it'll take us to get to Bella's?"

Fabia's friend, Bella Price, used to live in Castellgwyn, a village up the valley, but she'd moved up to Bangor some time ago to help run an artists' colony. Strangely she and Fabia had been friends since Fabia had had to give Bella a warning about possession of cannabis, but that was many years ago. She was a talented potter, but she also painted, and the last time Fabia had visited her had been to attend a week of artists' workshops. Bella had urged that Matt also come the next time Fabia visited and Matt had, at last, managed to get a couple of days off. They were both looking forward to spending a relaxing two days at Bella's rambling old bed and breakfast just outside Bangor.

"I think it'd be best if we go via Hereford and Shrewsbury," Matt said. "Mileage-wise it's further, but it's easier than going through the Beacons and Snowdonia. Should take just over four hours, give or take. If we leave at two, we should be there bang on drinks time."

"It seems a bit of a drive just for a couple of days."

"We can share the driving. And it's worth it. Didn't you say mobile reception is pretty patchy at Bella's? Think of that? No-one can get at us until we arrive home on Tuesday evening," Matt said, grinning. "I might even turn my phone off."

Fabia smiled across at him. "Wow! That'll be a first," she said. "But then, you can always tell the office you forgot to charge it, as usual."

* * *

Halfway through his solitary round of golf at Newport Golf Course early on Saturday afternoon, Ivor realised he was missing his phone. He wondered where he'd left it. He'd definitely had it with him when he was up in the gantry at the theatre, because he remembered a text coming through. Maybe he'd left it up there. He'd been so interested in Sally and Luke's activities on the stage, that he might have put it down without thinking. Damn! he thought. I'll have to go back. I really can't afford to have anyone pick it up, too much info on the damn thing. Luckily, he had a good memory for numbers so when he got back to the clubhouse, he used the phone in the bar and tried Sebastian Aubrey, but it went straight to voicemail, so he made another call. This one was answered.

"Have you got a stage door key?" Ivor asked on the second call. "I've lost my phone and I might have left it at the theatre … By the way, your wife was … No need to be like that … I wasn't serious. Okay, okay, just leave it in the usual place, I'll drop it back through your letter box."

Just under an hour later he parked down the road from the theatre and strode round to the stage door. He stooped to lift the lid of the electricity metre box and found the key hanging on a hook inside. Unlocking the door, he went in, flicked a few switches on the board by the door, and made his way to the back of the stage. Pulling himself up the ladder to the gantry, he searched around for his phone, muttering as he did so, and finally found it in a dark corner. As he grabbed it and prepared to go back down the ladder, he heard someone coming up. Frowning, he looked around as the person appeared at the top of the ladder.

"Hallo there, I didn't expect you to be here."

"I had to come and check up on a few odds and ends."

Ivor held up his phone. "I've just managed to retrieve it. I must have dropped it when I was here earlier. Great relief."

"I'm sure it is. You can't do without your phone."

"Absolutely." Ivor grinned. "Lots of useful stuff on here, as you well know. So, shall we go? You can take the key back, can't you?"

"Will do. After you."

Ivor edged past on the narrow gantry and put his foot on the first step of the ladder, began to make his way down, but something hit his head, one blow, then another. "Christ almighty!" he shouted. "Watch it!" His hands scrabbled to keep a hold, but a booted foot was stamping on his fingers. The phone flew out of his hand and landed somewhere in the recesses of the stage. Ivor hung for a moment by one hand, looking up at his attacker in agonised surprise. Then, with a jagged scream, he fell to the stage below.

Footsteps hurried down the ladder. A figure stood looking down at the splayed body, was about to bend, possibly intending to check what damage had been done, but there was the sound of someone coming into the foyer. The figure hesitated, searched around. No time. A moment later the stage door closed, and the key turned quietly in the lock.

CHAPTER 2

One of the things that Sebastian Aubrey was most proud of was the renovation of the Little Theatre in Pontygwyn. It had been built in the middle of the nineteenth century and had flourished through the Music Hall days and beyond, but it had fallen into disrepair in the late 1970s and was closed, derelict and boarded up, by the late 1980s. A few years after this, Sebastian and his wife had moved to Pontygwyn and, almost immediately, they'd become involved in the efforts to renovate the theatre. Sebastian had set up a fund-raising group and they'd successfully applied for a grant from the lottery. Through his contacts in the Chamber of Commerce, he'd managed to raise yet more funds, and he'd also persuaded the borough council to match any sum received from the lottery. And so, the renovation of the Little Theatre had begun.

Sebastian never tired of boasting that, without him, the theatre probably would have been pulled down by some property developer or other. Although his wife, Jean, never contradicted him, she felt that it had been a team effort and that her contribution, and that of some others, had been nearly as great. But pointing that out would just cause problems, she thought wearily. She did, however, complain to her close friend, Eve Kemble, just to relieve her feelings.

One of the celebrations that had been organised for the millennium had been a pantomime, Cinderella that year, and now it had become traditional that the Pontygwyn Players should put one on every Christmas. It was a very popular event.

Over the years it had become accepted that Sebastian and Jean would write the pantomime – although here again she felt her contribution was the greater – and that he should direct. Nobody had had the courage to suggest anyone else should take over the role of director, although several people, Eve included, felt they should be given a chance. As usual this year auditions had been held, the cast chosen, and rehearsals had begun in late October.

Sebastian, now retired from his job as an insurance broker, was the chairman of the trustees of the theatre and was wont to go down there between rehearsals, feeling that it was his own private domain. This Sunday afternoon was no different. That morning he'd told his wife that he wished to have a look at the accounts and would be toddling along, as he called it, to do a bit of checking. He was genuinely worried about them, having found a few small inconsistencies in recent bank statements.

"Can't you just use your laptop?" Jean asked.

"I prefer to be there, and anyway," he said, patting her on the shoulder, "it'll get me out from under your feet. I'll be back well in time for a G and T before dinner."

He strode off down Church Road, took a shortcut through the grounds of St Cybi's church, weaving his way between the ancient gravestones, and then made his way down the high street. Fifteen minutes after leaving home, he turned the corner into St Madoc's Road, strode past the Madoc Arms, and came to the Little Theatre. He stood looking at the frontage for a moment. Either side of the double front doors, which were painted bottle green, there were glass-fronted cases to display advertising posters, and beyond them were two tall arched windows which gave on to the foyer. He smiled in satisfaction. Truly a credit to me, he thought.

He unlocked the front doors and went in, closing them carefully after him, and made his way through to the small room behind the ticket office, put his laptop down on the desk, then went through to the auditorium. Turning on the lights, he inhaled the familiar smell, a mixture of plush upholstery, wood polish, and what else? Popcorn? Ice-cream? Greasepaint? It was hard to define.

He wandered down the centre aisle, looking around as he did so, soaking up the atmosphere. But enough of this. Time wasted is time lost, he thought, and he was just about to turn back when he noticed something unusual. There, in the gloom at the back of the stage, was what looked like a pile of clothes. He knew, when he'd closed up after rehearsal on Friday evening, that everything had been tidied away. He was always very firm about that. He felt annoyed. It just wasn't good enough, people coming in here without so much as a by your leave, strewing their garments about the place.

He was fully aware that others came in and out, and several people had keys. But he couldn't believe any of them would have left such untidiness behind.

He strode down the aisle and mounted the steps at the side of the stage. In the half-light it was hard to make out what he would find. Quickly he went backstage, flicked a few switches, and flooded the stage with light, then he went back and, as he did so, the pile of clothes stirred, and groaned. Heart beating fast, Sebastian knelt down and put his hand out.

"Good God, Ivor!" he exclaimed, realising who it was. "What on earth happened to you?"

Only one of Ivor Gladwin's eyes was visible, half open, and beneath his head an ominous pool of blood was spreading. His breathing was laboured, shallow. Sebastian watched as Ivor's mouth moved, trying to form words. He bent closer. "Ivor, old man, did you fall?"

"Agh... agh... up there... pushed off... I was... pushed..." A shudder went through his body, then he seemed to sigh, and was silent. His one visible eye stared, sightless, across the stage.

For a moment Aubrey crouched there, frozen in place, then he stumbled up and walked a few paces away, dragged a shaking hand down over his face then searched in his pocket for his mobile phone and dialled 999. Once he had got through to the police, relayed his information, been told to stay where he was and that there would be an officer with him as soon as possible, he cut off the call. He glanced over his shoulder at the still form, then scrolled down to another number. When the call was answered he said,

"Ellis? Aubrey here, I'm at the theatre. I'm afraid I have some terrible news."

CHAPTER 3

For Fabia and Matt it had been a restful two days, although Fabia hadn't felt very well, but she'd put it down to Bella's rich food. They'd crossed over to Anglesey and visited Beaumaris Castle, gone into Bangor to walk around the ancient streets and have a look at the cathedral, gone for a walk in the lush countryside around Bella's bed and breakfast, and spent two relaxing evenings catching up on all the gossip with Bella. It was when they stopped for a late lunch in Shrewsbury on their way home on Tuesday, that Matt thought to turn his mobile back on. Immediately it sprang into life and several messages came through, both voicemails and texts. Matt frowned as he listened to the first of the voicemail messages and said, "Oh bugger."

"Trouble?" Fabia asked as she took a bite from her sandwich.

"Looks like it," said Matt, giving her an anxious look.

Fabia frowned. "What's up?"

"The first one was from Dilys." Sergeant Dilys Bevan was one of Matt's closest colleagues. "There's been a death in Pontygwyn, at the theatre."

Fabia nearly choked on her food and had to take a gulp of wine to recover. "Who? How's Dilys involved?"

"She says a call came through late Sunday afternoon. That busybody chap you were talking about, Ivor Gladwin, he was found on the stage. It looks as if he fell from the gantry."

"Fell or was pushed?"

"What makes you ask that?"

"I don't know. It's just the way you said it, and he does – did – rather ask for trouble. Look at that business with Sally and Luke that I told you about – he definitely would have gone on winding them up if I hadn't intervened."

"And were there others that he targeted?"

"Oh yes," Fabia said, but she didn't elaborate.

"It seems he may finally have gone too far," Matt said, looking up at her. "Dilys says it looks like he was pushed. The voicemail was early Monday, then there's a text, also from Dilys, confirming that it's a murder investigation."

"Oh, Matt, how awful," Fabia said wearily. "Does she say who found him?"

Matt ran his thumb up the screen of his phone. "Yes, there's another one here from Dilys. He was found by Sebastian Aubrey, he's the director of the panto, isn't he?"

Fabia nodded.

"And Jess Foyle has taken the case," Matt said.

"Do you think she'll do a good job? She's not been in Gwent that long, has she?"

"I think she'll be okay. She only made inspector six months ago, but she's quite experienced. You don't work in the Met without learning a thing or two."

Fabia sighed. "What a shitty end to our mini holiday. Poor Cath will be up to her ears in it, being vicar, and the rest of them as well. I may sound a bit of a coward, but I feel like turning around and going back to Bella's."

Matt smiled at her. "You, a coward? Don't be silly, Fabia. But I know what you mean. At least I won't be involved this time, which is a relief."

* * *

When Matt got into work very early on Wednesday morning he was called up to his boss's office. Matt had never had an easy relationship with Chief Superintendent Charlie Rees-Jones and being hauled upstairs before he'd even had the chance to take his coat off didn't do much for Matt's mood.

Rees-Jones was sitting at his desk, his hawk-like face scowling as he brushed a hand across the thinning comb-over which did little to hide his bald patch.

"You wanted me, sir?"

"Sit down, Chief Inspector," Rees-Jones said, frowning across at his subordinate. "We have an awkward situation on our hands."

Matt raised his eyebrows but didn't comment.

"This death in Pontygwyn. Dr Curtis," Rees-Jones went on, referring to the local police surgeon, "has established – well she's about ninety per cent sure – that it's murder, and Inspector Foyle was put on the case right away. The SOCO team got going immediately and I'm sure they've done a thorough job. The victim, if victim he turns out to be–"

"It's still unsure, is it?" Matt interrupted.

"No, no, not really. Just wishful thinking on my part, I suppose." Rees-Jones gave him a sour smile. "The problem we have, though, is that Inspector Foyle has had to be taken off the case. Some fool drove into her yesterday afternoon and she's in hospital."

"Is she going to be alright?"

"I believe so, but she won't be back at work for a week, maybe two. So, I'm afraid I'm going to have to hand this one over to you. I haven't got anyone else available."

"But, sir," Matt protested. "It's a bit close to home for me."

"I realise that," Rees-Jones said, sounding irritated. "But you don't know the people from – what's it called? The Pontygwyn Players, do you?"

"Not well, no, but Fabia does."

"Well, you'll just have to rein her in. We really can't have her interfering. But, on the other hand," – he didn't meet Matt's eye as he went on, but concentrated on straightening two pens on his desk and adjusting the angle of some paperwork – "you never know, she may be able to give you a tip or two about the... the personnel. The victim was one of them." He glanced at a note on his desk. "He was due to play the dame in their pantomime, and another of the people mentioned on this list is Fabia as set designer."

Matt couldn't believe what he was hearing. In the past, whenever Fabia had become involved in a case Matt was working on, Rees-Jones had made it all too clear that he didn't approve. But here he was actually suggesting Matt should use Fabia's local knowledge. Matt resisted an urge to smile.

"Okay, sir. Well, shall I get on to it?" Matt put his hands on the arms of the chair, ready to push himself up.

"Do that. Sergeant Bevan has been working with Inspector Foyle, so she'll be able to bring you up to speed, and Carmichael is the team leader of the SOCOs. They should be nearly finished at the scene so you might be able to set up an incident room at the theatre."

"I'll ask Fabia if there's a suitable room," he said, straight-faced.

Rees-Jones made no comment. "We haven't had Dr Curtis's official report yet, you'd better get on to her about that."

As Matt got to the door, his boss said, "Chief inspector." He was frowning and, yet again, he didn't look Matt in the eye. "There's another thing." He stopped.

"Yes, sir?"

Rees-Jones seemed to come to a decision, sat back in his chair and said, "Not to worry. Anyway, get going, and keep me informed."

"Will do, sir," Matt said, making good his escape. As he hurried back downstairs, he wondered what the chief had been about to say. He shrugged. No doubt he'd find out at some point.

He strode back into the main office and, as he passed Sergeant Dilys Bevan's desk he said, "Come along, Dilys, bring me up to speed on this Little Theatre business."

* * *

Dilys, small, dark and neat, was someone he'd worked with for some years and they had a good relationship. She was a friend as well as a colleague, and a great fan of Fabia's, which endeared her to Matt, although he did sometimes feel that the two women were ganging up on him.

"How was Bangor?" she asked as she followed him into his office.

"Great," Matt said. "Bella sends her regards, by the way."

Dilys smiled. She'd met Bella Price when they'd been working on a murder case which had involved Bella's son. "She's a one-off, that one," Dilys said.

She pulled a chair round to his side of the desk and sat down, put down a sheaf of notes and opened up her laptop, then she rubbed her hands together and said, "Okay."

Matt smiled. "You always do that."

"What?"

"Rub your hands together and say 'okay' before you launch into an explanation."

"Do I?" she grinned. "How irritating."

"Not at all, it warns me that I've got to pay attention," Matt said. "Anyway, what have you got for me?"

"The victim is one Ivor Gladwin, sixty-one, unmarried, no known family. He lived in one of those 1950s semi-detached houses the other side of Cobett's Field in Pontygwyn. He was a car dealer, manager and part-owner of Gladwin & Shaw Car Sales and Rentals in Cwmbran. He used to work for the previous owner and bought him out about fifteen years ago, not sure where he got the money from. He's in partnership with the previous owner's son,

Hywel Shaw. All that information we got from the person who discovered the body, a bloke called Sebastian Aubrey–"

"Fabia says Aubrey was the main mover in getting the Little Theatre up and running again," Matt told her. "He's chairman of the trustees and he always directs the Pontygwyn Players."

"Quite something for an am dram group to have a theatre to work in."

"It is, isn't it? Fabia helps out with designing and painting the scenery."

"So, she'll know all the people involved in this panto."

"Yup," Matt said shortly.

"Could be useful, that," Dilys said, with a glance at Matt.

"Would you believe, the boss actually pointed that out too?"

Dilys gave him a startled look but all she said was, "Rightio then," and went on with her update. "Pat Curtis has done the post-mortem."

"With good grace?"

"Yes, in fact she was quite chirpy for once." The police surgeon was well known for her grumpiness, so this was unusual. "Unusually for her, Pat Curtis was quite forthcoming after her initial examination of the body, before it was moved. She said there was evidence that his hands had been damaged, a couple of the fingers were broken, and his hands were badly grazed, mainly on the top but there were some abrasions on the palms and under-surface of the fingers." She slid her fingers across the mouse on her laptop and brought up several photographs. "These were taken at the scene. She thinks he might have been holding on to the ladder from the gantry and someone, or something, hit his hands from above. There was no heavy object in evidence on the stage, unless it was cleared away, so I'd presume his hands were stamped on, but don't quote me on that, it's just a guess. However, Jess Foyle agreed with me when I suggested it to her. Look at that." She pointed to one of the photos. "And that." She pointed to another.

Matt leant forward and studied the screen. "Yes, you could be right, but this doesn't actually prove foul play."

"No, but he was still alive when Sebastian Aubrey found him, and he said a few words just before he died." Dilys pulled forward her notes and flipped through them. "Aubrey thinks he said, 'I was pushed off', and he said it twice."

"Did he mention any name?"

"No, unfortunately not."

"And death was due to?"

"A fractured skull and internal injuries caused by the fall."

Matt sat back in his chair, his face thoughtful, and Dilys waited patiently for him to speak. He frowned and chewed at his bottom lip, then sat forward and gripped the edge of his desk.

"We must get going on the interviews, but I also need to have a look at the scene."

"Inspector Foyle and the team have done some preliminary interviews, but we didn't get very far."

"The boss suggested we fix up an incident room once the SOCO team has cleared out. Let me just text Fabia and ask her if there's a suitable room." He did so, then turned back to Dilys. "Have you got a list of the people involved in the pantomime?" he asked her.

"Since he has no family, I think that's where we need to concentrate our activities, and on the staff at his work. From what Fabia has told me, he was a real wind-up merchant. She doesn't think he was actually into blackmail as such, not for money at any rate, although that has to be considered, but she says he loved to gather bits and pieces of information about people, stuff they'd rather not have known, and taunt them with it. Not a particularly pleasant individual, but that's no reason to bump him off."

She pushed a piece of paper across to him. "This is the list of the cast and others involved."

Before he could look at it, his phone buzzed. He glanced at the screen. "Fabia says the green room is big enough. Can you get someone, Dave Parry maybe, to organise that?"

When Dilys got back, Matt ran his finger down the names on the list then pointed to two of them. "This one here, Sally Cadogan, playing the lead, Fabia thinks she's having an affair with him." Matt pointed to Luke Melville's name. "What's more, Gladwin interrupted them on Saturday morning, not quite in flagrante but not far off. Fabia was busy painting the scenery and she had to intervene before he put his foot in it." Matt pushed a hand through his dark hair and grimaced. "This is going to be bloody awkward, Dilys, me living in Pontygwyn and knowing most of the suspects, if only by sight. I pointed that out to the boss, but he said there was no-one else he could spare. We're going to have to tread very carefully."

"We are, indeed, sir."

"Ah well," said Matt. "First let me read through all this and have a look at what Jess put into the system. While I'm doing that, could you organise for me to have a word with Sebastian Aubrey first, then we'll have to start on the others. Who's been involved so far?"

"Other than the SOCO team, Sharon Pugh and Tom Watkins, oh, and the new girl, Sara Gupta."

"Oh, by the way, I don't think dabs are going to be any use to us, the SOCOs said there were tons of them. Apart from a general sweep, they concentrated on the side struts of the ladder, but there really wasn't anything clear. I don't think there's any point in taking fingerprints, not at the moment."

"You're probably right. We'll hold off doing that for now, but we need to set up interviews with all these people. Sharon can speak to Fabia since they've not met before."

Dilys frowned and pursed her lips and Matt asked, "What's up?"

"I was just wondering," she said hesitantly, "if Sharon is the best person–"

"–to interview Fabia?" Matt finished for her.

"Yes."

"Possibly not, but she's the only one we've got who doesn't know Fabia personally, so needs must."

"I suppose."

Dilys got up and prepared to leave his office when Matt looked up and said, "Rather complicated all this, isn't it? Who'd have thought, another murder in Pontygwyn, and Fabia involved? At this rate I may have to move back to Newport, or get transferred."

Dilys gave him a grim smile. "Don't you dare," she said.

CHAPTER 4

Ever since the news of Ivor's death had reached her, Sally Cadogan had been in a state of panic. On Sunday afternoon, before she'd heard about it, she'd gone for a long walk through the drizzle, up through the thick woods near Cwmcoed Farm, where she and Luke Melville had managed to meet up and spend a stolen half hour together, hidden by the thickness of the trees. He'd tried to reassure her, but this time it hadn't worked. They'd gone their separate ways about four o'clock and she had walked slowly back, managing to spin her return out to about an hour, but in the end, she'd dragged her reluctant footsteps back to the house in Parc Road that she'd come to hate. Dusk was falling as she let herself in.

Her husband, Ellis, had come out to the hall directly he heard the front door close. "Where the hell have you been?"

"I've been for a walk. I always go for a walk on Sunday afternoons."

He'd held up his wrist with his watch facing her, thrust it towards her face. "For over two hours? In this weather? Come off it, woman."

"I have, Ellis. I don't mind a bit of rain."

"You look like a drowned rat," he said, glaring at her. "Go and get yourself sorted out, then come straight back down. I need to speak to you."

Heart sinking, she'd taken off her coat and hung it on the coat stand above the two pairs of neatly stacked Wellington boots, then she'd trudged upstairs to change her rain-soaked jeans. While she'd done so, she went through all the things that could have put him in such an awful mood. What had she done that could generate this reaction? She'd been so careful not to get on the wrong side of him lately. The more she had to hide, the more careful she'd become. Then she remembered the awful moment when Ivor had walked in on her and Luke on Saturday morning. Had he spoken to Ellis? She wouldn't put it past him. Please, God, don't let him have done so.

Feeling sick with apprehension, she'd come back downstairs to find Ellis pacing up and down the sitting room. His mouth was clamped into a thin line and his pale blue eyes were more glassy than ever. He turned to glare at her, and she felt the familiar cold fear that always gripped her when he was like this.

"What has happened, Ellis?" she asked, trying to keep her voice even as she spoke. If she showed the fear she was feeling, it always made him worse.

He stared at her for a moment then snapped out, "Ivor Gladwin was found dead on the stage of the Little Theatre this afternoon."

This wasn't at all what she'd expected Ellis to say. "Oh my God!" she gasped. "How– how did he–?"

"How the hell should I know?"

"I thought you might–"

"Sebastian found him," Ellis went on. "He called the police. He says it looks like he fell, or was pushed, off the gantry."

"H-how was he killed?" she'd stammered.

"They're not sure yet." He'd resumed his pacing. "Sebastian found him lying on the stage. He phoned the police and then he phoned to tell me, that must have been just after half past four." Suddenly he stopped directly in front of her. "So where were you at that time?"

She'd felt an icy chill run through her, tried to step back, but the sofa was behind her. "I– I was on my way back from Cwmcoed woods, I was…" Her voice petered out. It was impossible to tell him she'd been with Luke.

His eyes had narrowed. "And did you know Ivor was going to be at the theatre today?"

"What do you mean, did I know?" Sally snapped, too shocked by his question to be careful. "Why should I?"

Something in her tone of voice must have brought him up short. To her surprise he stepped back, looking a little unsure of himself. She'd taken advantage of his hesitation. "What are you suggesting, Ellis?"

"Nothing, nothing. I just wondered if you'd seen anything suspicious, on your walk."

"What on earth would I have seen? I went down via the bridge and then through the park, so I wasn't anywhere near the theatre. There were some other people out walking, but no-one I knew."

At that moment they'd been interrupted by Ellis's mobile phone and, when he answered it, Sally had taken the opportunity to escape to the kitchen. With shaking hands, she'd switched on the kettle and, while she waited for it to boil, she'd gazed out of the kitchen window, unseeing, all the time listening to Ellis's side of the conversation.

"Sebastian, what's happening? … So, we have no access until they're finished? How long do you think that'll take? … Did they say anything about how he died? … That's par for the course, they're not going to let us know what they're up to." He'd sounded scathing. "Why?" His tone had sharpened. "What? All of us, the whole cast and crew? … Well, I suppose so, we'll just have to wait for them to contact us." A moment later he'd said, "This is a disaster for the pantomime and the theatre, you realise that?" Sebastian had obviously protested at the suggestion he might not have done so. "Of course, of course, I didn't mean … okay, thanks for the heads up, Sebastian, keep me posted." And Ellis had ended the call only to tap in another number. "It's me," she heard him say. "Have you heard about Ivor? … This means the police will be crawling all over everything … we'll have to be careful … have you any idea who– ? … No, of course not, the way he behaved the list of suspects is going to be a mile long … phone me if you hear anything."

Quickly Sally had turned back to the kettle, switched it on again, got out mugs and clattered them on to the worksurface and made tea. She hoped desperately that he wouldn't realise she'd been eavesdropping. Who had he been speaking to on that second call? And what did it all mean? As she'd stood there, stirring the teabags in the mugs, a thought occurred to her that caused nausea to churn in her stomach. When had Ivor been killed? And where had Luke been at the time?

Now it was Wednesday morning and she was waiting for a police officer to come and interview her. She was still trying to decide whether she should tell them where she'd been on Sunday afternoon, and who she'd been with. If Ellis insisted on being present during the interview, it was going to be very difficult to tell them the truth. But perhaps the police would insist on seeing them separately. She desperately hoped so.

* * *

At the station Matt went out into the stairwell to call Fabia uninterrupted. She picked up immediately. "What's happening?" she asked. "Have you had time to look at Jess's notes yet?"

"I've read through them all, and we've just received Pat Curtis's report. It's what we thought, he was almost certainly pushed off the top of the ladder. It looks like Dilys was right, someone stamped on his fingers."

"Has his phone been found?"

"What?"

"His phone? Have you found it? Given the way he used to behave, it could contain some pretty useful information."

"I know that, Fabia," Matt said, sounding annoyed. "And no, it hasn't been found." There was a pause, then Matt said slowly, "Which is a bit odd, isn't it?"

"Yup," Fabia said, triumphant.

"Smug, or what?" Matt said, smiling.

"That's me."

"Anyway," he said, changing the subject. "There'll obviously be an inquest, but it won't take long, a case of wilful murder by person or persons unknown and an adjournment, because we're hardly likely to have found out who did it by then. Not unless someone comes forward and confesses."

"And I'd say that's unlikely."

"One can but hope." Matt paused, then changed the subject. "Dave Parry's organising the incident room, your suggestion was a good one."

"Has Sebastian Aubrey been told? He's the chair of the theatre's management committee and a trustee. His wife acts as secretary."

"Who else is on that committee?"

"Ellis Cadogan is treasurer, Geraldine Humphries, Eve Kemble and Oliver Talbot are committee members, and so was Ivor. Peony Smith usually looks after the ticket office but, since she got a larger part this year, Cath said she'd look after the bookings. That reminds me, I must phone Cath and bring her up to date on what's going on." Fabia sighed. "This is so bloody awful, Matt. What can I do to help? Am I allowed to?" she asked, knowing that she'd be trying to do so whatever Matt said.

"Never mind you being allowed, Charlie Rees-Jones actually suggested I involve you!"

"No! Did he?"

"I nearly fell off my chair," Matt said. "But since we have official permission, could you make a list of everyone involved in the Players, with a few notes about each, and maybe do one of your mind maps for me. Dilys has a lot of time for them," Matt said.

"And you don't?" Fabia asked.

"Well, they are useful," Matt conceded, sounding apologetic. "It'd be really helpful if I have a clearer idea of the personalities and their relationships. I know a bit, obviously, because you've talked about them, but I may not have listened to everything you've said."

This time she laughed. "You mean you don't hang on my every word?"

"Depends what you're talking about, now if it's food, or how much you love me, or how soon we can go upstairs to—"

"Shut up, Matt."

But he was soon serious again. "I'm going to send Sharon Pugh to talk to… interview you about what you know, etc. I have to make it official, and at least it's better for her to do it as she's not a friend of yours and doesn't know so much about our background. Better to keep it that way, I think."

"Okay," Fabia said, not sounding very keen on this idea. "She surely knows I used to be in the force, though, doesn't she?"

"I suppose, but not the gory details."

"An appropriate phrase at a time like this."

"Fabia!" Matt exclaimed.

"Sorry," she said, "defence mechanism."

"Will you be at home around half eleven?"

"I can be."

"Good, I'll send her round. And I'll see you later, probably much later." And Matt went back into the office to speak to Sharon Pugh.

* * *

Fabia was busy working in her dining room cum studio when the doorbell rang. Two years ago, she'd been commissioned to illustrate a series of children's books. She was now on the fourth in the series and her agent was pushing for her to send the completed drawings. She stood there for a moment, studying what she'd done so far, then put down her pencils and paints and stepped away from the drawing board, took off her paint-spattered overalls and tried to tidy her hair. The doorbell rang again as she made her way to the front door.

The woman standing on the doorstep was tall and efficient-looking, her brown hair falling straight around her head, her rather thin lips unsmiling.

"Ms Havard?" the woman asked. "I'm Detective Sergeant Pugh, Chief Inspector Lambert asked me to come and have a word with you."

"Yes, he told me, come in." Fabia's heart sank. She wasn't at all sure she'd take to this rather cool, prim-looking person with her hard eyes and thin lips.

But behind her stood a familiar figure, DC Tom Watkins, someone Fabia knew well. Fabia wondered if Matt had chosen him deliberately to accompany Sharon Pugh. He could have thought Tom's fresh-faced openness would make the interview easier. Bless him if that was the case.

Fabia gave him a broad smile. "Hallo, Tom, good to see you."

"Morning, ma'am." His lips lifted in a rather rueful smile, and Fabia noticed DS Pugh glance at him, frowning. Maybe she didn't approve of this form of address. Oh dear, Fabia thought, this could be difficult.

"Come into the kitchen, I'll put the kettle on," she said, and led the way down the passageway. "Coffee? Tea?" she asked when they got there.

"Not for me, thank you," Sharon Pugh said.

But Tom Watkins accepted. "Coffee please, black," he said with a tinge of defiance in his tone. Fabia had to turn away to hide a smile.

Once they'd settled round the table, Tom, with slow deliberation, took out his notebook and flattened it on the table. Sharon Pugh gave a sigh of irritation and looked across at Fabia.

"Ms Havard," she said, "I gather you knew the deceased, Ivor Gladwin."

"Yes. I've known him for a while, ever since I first became involved in designing sets at the theatre."

"And that would be how long ago?"

"Well, the first one I did for the Players was the panto last Christmas, that was Babes in the Wood, and then I did the sets for a play they put on in the summer, so this is the third production I've been involved in."

"Did you know any of the Players before?"

"Yes, I did."

"Can you tell us who?"

"Do you want me to go through the cast and tell you how I know each one?" Fabia asked sweetly. There was no way she was going to tell Sharon Pugh that Matt had asked her to make notes about them all, and she certainly wasn't going to mention the mind map. Fabia was pretty sure that wouldn't be approved of one little bit.

"That would be useful," Sharon Pugh said, then added, "thank you." It sounded like an afterthought.

"The Aubreys – that's the director and his wife – I've known them ever since I moved to Pontygwyn. They're quite prominent in the community. He was one of the main movers when it came to the restoration of the theatre. I believe he was the one who discovered the body."

"How did you know that?"

Fabia, annoyed with herself, had no choice but to give her a truthful answer. "Matt Lambert told me."

"Aha," said Sharon, as if she'd caught Fabia out.

Fabia simply looked across at her, eyebrows raised, then went on. "I've known several of the others for some time too. Eve Kemble and her husband have lived in Pontygwyn for some years, and Geraldine Humphries is a close friend of mine. I also know Sally Cadogan quite well, though I don't know her husband that well. The others are what you might call, acquaintances. I do, however, know Cath Temple very well indeed, she's the vicar at St Cybi's. She's prompt."

Sharon frowned. "She's what?"

Fabia was surprised she didn't know and showed it. "She sits in the wings with the script and prompts anyone who forgets their lines."

"I see," Sharon said, dismissively. "Can you think of any reason why any of them would want to harm Mr Gladwin?"

Fabia put up a hand to pull her hair back from her face and twist it into a knot to try and give herself time to consider her answer. She glanced at Tom who looked up from his notes but didn't comment. What should she say? Ivor Gladwin was a nasty little snoop who loved to needle people. I could give you a list a mile long of people who'd have liked to see the back of him, she thought. Into her mind came a picture of Sally and Luke standing awkwardly on the stage, and Ivor grinning.

Sharon Pugh was sitting with her hands on the table. As the silence lengthened, she began to tap her fingers on the scrubbed pine, obviously impatient for Fabia to answer her question.

"I can't think of anyone specific," Fabia said, pushing thoughts of Sally and Luke out of her mind, salving her conscience with the fact that she'd already told Matt about what she'd overheard. "Ivor enjoyed winding people up. He loved to push people's buttons and watch them squirm. I'm not sure he would actually have gone in for blackmail as such, I don't think he would have had the courage. Bullies are usually cowards, aren't they? But I do think he might have demanded favours for keeping quiet about things he found out."

"What sort of things?"

Fabia shrugged. "Everyone has their secrets, things they'd rather not have publicised. I'm sure you have?" she added provocatively, but all she got in response was a slightly scornful look. Maybe not, she thought. "I don't think it's for me to guess at what he may have picked up. And I couldn't honestly say I know anything specific. I do, however, know that he had a habit of hinting that he knew this or that about a person, and then he'd grin at them and wait for a reaction. He did it to me."

Tom gave her a sharp glance then looked at his colleague, but he didn't say anything.

"In what way?" Sharon Pugh asked.

"He knew that I'd been a superintendent of police and that I had to take early retirement for personal reasons. I'm sure you've done your homework, sergeant, and that you're fully aware of the background. He used to try to wind me up about it, but I'm afraid, in my case, it didn't work." Fabia gave a wry smile. "I have a thicker skin than most, I suppose, and Ivor's jibes about my past and my relationships had little effect on me. Unfortunately, that probably wasn't the case for everyone."

The silence stretched out, then Sharon asked, "Are you sure you can't be more specific?"

"I am. I don't think speculation on my part would be helpful at the moment." And, thought Fabia, if I was going to speculate, I'd be talking to Matt not you, my girl.

"So, you have no idea who, of your friends and acquaintances, may be responsible for Gladwin's death?" Her tone was slightly scornful, as she had doubts that Fabia knew nothing.

At her tone, Tom Watkins shifted uncomfortably, swinging his pen back and forth between his fingers.

"No idea at all," Fabia said, and waited, content to leave the ball in the sergeant's court.

Sharon Pugh's eyes narrowed, and she seemed to be considering her next move, then she smiled. "Well, if you do remember anything useful – that would be useful to us, I mean, please don't hesitate to contact me."

"Of course, I will," Fabia said sweetly. "Or I'll just speak to Matt when he gets home or contact Dilys." She turned on her chair. "Or tell you, Tom."

Then she felt guilty as Tom seemed to be struggling with a mixture of amusement and embarrassment.

Abruptly Sharon got up from her chair. "Thank you, Ms Havard, I think we have all we need," she said coldly as she hitched her bag on to her shoulder.

Fabia raised her eyebrows questioningly at Tom, who gave a slight shrug.

As she escorted them to the front door, Fabia said, "I do hope you're enjoying working in Wales. I gather, from Matt, that you came to Gwent from the Lincolnshire force."

"I did."

"Well, we're a bit different round here. I'm sure you'll get used to our ways."

Sharon Pugh's lips tightened as if she was stopping herself from commenting, then she gave a curt nod. Tom smothered a grin. And Fabia went back inside, feeling as if she hadn't dealt with that interview very well.

CHAPTER 5

Luke Melville was used to being in control, and this feeling of events spinning out of control was not one he enjoyed.

He'd jumped at working undercover, particularly as it had meant he could return to South Wales, but things hadn't gone to plan, and now Ivor Gladwin's death had complicated matters even further. On Monday he'd contacted head office and told them about the murder. His boss had urged him to continue to keep a low profile but, if necessary, he was to go and speak to Chief Inspector Lambert, bring him up to speed. Luke was not looking forward to doing that. He wouldn't blame Matt for being angry that he'd not taken him into his confidence weeks ago, particularly as Matt's boss hadn't chosen to tell him either. He'd got the impression Chief Superintendent Rees-Jones and Matt didn't get on all that well. He grimaced. His opinion of Matt's chief wasn't particularly high, whereas he had a lot of time for Matt.

And then, of course, there was Sally. He'd not told his boss about their relationship, fully aware of the fact that he'd be in serious trouble, possibly even recalled, if his superiors found out about it. Ivor walking in on them on Saturday had been a disaster. And Ivor could have told Ellis, or anyone else for that matter, about what he'd seen and heard. Luke swore, calling himself all kinds of a fool for not being more careful. He cared for Sally. He didn't think he'd ever cared so deeply for anyone before. But he knew he should have nipped the affair in the bud before it got anywhere. What a fool he'd been! And what about Fabia Havard? He'd wondered if he should pop round and talk to her but decided against it. Although he was pretty sure that she'd keep things to herself – he knew she was fond of Sally and wouldn't want to cause problems for her – it hadn't seemed fair on Fabia.

Round and round it went, and he still hadn't decided what to do. He knew the local police would be coming to interview him, they'd be speaking to everyone involved in the theatre and the pantomime, so he would obviously be on their list. He may not be part of the cast, but he'd promised to act as stage manager and help build the sets. It had meant he could keep a closer eye on his targets and had seemed a good idea at the time. Would it be better to go and see Matt at home, make it informal to begin with? That idea appealed. And given Fabia's past connection with the police, he'd feel okay with including her in the conversation. With her there, Matt might be less inclined to jump down his throat. He gave a twisted grin, mocking himself for being a coward.

Half an hour later he came to a decision. He scrolled down to a number on his phone, punched it in, but Matt didn't pick up. He selected another number and, this time, he got an answer.

"Hallo, Luke." Fabia sounded a little surprised to get his call.

"Fabia, um, I suppose Matt's at work."

"Yes, up to his ears in investigating Ivor's death."

"Has he been put on to that?"

"I'm afraid so." But Luke didn't think she sounded as if she minded. "The person who was in charge has been in a traffic accident," she told him, "so she's been taken off the case. As they're so short-staffed, Matt's boss ended up asking him to take it on. Not an ideal situation, but needs must."

Mind racing, Luke realised this made it even more important that he should speak to Matt. "I was wondering, would it be possible for me to come around and talk to the two of you later on?"

"I don't see why not," Fabia said, sounding curious, "but why don't you give Matt a ring and speak to him?"

"I've tried, he's not answering."

"Ah. He's hopeless at keeping his phone charged."

"What sort of time do you expect him home? It's quite important."

"Probably late," Fabia said. "Is it to do with the investigation?"

"Sort of," Luke told her.

"Look, leave it with me. I'll get hold of Matt and ask him when he expects to be back. I'll let you know."

"Thanks, Fabia, that'd be great."

He ended the call and immediately started wondering if he'd done the right thing, then called himself a fool. He wasn't used to being so unsure of himself.

* * *

Fabia stood by her drawing board looking at the screen of her phone as if it could answer the questions in her mind. Why did Luke want to speak to them? Was it about Ivor's death, or something else?

She'd always thought there was more to Luke than met the eye, but she'd never been able to put her finger on exactly why. He'd not been in Pontygwyn long, only about six months. He'd told everyone he wanted to return to his roots, that his mother had been brought up in Pontygwyn and, when he became tired of life in London, he'd decided to come home. She wasn't sure this was the whole story. Instinct told her there was more to it. She knew he had managed to buy back his old family home, Nant Fach Farm, a few miles west of Pontygwyn. In spite of its name, Little Brook, it was a not insubstantial farmhouse named after the trickling stream that bordered the land, a small tributary of the river Gwyn. Fabia had checked all this online. When he was asked what he did for a living, Luke had always been rather vague, implying that he was a freelance financial advisor and worked with his clients from home. As to joining the Pontygwyn Players, he'd told Fabia that he felt it was a good way to meet people and that he'd been a member of an amateur dramatics group in London who put on productions at a small theatre in Palmers

Green. Grinning, he'd suggested he might have been some kind of thespian in a past life.

Fabia had also checked on the theatre in Palmers Green, and there it was, large as life. At this point she'd told herself to stop being so suspicious and nosy and leave the poor man alone. She hadn't told Matt about her researches, afraid he'd laugh at her, or accuse her of being too interested in a good-looking newcomer to the town. He gave her enough grief over being friendly with Tony Vaughan next door. But now all her questions about Luke resurfaced, particularly in the face of the encounter she'd witnessed between him and Sally, and then Ivor's death. All this may be interesting, but it was also worrying.

She was just about to try Matt's phone when she heard the front door open and his voice call, "Fabia?"

She came out of the dining room in time to see him and Dilys making their way to the kitchen. "Hallo, you two, what are you doing here?"

"We thought we'd come and grab a sandwich," Matt said. "Have you eaten?"

"Yes, I had a mug of soup while I worked."

"We've just been to have a word with Sally Cadogan," Matt told her.

"And her awful husband," added Dilys.

Fabia grinned as she followed them down the hall. "You didn't take to Ellis, then?"

"Not one bit," said Dilys.

Matt was busy getting out bread, cheese and a packet of ham. Fabia got out pickles and took a cucumber from the vegetable wrack and handed it to Dilys. She switched on the kettle. "I'll make you some coffee. There's a knife there for the cucumber, Dilys."

As they busied themselves Matt said, "We didn't get much information out of either of them. I think she would have told us a good deal more if her husband hadn't been there, but every time either of us asked her a question, he answered it."

"That really annoyed me," said Dilys. "I hope I didn't show how irritated I was."

"You were your usual cool self," Matt told her.

When they were all sitting round the table Fabia said, "By the way, talking of not taking to people, I can't say I liked your new sergeant much."

"No?" said Matt, non-committal. "She's very efficient."

"That's as may be, but she certainly doesn't approve of me."

"What makes you think that?"

"Oh, I don't know, her attitude. Never mind." Fabia decided not to pursue it. "Has the time of death been established yet? I left the theatre at about a quarter to one, not long after Sally and Luke – oh, by the way, Matt, Luke phoned this morning. He wants to come and talk to you. He said it was important. I told him I'd let him know when you'd be home."

Matt glanced up at her, frowning. "I wonder what that's about?"

"He didn't say."

Matt's frown cleared. "Maybe he's got some useful information."

"Could be. He said he tried your mobile, but there was no reply." Fabia gave him a stern look. "When did you last charge it?"

Matt didn't reply but Dilys grinned and said to Fabia, "In the car just now."

"You're hopeless, Matt. Anyway, what time shall I tell him?"

"I'll try to make sure I'm home by eight."

"And talking of phones, have you found Ivor's yet?" Fabia asked. "Info on that could be very useful."

Matt gave her a look under his brows which said, 'do you think I haven't thought of that?'.

"I know, I know," Fabia said, responding to the look. "Why I ask is that he used to have a habit of taking random photos at rehearsal, particularly if it was of something that would embarrass people, like the youngsters, Lewys and Peony. Sebastian had to have a word with him about it, so there might be useful stuff on it."

"The trouble is we haven't found it yet. He didn't have a phone on him, and the search at his house turned nothing up, not a laptop, an iPad or a phone, which I find strange. Jess Foyle told Dilys she thought someone had searched the house, and if that's the case, then we probably won't find any of his devices."

"What made her think that?" Fabia asked Dilys.

"She didn't know for sure, she just said it was a feeling – drawers that were slightly open, a photo of Gladwin receiving some kind of award was on a bookcase in the sitting room and she says it had been moved, the mark in the dust on the shelf didn't match its position. She also said there were several marks in the dust which looked as if someone had put a hand on the furniture, but there were no fingerprints to coincide with those marks."

"Sharp," said Fabia, admiringly.

"She is," Matt said. "She also ordered a comprehensive search of the theatre, obviously, but that didn't turn up anything either. I think I'll arrange another one."

"I'll sort that out, sir," Dilys said, making a note on her phone.

"Thanks, Dilys."

"And another strange thing," Matt told Fabia. "He didn't have any house keys on him. They had to break into his house in order to do the search. They did find what looked like a spare set hanging by the kitchen door, but that's all."

"What else did that search turn up?" Fabia asked.

"Very little. There was a desk in this sort of study room with very little personal stuff in it, just papers relating to his job, same with a filing cabinet. And there were no family photos or anything of that sort, other than the one of him getting the award. It was all rather clinical and gave very little clue to his background or his personal life."

They went back to speculating on the time of death. "Before he left the theatre, Ivor muttered something about going for a game of golf," Fabia told them. "I should have told you before."

"Yes," said Matt, "you should."

"Sorry," Fabia said, grimacing at him.

"Did he say where?"

"No, but there are several possibilities," Fabia said. "Newport, Tredegar Park, or possibly the Celtic Manor. One of the others in the Players might know if and where he was a member."

"Can you get someone to do a bit of research on that, Dilys," Matt said, "find out if anyone saw or spoke to him?"

"Will do," said Dilys, taking out her phone and making yet another note on it.

"Sebastian Aubrey says he discovered the body just after half past three," Matt said, "which is probably about right as his call to the emergency services was recorded at three forty-five. If Gladwin did play a round of golf, it doesn't give an enormous window of opportunity for whoever pushed him off the ladder. Say he got back to the theatre, for whatever reason, at about three, it only gives us about half an hour to play with. We've set up the door-to-doors to check if anyone saw him, but nothing's come in yet."

"Did you get anything useful from the Cadogans?" Fabia asked.

"Not a lot, but it's early days. Sally says she was out walking on her own most of the afternoon, so no alibi there, and Ellis says he was with Morgan Conway, rehearsing one of the song and dance routines from the pantomime, he plays a character called Wishee Washee." Matt grimaced. "Is there really a character in this panto called that?"

"Yes," Fabia smiled at him. "He's Aladdin's less intelligent friend."

"That follows when it comes to— no, I shouldn't say that. Apparently, Morgan's not very confident about his singing. Is that the impression you get, Fabia?"

"Definitely, poor chap, and Ellis is a perfectionist, and quite a hard task master as musical director," Fabia told him. "It could just be that he wasn't satisfied with what Morgan was doing. He could have asked for a private rehearsal to avoid Morgan getting stroppy, he doesn't take direction very well."

Half an hour after they'd arrived, Matt and Dilys got up to leave. "Must get back," Matt said, giving

Fabia a quick kiss. "I'll do my best to get home in time for Luke. Keep him talking, will you, if I'm late?"

"Your word is my command, sir," she said. "See you soon, Dilys." And she lifted a hand to wave as they went down the path.

* * *

Later in the afternoon Fabia's work was interrupted again, this time by a call on the landline. It was Jean Aubrey sounding breathlessly worried. "Oh, Fabia, this is so awful. Sebastian and I are devastated by Ivor's death. It's such a tragedy."

Fabia, fully aware of how difficult Ivor could be, wondered if Jean was being a little disingenuous, but she wouldn't have dreamt of saying so.

"I know, Jean," she responded, "how are you and Sebastian holding up?"

"Well, I have to say..."

There was a pause and Fabia wondered what was coming next.

"We were so relieved when we heard that your Matt has taken over the investigation," Jean said. "At least we can be sure that he'll be... er... he'll be thorough and also considerate of how much this has hit our community."

"He'll do his best," Fabia said, "but he is, first and foremost, a police officer. It's awkward for him to be investigating so close to home, but that won't make any difference to his thoroughness."

"No, no, of course not," Jean assured her. There was a pause, then she said, "Fabia, I wanted to ask your advice."

Fabia's heart sank. "I'm not sure–"

"Sebastian and I have been talking about the future of the pantomime. What we wanted to ask you was, have you any idea how long it will take Matt to discover what happened? The thing is, we'll have to find another dame, and that could present problems."

Fabia could hardly believe what she was hearing. She knew full well how obsessed both of the Aubreys were with the Pontygwyn Players' productions, and with the Little Theatre, but surely this was taking it a little too far? And how on earth did Jean think she could give her an estimate of how long the investigation would take? What was more, didn't she realise that they were all suspects? She'd have to make it clear she was not involved in the investigation in any way.

"Fabia? Are you there?" Jean said.

"Yes. Sorry. Look, Jean, I have no idea how long it will take to find Ivor's killer." She said this very firmly. Maybe she could shock Jean into getting her priorities right. "You must realise that Matt and his team will have to question everyone, that's a given in a murder investigation, probably several times over. In the circumstances, since one of the cast might be involved, don't you think it would be best to cancel the pantomime now, rather than let things drag out?"

"Oh no! It can't have been one of us." It was a wail of protest.

Fabia wondered how to express what was in her mind. "Jean, you have to admit that Ivor was inclined to... to get on the wrong side of people."

"What do you mean?"

Fabia found it hard to believe what she was hearing. Had Jean been completely blinkered? She sighed. "When a person spends a lot of time winding people up and attempting to expose their secrets, they're not going to be popular, are they?"

Jean didn't respond immediately, but then Fabia heard her take a deep breath. "I know what you mean, Fabia, but it was all meant in fun. He wasn't serious."

"That's as may be, but someone might have taken him seriously."

"Oh, I don't think so" – she was obviously going to stick to her blinkered view of Ivor – "and I'm absolutely sure Ivor would not have wanted us to cancel, the pantomime meant so much to him."

"But I still think it has to be considered."

"Do you really think so, Fabia?" But Jean didn't wait for an answer to this question. "We'll have to speak to the rest of the Players."

"That'd be best," Fabia said. "Let me know what you decide."

Fabia slowly put down the receiver and stood frowning, looking out of the kitchen window, going over what Jean had said. If she and Sebastian were that obsessed with the pantomime, surely neither of them would have harmed Ivor, would they? Unpleasant he may have been, but he made a very good dame and always drew the crowds. And the Little Theatre, and all it stood for, was of such importance to them. But what if he'd found out something about one of them that they wanted to keep hidden?

Before she could pursue this thought, her phone rang again.

"Fabia, darling."

She recognised the deep voice and felt a little guilty. "Hallo, Gerry, how are you?" she said, wishing she'd phoned her friend, Geraldine Humphries, days ago. With her history, she'd be more affected by the situation than most. But then Fabia began to make excuses for herself. Since she and Matt had got back from Bangor, she'd been so busy trying to get the illustrations for the book finished, she'd hardly had time for anything else. But she still said, "I'm so sorry I haven't called you before. I really should have. This is all pretty shitty isn't it?"

"It is, rather," Geraldine said, her voice calm, but Fabia wasn't taken in.

"You sound stressed. Weren't you due to visit Frank at the end of last week?" she asked gently.

"Yes, I drove up on Friday. He seems okay. He's got a new psychiatrist and they get on well, which is always a good thing."

"But I don't like you making that drive on your own," Fabia told her. "Next time why don't I come with you? I can always drop you off then pop into Bracknell or Farnborough to have a look around, or sit in the car and read."

"Don't be silly. I'm used to it, after all I've been driving up and down the M4 to visit him for so many years now." There was a pause, then Geraldine said, "Fabia, I've been meaning to ask you, did you know that Ivor knew about Frank?"

Suddenly Fabia felt cold. Surely not even Ivor would wind Geraldine up about the fact that her son was in Broadmoor. That would be the absolute pits, even for him. But no, he might have. And then the chill increased. What if Geraldine – no, that was ridiculous.

"Are you sure? I thought I was the only one who knew. I haven't even mentioned it to Matt." She paused, then added, "Although it might be a good idea to say something when the police come to interview you."

"What, again?"

"Yes, love, they're going to interview everyone involved in the pantomime," Fabia told her. "Matt has had to take over as SIO and he wants to go over things himself."

"What's an SIO?"

"Sorry," said Fabia. "Senior investigating officer. The woman who was in charge was injured in an accident and she's off for two weeks, and they didn't have anyone else."

"Oh no!" Her reaction seemed extreme, but then, a moment later, she just asked, "Does he mind?"

"No, not really. But it could be a bit awkward. Obviously, he couldn't interview me, so I had the third degree from one of his colleagues earlier today. She's new; a detective sergeant called Sharon Pugh. I did not take to her."

"What was wrong with her?" Geraldine asked.

"Well, she didn't seem to approve of Tom Watkins calling me ma'am. I've met Tom several times and I think she felt we were being too familiar with one another, although ma'am isn't exactly– anyway, perhaps she thinks my murky past hides more than I'm admitting to. I don't know, maybe she fancies Matt and thinks I'm too old for him."

"Don't talk nonsense," Geraldine said briskly.

Fabia realised she'd been distracted from what Geraldine had said about Ivor. "But Gerry," she said, "what made you think Ivor knew about Frank? Did he say anything specific?"

"It started off with his saying something last week at rehearsal. He remarked that sons can get out of control and gave me such a look that I felt sure it was aimed at me. I'm sure he knew. How do you think he found out?"

"I doubt that he did know," Fabia said, hoping she was right.

"But that wasn't all. He came up to me backstage. You know the way he used to creep up on you, invade your space, and start talking quietly with that stupid little smirk on his face?"

"I remember it well," Fabia said, not bothering to keep the disgust out of her voice.

Fabia could hear Geraldine take a deep, shuddering breath. "He said 'how's Frank then?' I just couldn't believe it. I pretended not to understand. But he went on muttering about how much I must want to keep it all under wraps, and that he wouldn't say anything, not if I'd be nice – and that was the point we were interrupted, so I don't know what else he would have said."

"Oh, Geraldine, you poor thing," Fabia said. "What a horrid little shit he was."

"I know, but Fabia, the thing is, I was—" There was a pause and then Geraldine went on, "It's all so awful. It brings it all back. You know, the yellow and white tape round the theatre, and police all over the place, and now you say they're going to pitch up on my doorstep yet again."

Fabia was sure that Geraldine had intended to say something quite other but then changed her mind. "Gerry, you said the thing is, the thing is what?"

"Did I? No, it's just that it's getting to me, the similarities."

Fabia didn't press her. It didn't seem fair. "If you like, I can say something to Matt? Maybe suggest he come to speak to you himself." Then she changed her mind. "Actually, maybe not, he knows you too well, but I can check up on who he'll be sending, he'll probably tell me."

"Would you? And I'd be grateful if you'd tell Matt about Frank, sort of prepare him."

"Are you sure?"

"Yes," Geraldine said decisively.

"Okay," Fabia said, then added, "Did you take my advice and tell Oliver?"

"No, I chickened out."

"Here's an idea. Give Oliver a call, drag him off to the pub, and talk to him. He cares about you, Gerry."

"We're just friends," Geraldine said, but she sounded pleased.

"That's what I used to say about Matt."

Geraldine gave a shaky laugh. "I see what you mean. I suppose I could give him a ring."

"Do that, and Gerry, I know it's a bit pointless saying this, but try not to worry."

There was a weary sigh from the other end of the line. "Totally pointless, darling, but there you go."

And Fabia was left thinking that there had been a whole lot more that Geraldine had wanted to talk about, but she'd changed her mind.

CHAPTER 6

Peony Smith and Lewys Bennion sat in a secluded corner of The Oaks pub. The place was crowded for a Wednesday evening as there was a birthday celebration going on by the bar. The two of them took little notice, they had their own preoccupations. They were the two youngest members of the cast of Aladdin, and had struck up a close friendship during rehearsals, which hadn't gone unnoticed by Ivor Gladwin. He'd teased them unmercifully, calling them the 'little lovebirds', asking Peony if Lewys was good in bed, remarking to Lewys that he should be ashamed going out with an underage girl. When Peony had risen to the bait and protested that she was nearly twenty, Ivor had opened his eyes wide. 'Ah, a baby snatcher, eh? Busy teaching Lewys how it's done, are you?' he'd said, moving his hips back and forth suggestively. And there'd been much more.

Peony, prone to blushing at the drop of an innuendo, had hated the way her face flooded with red at every jibe. And Lewys, shy and unsure of himself, had found Ivor's behaviour equally embarrassing. But in a strange way it had drawn them together and Lewys, for one, hoped their friendship would develop into much more.

"It's so awful, Lewys," Peony said. "I know I should be sorry for Ivor and all that, but I just can't bring myself to, like, feel sorry for him now he's dead. He was such a shit!"

"I know. I said something like that to my mam and she told me off, said I shouldn't speak ill of the dead."

"Sod that. I'm not being funny but, well, everyone knows what he was like, but I wouldn't have harmed him," Peony said earnestly. "Still, someone must have. I've heard the way he speaks to people, makes them angry and uncomfortable. I'm sure it must be something to do with the way he behaved. Maybe he went too far, what do you think?"

"I suppose he could have," Lewys said. He took a gulp at his pint and frowned across at her. "He certainly used to annoy me, but I wouldn't do him any harm just because of that."

"No, of course you wouldn't, but who do you think was responsible?"

Lewys shook his head. "I've no idea. I've been going over and over it. I mean, when he wasn't winding people up, he was bloody chopsy, always arguing with Sebastian and Ellis, thinking he knew better than both of them. That certainly used to annoy them, but it must have been something much worse than that." He glanced at her as if wondering if he should say what was on his mind. "You know, I overheard him having a go at Eryn the other day when she was trying to sort out some steps in that stupid dance he does. He said something about her having the hots for Luke and didn't she realise that Luke was looking in quite another direction."

Eyes round and questioning, Peony said, "What do you think he meant?"

"I'm not sure, although I do think Sally and Luke are quite friendly, don't you?"

"Oh no!" Peony said. "I don't think she'd dare, not with Ellis like he is. Once I overheard him tell her she was a useless bitch, can you believe that? I felt really sorry for Sally, poor love."

"He can be just as much of a shit as Ivor was," Lewys said. "I could see Eryn was tamping when he had a go at her. I'm surprised she didn't trip him up."

"I would have!" exclaimed Peony, then slapped a hand to her mouth. "Oh dear, I shouldn't have said that either. It's so difficult. I'm just never going to be able to be nice about him just because he's dead."

"And another thing," he said, "Ivor and Morgan were having a barney in the green room on Saturday. I walked in on them and they both looked as if they'd been at it hammer and tongs, didn't even notice me at first."

"What were they arguing about?" Peony asked.

"Something about Ivor knowing what was going on. I think he said, 'he owns a few doesn't he, all over', or maybe he said she, I didn't catch all of it. Morgan looked really confused and sort of cornered, he gets that way, doesn't he? He said something like 'you keep your mouth shut or else', then they noticed me, and Ivor gave Morgan one of those grins and scarpered."

"Lewys! You'd better tell the police what you heard. It could be important."

"I suppose. Have they been to speak to you again?"

"Not yet. Do you think they will?"

"Of course, they will, Peony. They'll go on and on until they find out who killed him. I heard that Fabia's partner, Matt Lambert, is in charge."

Peony grinned at him. "I wouldn't mind being interviewed by him," she said.

Lewys didn't return her smile.

"Sorry, not appropriate," she said. "But you must admit he's lush."

"Not my type," said Lewys, trying to make a joke of it and wishing that she'd say that about him.

* * *

Fabia had contacted Luke and told him Matt would be home by eight o'clock. As it happened, Matt managed to get back half an hour before and they had just finished their meal when Luke arrived. Matt took him through to the sitting room, and Fabia followed with a bottle of wine and glasses. As she put them down on the coffee table, she noticed that the atmosphere in the room was tense. She glanced at Matt, who was frowning, and at Luke, who was sitting forward in his chair with his hands clasped between his knees.

"Why don't you pour the wine, Matt, while I sort the fire out." Hopefully, she thought, alcohol and warmth will help to relax everyone.

Once flames were licking at the logs she'd placed on the sluggish embers, she settled back beside Matt on the settee. The direct approach, that's what we need, she thought. "So, Luke, what was it you wanted to run past us?"

He looked at her, then away again. "I suppose you've heard that my mother's family came from Pontygwyn?" he said, staring at the flames as he spoke.

"Yes," Fabia said. "Your house was her family's farmhouse, wasn't it?"

"Way back it belonged to her family, yes, but that isn't the main reason I came to Wales. I was sent to do a particular job. The fact that the house was on the market just at the right moment was a lucky coincidence. I'm… er… more or less in the same line of business as you, Matt."

Matt didn't comment, just waited for Luke to go on.

"I'm with the National Crime Agency."

"You're what?" Matt snapped, leaning forward.

Luke put a hand into his inner pocket and brought out a warrant card which he handed over. Matt studied it carefully, then handed it back. "Okay, explain," he said, tight-lipped.

"I've been seconded to Gwent on a particular job. They wanted someone who wasn't a familiar face in the area but, because of my Welsh background, they thought I'd fit the bill and it'd make a good cover story. My remit was to bed down in the community, get to know people, and keep my ear to the ground."

Matt's frown had deepened. "Who knows about this?"

"Your chief super, Rees-Jones, and my bosses at headquarters. Other than that, no-one."

"And you didn't think to tell me you were working on my patch?" Matt demanded.

"I– I was told not to. Rees-Jones said you had enough on your plate without having to become involved in my activities."

"Hah! That sounds just like the kind of crap he'd be spouting."

Fabia could feel the anger vibrating through Matt, and she thought it best to intervene, give him time to get control of himself.

"And what is this job you've been sent to do?" she asked. Her tone was cold, and her expression would have put the fear of God into a lazy recruit back when she was in the police force. She too felt as if they'd been taken for a ride. Her past experience told her these undercover jobs had to be done, but she was still angry. There's absolutely no reason she should have been told, but Matt was quite another matter.

In spite of Fabia's tone, Luke sounded relieved at her intervention. "I've been working on a people trafficking ring. They bring people, mostly women, in from Romania, Belarus and sometimes further afield. Some are forced into domestic slavery, others into working in nail bars, mainly in South Wales but also some in Hereford and Bristol. It's all very well planned and, so far, they've managed to escape our net. The reason I ended up down here is that, at the end of last year we managed to interview two women who were trafficked from Romania, they managed to make contact and they're now in the care of social services, but they knew little about the people heading up the organisation. They answered adverts for jobs, thinking they were legitimate, and were met at the airport and driven away in vans where they couldn't see out, so there's no point in asking them what route was taken."

"Which airport?" asked Matt.

"Bristol. The people, both men, who picked them up took them first to a hotel in Cardiff, were they were told to hand in their passports, given some spurious reason, immigration issues or whatever. Then they were told the jobs they came to do had been taken and they would be working as domestic servants, one in Bristol, the other in Cardiff. These two women were a little more savvy than most and managed to contact the police, but when the hotel was raided there was no sign of the two blokes who picked them up and the manager denied all knowledge of them."

"So why were you sent to Pontygwyn?"

"Because we believe the outfit is based in this area. Several things point in that direction. It's near enough to Newport, Cardiff and Bristol without being too obvious."

"Were there other indications?" Fabia asked.

"Yes, there were. There's a registered charity, it was set up to help women in abusive relationships, but we're not at all sure that it isn't a cover for other activities, that's being researched by head office at the moment." Luke ticked off several further points on his fingers, then added, "It seems to be a well-organised set-up. We've been working on it for some time but haven't made any headway. But now there's been a development."

Matt gave an exasperated sigh. "What kind of development?" he asked.

Fabia glanced at him. It was obvious to her that he was making a great effort to keep control of his temper. Hardly surprising, she thought, I'd be seriously pissed off in his situation.

Luke went on. "We think drugs might be involved as well. There seems to be a pretty efficient dealer based around here, but I haven't managed to find out who they are and how they're passing them on."

"How did you find that out?" Matt snapped. "Have you contacted our drug squad?"

"Not as yet. It's all smoke and mirrors at the moment, and I didn't want to get distracted from the main investigation into the trafficking."

"I wouldn't advise you to go much further before involving them," Matt told him. "We have a major drugs problem in Gwent and not nearly enough personnel to deal with it. They need any help they can get, and they won't appreciate being kept in the dark any more than I do."

"I realise that, sir."

"So why, all of a sudden, am I to be put in the picture?"

Luke didn't give him a direct answer. "Look, sir."

Fabia noticed he'd begun to address Matt as a senior officer, but she didn't think this would get him out of the hole he was in.

"I'm truly sorry about this," Luke went on, "and I would have much preferred that you be told right from the start, but there it is. And I'm stretching it a bit telling you both, but no-one instructed me to keep it from Fabia when they said I could come and speak to you." He gave Fabia a quick smile, but she didn't return it. "My remit was to watch and wait. We're not after the small fry, here, the ones that do the meeting and greeting at the airport, etc. The people I'm after are higher up the pecking order. The ones who organise the hiring of vans and plan the journeys, and deal with the money made from the trafficking and launder it."

"And you think they're local, to Pontygwyn even?"

"Yes, I do. And I think your investigation into Ivor's murder might overlap with mine."

"Oh, for fuck's sake!" exclaimed Matt. He stretched out and grabbed the bottle of wine, poured some into his glass then handed the bottle to Fabia who refilled her own.

Luke put his hand over his own glass. "Driving," he said, with a rueful smile. "I'm in enough trouble already without being stopped for being over the limit."

She nodded and smiled, her anger dissipating a little. "Talking of being in trouble," she said, "what about Sally?"

Luke sat back in his chair and groaned, put his hands up and dragged them down his face. "Oh Lord. Of course, you know about that?"

"I'm observant," Fabia said. "And I could hardly miss it after Saturday morning."

Luke gave her a rueful smile. "True." But the smile soon faded. "Falling for her was one of my biggest mistakes."

"What do you mean, mistakes?" Fabia snapped, all her anger returning. "I don't think she'd appreciate being described like that. For goodness sake, Luke, have you no idea what she's going through with that awful husband of hers? Don't you know how fragile she is?"

"No, no, no. That's not what I meant," he said, his tone agonised. "The mistake I made was to fall in love with her, absolutely head-over-heels the first time I saw her. Nothing like it has ever happened to me before. I should have stepped back, controlled myself, asked to be recalled, whatever. But, by the time I realised how much trouble I was in, I just couldn't bring myself to– to leave her."

Memories from her past rushed in on Fabia. Years ago, before she'd met Matt, she'd had an affair with a fellow police officer. At the time she'd thrown caution to the winds, known that it was a big mistake, but ignored the alarm bells. Now, reluctantly she had to admit she understood Luke's situation. But she'd learnt her lesson long ago. Matt glanced at her and she knew he was aware of what she was thinking. He knew all about her past. She put out a hand and touched his with her fingertips.

"And to add to my problems," Luke said, "I thought I might finally be getting somewhere with my investigation."

Fabia noticed he referred to the problems as his. Surely, they went further than that, given Sally's involvement? But she didn't comment.

Luke went on. "Funnily enough, Ivor had been instrumental in pointing me in what I thought could be the right direction. His habit of dropping little hints about people's secrets came in useful. You know what he was like, Fabia."

She nodded. She certainly did.

"He'd look at someone during rehearsals," Luke said, "or at the pub, and make some pointed remark. They'd try to ignore him but flush up, or stumble on their words, or give some other sign they'd heard his jibes, and then he'd change the subject, but with that smug, knowing look. The number of times I wanted to punch his fat little face!"

"But you resisted the temptation to go for him?" Matt asked, his tone sarcastic.

Luke looked at him, eyes wide. "I certainly did, sir," he said. "And I made damn sure he had no idea I was watching him."

"Okay," said Matt. "I'm inclined to believe you. But, given the circumstances, and what Fabia told me about Ivor walking in on you and Sally last Saturday, thousands wouldn't."

"I know, I know." He put his hands up to his face again. "Look, sir. I fully realise I've screwed up, and I may have to step down, admit defeat, but please can we keep going on this? I feel as if I'm so close. I really don't want it to go tits up at the last moment."

Matt sat back. Eyes narrowed, he looked across at Luke. Fabia waited, knowing how she'd like to respond, but aware that it was up to Matt. The seconds ticked by, then Matt said, "Okay. You'll have to tell me what you've got so far, and I have to tell Rees-Jones that you've put me in the picture. Actually" – he gave a quick grin – "I might enjoy doing that. So, who are your main suspects?"

Luke told him. Matt's eyebrows rose and Fabia frowned, incredulous.

"That's a pretty wide field," Matt said. "You'd better give me access to all your notes, and I'll go through them."

"I'll have to clear it with–" The look on Matt's face stopped Luke in his tracks.

"Well, maybe not," Matt said.

"Wow, Matt! Not sticking to the rule book?" Fabia said, teasing. "There's hope for you yet."

"Shut up, you," Matt said, but he smiled at her.

Luke was looking worried. "The thing is, sir, I don't want them put off when they're being interviewed about Ivor's death, but I'm obviously fully aware that you have a job to do."

"I do indeed," Matt said, eyebrows raised a little haughtily, then he relented. "We'll do our best to keep your activities out of it, but I do have a killer to find and I'm not going to sacrifice my investigation for the sake of yours. I hope that's understood."

"Yes, sir."

"But why don't we work together. If I come across anything that I think would be useful to you I'll let you know, but only on condition you do the same for me."

"It's a deal," Luke said and held out his hand. Matt shook it briefly, then Luke rose from his chair.

"I must get going. Thank you both for being so understanding."

"I don't think we had much choice," Matt said.

Fabia said, "No problem." But as she came back into the sitting room, she looked across at Matt. "I don't know why I said that. No problem! Who am I kidding?"

CHAPTER 7

The green room at the Little Theatre had been cleared
of its battered armchairs and occasional tables. Under
Dave Parry's instructions, tables and upright chairs
had been brought in, computers had been linked up
and two or three whiteboards had been placed against
the wall. Stuck to one were photos of the scene of the
crime, to another, photographs of all those involved
in the pantomime. The third was blank and ready for
use when needed. From the church hall Cath, at
Fabia's instigation, had provided a larger kettle than
the one that had been by the sink in the corner of the
room, Fabia knew how much coffee and tea would be
consumed as they worked. Luckily there were plenty
of mugs and glasses in the cupboard above to cater
for all contingencies.

Once everyone was gathered, except Matt who had
a meeting with the chief superintendent, Dilys passed
on Matt's instructions.

"Okay, listen up people," Dilys said. "The boss
wants another search of the whole of the stage area."

There was a half-hearted groan of protest. "Sorry, folks, but it's got to be done. This time the search is specific, we're looking for the victim's mobile phone. Okay, get to it."

The place was flooded with light and, half an hour later, two officers were crawling along the catwalk above the stage, several others were searching around in the wings and in amongst the various pieces of scenery propped backstage, and two others were searching the auditorium.

Suddenly a shout went up from the gloom of the wings. "Sarge! I think I've found something." The young PC, a recent recruit called Sara Gupta, had a triumphant look on her face.

Dilys, who had been overseeing the activity, went quickly into the wings on the left-hand side and joined her. She pointed to a substantial crack in the floorboards. "Down there, Sarge, I think I can see something."

Dilys crouched down and shone the light from her own mobile phone down into the gap between the floorboards that Sara was indicating. Up-ended, just out of reach, was what looked like a very slim mobile phone.

"That looks the business. Well done, Sara," Dilys said. "Stay here and I'll fetch Dave Parry. We might need some brawn to lever up this floorboard."

Within minutes Dave was crouching down to look. "I think you're right. I'll get that out, easy, and we can give it to Aidan to work his magic on."

DC Aidan Rogers was a computer geek who had worked on several cases with Matt and Dilys. He seemed to be able to ferret out information from any device that he was given to work on. A simple mobile phone would be a doddle. A few minutes later the phone was retrieved and handed over to him.

***

Matt arrived an hour later, frowning as he marched into the room, but he cheered up when told of Sara's discovery. "Well done," he said to her, but a moment later the frown had returned.

Dilys glanced at him then asked quietly, "Trouble, sir?"

"You could say that," Matt replied. "Let's go into the auditorium and I'll bring you up to date."

As they went Dilys filled him in about the golf club Ivor had used. "He wasn't a member at any of the ones we thought of; it was Newport Golf Course where he played. I sent Tom to have a word. It seems he used to play on his own most of the time. The pro said he saw him, briefly, on Saturday afternoon, but not to speak to, he said it was early afternoon but wasn't any more precise than that."

"That doesn't really get us any further, but never mind, just as well to have checked."

They settled themselves in two of the seats halfway down the auditorium.

"Luke came around to see us last night," Matt began.

"At this rate we'll be moving all our activities to Morwydden Lane," Dilys said, grinning. "Actually, that's not such a bad idea. It's just as well the chief suggested you involve Fabia."

Matt grinned back. "I know," he said, then went on to tell her what Luke had told him and Fabia. This wiped the smile from her face.

73

"What a bloody cheek, not telling you what he was up to!" she exclaimed.

"I suppose. I was pretty angry at first, but I've been thinking about it and, since he was under orders, it did make things difficult for him. That's why I went in to see the boss first thing, he needed to know that I'd been put in the picture, finally. I rather enjoyed telling him. He seemed a tad embarrassed."

Dilys gave a grim smile. "And did he explain why he hadn't told you?"

"A lot of waffling about the need to know and how busy I've been. I'm still not sure why he kept me in the dark, but I have a sneaking feeling he was afraid I'd tell Fabia and that she'd blab, which annoys me somewhat."

"I should say so. Fabia would never do a thing like that."

"I know that, you know that, but Rees-Jones obviously doesn't. I didn't tell him about Luke's involvement with Sally. I didn't want to drop Luke in it. In spite of the fact he's encroached on my patch and kept me in the dark, he's a tidy sort of bloke."

"And you say he hinted at those he thought might be involved in laundering the money from the trafficking."

"Yes," Matt said, and gave her the names.

"Interesting. That definitely means that his investigation overlaps with ours," Dilys said. "Do we haul each of them in under the guise of interviewing them about Gladwin's murder?"

"I think we'll have to, but I promised Luke we'd tread carefully. Neither of us wants them warned off. Let's see what we get out of that mobile phone. If it turns out it belonged to Gladwin, which I think it probably will, it should be useful. We also need to put a call out for the missing laptop and iPad, because I cannot imagine he didn't have either, although that'll be like searching for a needle in a haystack. The thing is, I can understand the absence of a computer on his desk, but don't you think he would have had a laptop instead?"

"You would have thought so," Dilys said. "We'll have to interview the staff at his garage, sooner rather than later, and search his office. That hasn't been done yet."

"Bugger. You're right," Matt said. "Can you get that sorted?"

"Will do."

"It's as if we've lost two or three days because of Jess Foyle's accident."

"Well, we have, to all intents and purposes."

"I suppose," Matt said. "The next thing I want done is for one or two of the team to do a search on all the names of the cast and crew, see what they can turn up that might have been of interest to Gladwin and his snooping. Anything, however trivial, I want to know, and I want them to go way back. You're certainly not going to be lazing around doing nothing."

"Do we ever," she said with a smile. "I'll set that up. What else?"

"That's about it for now, Dilys. Let's get back to the green room, see if anyone's turned anything up."

As they walked back down the aisle to the side door which led through to the backstage area, Dilys asked, "Why's it called a green room?"

"No idea. I'll have to ask Fabia."

* * *

75

Cath Temple was catching up with a string of e-mails on the computer in her study when the vicarage doorbell rang. She pushed herself up from her chair, wondering who it could be. She wasn't expecting anyone, but then being a vicar, she always had a metaphorical – and actual, for that matter – open door for her parishioners.

When she opened the front door, Sally Cadogan was standing on the doorstep, her face white and streaked with tears. "Please, can I come in?" she asked, her voice cracking as she spoke.

"Of course," Cath said and put out a hand to pull her into the hall. "Come into the study."

Sally followed Cath into the shabby but comfortable room. Books were piled everywhere, and various boxes of pamphlets and hymn sheets were stacked in one corner. A cassock hung on the back of the door and there was a small mirror with bits and pieces of make-up and a hairbrush on the bookshelf beside it. On the walls were framed photographs, some family groups, one of Cath Temple in a university gown, another of her in full vestments. Opposite the desk was a sofa covered in a bright-coloured throw, and an ancient armchair stood to one side, a coffee table separating the two.

"Sit down, Sally, and I'll get us some tea, then you can tell me what's up, okay?"

Sally nodded, seeming comforted by the homeliness of the room.

When Cath got back with a tray laden with mugs, sugar, milk and a plate of biscuits, Sally was sitting on the sofa, her head against the back, her eyes closed. Cath placed the tray on the table and sat down in the sagging armchair.

"Do you want milk and sugar?" she asked.

Sally opened her eyes and said, "Both please." She took out a crumpled tissue from her pocket and blew her nose. "I'm sorry about this. I just couldn't think where else to go. I was shopping and I couldn't remember what I was in Spar for, my mind was a blank. I just picked something at random, and then I dropped my purse and the money went everywhere, and the woman behind the till was getting impatient, and the others in the queue were all looking at me. I just ran out of the shop, but I couldn't face going home, so I came here."

"There's absolutely no need to apologise," Cath said, handing her a steaming mug of tea. "Now, tell me how I can help."

"It's Ellis. I– I'm so afraid…" Her voice petered out as she bit at her lower lip.

After seconds had ticked by and Sally said no more, Cath prompted, "Afraid of what?"

"That he's responsible for Ivor's death," she said in a rushed and agitated whisper.

"But why would you think that?" Cath asked. As she'd intended, her quiet tone seemed to calm Sally down.

"I overheard him talking to someone on his mobile." She reddened. "I often listen to him, it's one of the ways I can work out what mood he's in and what way I must, well, behave. He thought I was upstairs having a shower, but I was getting my breakfast in the kitchen. I don't know who he was talking to, but he said something about its being good riddance and at least there would be no more of Ivor's snooping now. Who do you think he was talking to?"

"I've no idea. But none of this means that Ellis was involved." It occurred to Cath that Ivor might have realised Ellis was abusive to his wife, but she wouldn't have thought that was the kind of thing Ivor would be that bothered by. She chided herself for being uncharitable. "Granted, it's not a particularly appropriate or nice thing to say in the circumstances, but that's all."

"And then, last Sunday, I heard him talking about the police being all over the place and he told the person they'd have to be careful. He asked when the next consignment would be coming in and said it should be delayed. A consignment of what, Cath?"

"I really have no idea, Sally. And as to being careful, that could mean anything. Do you know if Ivor had threatened your husband in any way?"

"No. What could he have threatened him about?" Then Sally put a hand up to her mouth. "I suppose he could have found out about Ellis's gambling."

"He gambles?"

"Yes, online, and he's lost lots of money. That's why I had to go back to working full time, to try to pay off the debt. He says it's my fault that he gambles, that he has to take his mind off– off–"

Cath frowned, waiting for Sally to go on, but she didn't, just said, "But surely, lots of people gamble, and how would Ivor have known about it?"

"I don't know, Sally. Have you any idea who Ellis was talking to on either call?"

"None at all." Sally said a little too quickly. Cath wondered if she was telling the truth. "And I can't possibly ask him," Sally went on. "He'd be so angry that I was listening."

"And you think, because of what you heard, Ellis might have had some part in Ivor's death?"

"No! Yes! Oh, I don't know. But that's not the worst of it."

Cath waited for her to go on.

"You see, he also told whoever it was that he was going to deal with... deal with–" She drew her breath in on a ragged sob. "With Luke. And if Ellis killed Ivor, don't they say that murderers find the second one easier to do?"

Cath's mind was racing as she tried to decide how to respond. She needed to persuade Sally to go to the police with her fears, but she was pretty sure that if she suggested it, Sally would shy away from the very thought. She'd had her suspicions that Sally and Luke were more than just fellow members of the Pontygwyn Players – Cath didn't miss much, one way and another, but this was the first time she'd had any kind of confirmation. She took a deep breath, reached out and took Sally's hand. "Why would Ellis want to deal with Luke?"

"Because he and I are... particular friends." Sally wouldn't look her in the eye.

"Sally, love, I may be a vicar, but I live in the real world." She gave a rueful grin. "If I told you about some of my own past escapades, they'd make your hair curl even more than it does already, so whatever you say isn't going to shock me."

Sally gave her a watery smile. "We're in love."

"And does Ellis know about this?"

"Oh God, no!"

"Then why would he talk of dealing with Luke?"

"I don't know. Well maybe he suspects, and he'd kill me if he–" Sally suddenly leant forward to put her mug on the table then got up. "I must go. Thank you so much for listening. I'm probably over-reacting. Yes, I'm sure I am."

"I don't think you are," Cath said. How could she mention going to the police without frightening her off? Then she had an idea. "Look, Sally, how about having a quiet word with Matt Lambert?"

"Oh no, I couldn't."

"I really think you should," Cath urged. "All this may mean a lot more to Matt than it does to us."

But Sally shook her head vigorously and her eyes filled with tears. "I can't. I can't."

"Then how about talking to Fabia? I know she's not in the police force any more, but she would be able to advise you what's best to do. And she might be able to pass on your fears to Matt. What do you think?"

Sally stood, hesitating, for a moment. "I'll think about it," she said.

That wasn't good enough for Cath. She was sure that, once Sally left the vicarage, she'd do her best to push all thoughts of what she'd heard into the back of her mind, if only for her own sanity's sake. "I could give Fabia a ring now. She could be here in a matter of minutes. How about it?"

Sally glanced at her watch. "I'm sorry, Cath, I have to get back. Ellis said he'd be home for lunch and if I don't have it ready it'll put him in such a bad mood."

"In that case," Cath said, grasping at straws, "will you let me pass on what you've told me to Fabia? Then I could let you know what she says."

"Alright," Sally said slowly. "But you mustn't phone me on the landline. I'll give you my mobile number." She dictated it and Cath tapped it into her own phone. "Ellis has been threatening to take my phone away from me," Sally added, "so, if he answers it, can you make up some innocuous reason for phoning?"

It occurred to Cath that Sally said this as if it was something quite normal for a husband to threaten to do. She felt her anger increasing, not with Sally but with her husband, but it would be counter-productive to express it. She must remain calm.

"Of course, no problem. I can always make it a query about music or something else to do with the pantomime."

Sally reached out and gave Cath a hug. "Thank you so much for listening. I feel much better now."

"No problem, that's what I'm here for."

Cath saw her out and then went back into the study, picked up her mobile phone from the coffee table, and tapped out Fabia's number.

CHAPTER 8

Several police officers were gathered round a table at one end of the green room. Matt and Dilys were there, with Sara Gupta, Dave Parry, Tom Watkins and Sharon Pugh. Matt had allocated each with one or two of the people involved in the pantomime to research, and also those that Ivor Gladwin had worked with, and they were now gathered to share their information.

"Okay, let's have what each of you has turned up," Matt said. "Sharon, you first."

"I've been researching Ellis Cadogan," she said. "Originally, he trained as an accountant then swapped careers, did a music degree, and ended up teaching music at St Madoc's school, but he left teaching, voluntarily it seems. I did, however, find an interesting piece from the South Wales Argus archives." She ran her finger across the mouse on her laptop then read from the screen. "It states that the parents of a student complained to the school that their child was being bullied by Cadogan, accused him of shutting the piano lid down on this kid's fingers. They threatened to sue, but it was settled out of court. That put paid to his teaching career. I think that's the point at which he got the job as an accountant with a chain of music shops, but he's still teaching music privately. There's an advert for his services online and he has a Facebook page. He and his wife have been married for twelve years, she's ten years younger than him and she works as a receptionist at the surgery in the high street."

"When did he leave teaching?" asked Dilys.

Sharon looked at her screen again. "In 2012."

"I'm surprised they stayed in Pontygwyn after a scandal like that," Matt said. "You'd have thought they'd want to move as far from St Madoc's as possible."

"Maybe he didn't think he was culpable," Sharon said, then added with a touch of scorn, "some parents are pretty flaky about their little dears."

Dilys gave her a sharp look but didn't comment. "I suppose Ivor Gladwin could have wound him up about it all," she suggested.

"But that's hardly a motive for murder," Matt said.

"And anyway," said Sharon, "when Inspector Foyle did that first interview, Ellis Cadogan said he was with Morgan Conway on Saturday rehearsing Morgan's songs for the pantomime, and Conway confirmed this, so that effectively gives them both an alibi."

"Has anyone checked this out with Conway's sister?" Matt asked. "What's her name? Carmen Lloyd, runs that hairdressers in the high street and she lives with her brother, doesn't she?"

Sharon simply said, "I haven't, but someone else might have."

They all shook their heads.

"Better get that checked out then," Matt told her firmly.

"Okay," she said, seemingly unaware that Matt was a little annoyed at the oversight. "Do you want what I've turned up on Cadogan's wife?" Sharon asked, sounding impatient, then she glanced at Matt and added, "Sir," as an afterthought.

Dilys frowned, she'd have to have a word with Sharon if her attitude didn't improve. Others had started to remark on her rather brisk and unfriendly manner, and Tom Watkins reported to Dilys that she hadn't, in his words, been respectful towards Fabia when they interviewed her. Dilys had taken this with a pinch of salt, knowing that Fabia was a favourite of Tom's, but she'd still have to keep an eye.

"Okay," Matt said, in answer to Sharon's question. "Have you turned up anything useful on Sally Cadogan?"

"No, not really." She seemed completely unaware of how she was coming across. "She's been working at the surgery for some years. She's a singer and has one of the main roles in the pantomime."

Matt opened his mouth to say something, then seemed to change his mind. Dilys wondered what he was thinking.

"Tom, you were researching Eve Kemble and Oliver Talbot, what have you come up with?"

"Eve Kemble, she's a bit of a mystery. She and her husband are pretty well off. She used to work in theatres in London, apparently. I turned up an article from the Argus about her having worked with the

Royal Shakespeare Company, but there was nothing about why she's now living down here. As you probably know, she's in charge of the costumes for the panto, bit of a come down, that. I expect you know more about her than I've managed to discover," Tom said, then coloured a little. "Sorry, sir, what I mean is that she knows Ms Havard, doesn't she?" And his colour deepened.

Matt gave him a rueful smile. "Not that well. Fabia has mentioned that there have been rumours about their moving to South Wales, but she didn't tell me what. She thinks Eve has ambitions to be the director of the Players productions, considers herself better qualified, but that Sebastian Aubrey won't relinquish control. That could be a bone of contention, but I wouldn't have thought it's relevant to our investigation. What about Oliver Talbot?"

Tom relaxed. He had more to offer on Talbot. "I turned up quite a lot on him. Several years ago" – he glanced at his laptop screen – "2014 it was, he was a partner in a firm of solicitors in Cardiff. One of the other partners blotted his copybook, a bloke called Emrys Fenton. This Fenton was found guilty of falsifying evidence on behalf of an important client, some bigwig property dealer who'd been accused of killing someone in a hit and run. Although Talbot was cleared of all blame – he and another partner had no idea this had happened until Fenton was arrested – the practice never really recovered from the scandal. Mud sticks."

"That rings a bell," Matt said. "I think John Meredith spoke up on behalf of Talbot and helped him clear his name."

"You mean the John Meredith that just got married to Fabia's friend, Anjali?" asked Dilys.

"Yes. I remember him talking about it, but I hadn't made the connection." Matt pushed his hair back from his forehead and leant back in his chair. "If Gladwin knew about this, he might have been winding Talbot up about it. But I wouldn't have thought that was sufficient motive either, unless, of course, Talbot was actually involved."

"Do you want me to do a bit more research on that hit and run?" Tom asked.

"Yes, you'd better do that."

"Rightio, sir."

Matt turned to Sara Gupta. "Did you find out anything useful about Morgan Conway, Sara?"

"No, sir, I'm afraid I didn't," Sara said, looking embarrassed. "He's a taxi driver, lives with his sister, Carmen Lloyd, who owns and runs the hairdressing salon, Cut & Curl in the high street. They live in one of the fancy flats in that new block on Sycamore Road, she must be doing well because I doubt that Conway makes much with his taxi. When we" – she glanced at Tom Watkins – "interviewed him he said he's from round here, and was introduced to the Players by Ellis Cadogan, who doesn't drive so uses his taxi quite often. He said he used to go to the pub with Ivor Gladwin and that he was, how did he put it, a top bloke, which is a bit different to what most of the others have said. That's all I've got so far, I'm afraid."

"Not to worry," Matt said, smiling at her, "just keep digging."

"Will do, sir."

"And, Dave." Matt turned to Dave Parry who'd sat quietly listening to what everyone else had to say, his solid bulk overflowing the plastic chair he was sitting on. "Did you get anything from his work colleagues?"

"They said the same as others have said, that he was a bit of a joker, that he enjoyed winding people up. One of the women said that he was inclined to overstep the mark, a bit too nudge nudge, wink wink, for her liking, she said." He looked down at the notes he had in front of him, Dave preferred to work with pen and paper rather than on a laptop. "There was one thing, though. His partner, a bloke called Hywel Shaw, said that Ivor had mentioned turning up some information on a scam that was being run locally, but he didn't go into detail, said it was something to do with immigrants, but that was all. Gladwin implied he knew who was behind it, had found out a few things through the business, and that he was going to go to the police."

"When was this?" Matt asked.

"A couple of days before he was killed," Dave told him. "He said he didn't know whether it was legit or just Ivor being imaginative, as he put it."

"I'd like to have another word with this Shaw."

"And, sir, can we get a search warrant for Gladwin's office? It occurred to me that he might have kept his laptop and iPad, whatever, in his office rather than at home."

"Good idea. I'll organise that," Matt said, getting up. "Okay folks, good work."

They all gathered up their notes and laptops and went back to work.

* * *

Morgan Conway wasn't working on Thursday morning. He didn't have any bookings until two in the afternoon. Once his sister, Carmen, had gone off to work, he couldn't settle to anything. He paced up and down the flat, desperate to find out what was going on and wondering who to contact for information. Earlier he'd walked briskly past the theatre, keeping to the opposite side of the road, and seen all the tape draped across the entrance, and the police constables guarding the front and stage doors. He'd considered going to talk to one of them but decided against it. Too risky. He went on home, none the wiser about the activities at the theatre, and resumed his pacing. A couple of times he'd taken out his phone, frowned at the screen, scrolled through the numbers, then changed his mind. Oliver Talbot? No, he didn't feel he knew him well enough. Sebastian and Jean? They might know what was going on, but they'd probably go on and on about the pantomime. Ellis Cadogan? He tried the number but got no response. What about Tony Vaughan? He was a good chap, Tony. They often had a pint together at The Oaks and they were in the same darts team. Tony always behaved as if they were friends. What's more, he lived next door to Fabia and Matt. Yes, he might have more information than most.

Morgan scrolled down to the number and punched it in before he could change his mind.

"Tony? Morgan here," he hesitated, then rushed on, "I'm not gonna lie to you, I'm very worried about this business with Ivor."

"I think we all are," Tony said.

"Of course, of course. Have you heard anything more?"

"More than what? I mean, it's a murder investigation. There'll be an inquest."

"What happens at an inquest?" Morgan asked.

"They go through what happened, Sebastian will have to be there to tell them about finding the body, the police will give evidence and will probably ask for an adjournment. After that the investigation will continue."

"They won't want any of us to be there, will they?" Morgan felt panic rising.

"No, I shouldn't think so. Don't worry, mate. We should know more after that. Like I said, it'll probably be adjourned until the police have done their stuff. Have you heard the local news?"

"No, I haven't." Morgan walked into the kitchen and turned the radio on, tuned it to a local FM channel, but then turned it down again in order to hear what Tony was saying.

"The police are asking anyone who has information to come forward."

"I know. I had a visit from a couple of them, but I don't think they were particularly pleased with what I had to tell them. Do you know anything that'd be useful to them?"

"I suppose Ivor did make a habit of getting on the wrong side of people," Tony suggested. "I did mention that, but they seemed to know about it already."

"Surely that's no reason to kill him, poor old chap," Morgan said, then added. "I wondered if you'd heard anything from your neighbours."

"Matt and Fabia?"

"Yes."

"No, not really. I gather Matt Lambert has taken over the investigation," Tony told him, "which could be a plus, could be the opposite. I'd have thought it'd be a bit difficult for him, given that he lives locally. On the other hand, he knows most of us so that could be helpful, I suppose."

"Do you think so?" Morgan asked, with a worried frown, then added, "Poor chap. I don't think that's a job I'd like to do."

"I dare say he'll be coming back to all of us to find out everything he can," Tony said. "If I hear anything further, do you want me to let you know?"

"Would you? I want to do anything I can to help. I mean, Ivor could be a bit of a pain sometimes, but no-one deserves to be killed just like that."

When he ended the call, he stood staring at the blank screen of his phone for some time, then he turned up the radio, hoping there'd be more on the ten o'clock bulletin.

* * *

Fabia and Cath sat opposite each other at Fabia's kitchen table.

"The thing is, Fabia," Cath said, "I really think Sally ought to speak to Matt but I'm pretty sure I'd not be able to persuade her to do so. She did agree that I could pass on what she told me to you, though, so what do you think?"

"It's such a mess, Cath," Fabia said, wishing she could tell Cath what Luke had told them. "I mean, I'm sure Luke can look after himself, but I will have a word with Matt if you like. He and Matt have become quite good friends." That's as much as she felt she could say.

"But what if Sally's right, and Ellis did have something to do with Ivor's death?"

"I wouldn't have thought he did. Most abusers are cowards, deep down. I would have thought whoever killed Ivor must have lain in wait for him, and you'd have to have courage, however warped, to do that."

"I suppose."

"I'll pass all this on to Matt," Fabia told her. "Do you think, if I invited Sally round here for coffee or something, and Matt happened to be home, she'd talk to him?"

"She might feel a bit highjacked."

"True. I'll think about it."

"The other thing was she said something about him threatening to take her mobile away, and that she had to get back to get his lunch because, if she didn't, he'd be angry. In my book that amounts to coercive control, but I didn't see any signs of physical harm. But then people hide the bruises, don't they? Abuse isn't all about being hit."

"Absolutely not. What is it with these men?"

"And occasionally women, Fabia."

"I know, I know." Fabia sighed. "Look, leave it with me and I'll have a word with Matt when he gets home."

Suddenly Cath changed the subject. "I do love it when you talk about Matt getting home!" Cath said, smiling across at her, but a moment later there was a wistful note in her voice. "I do envy you sometimes, having a lovely man to keep you warm."

"Oh Cath, love. Your problem is you're married to your job. But there's nothing to stop you going online and having a search around."

Cath grimaced. "What? 'Vicar looking for love' doesn't sound all that appealing. No, I don't think so. Don't take any notice, I'm being silly. I have quite enough on my plate without complicating things. Anyway, I must get going, I've got a confirmation class after lunch."

Fabia got up to go with her to the front door. "Can you just run what Sally said past Matt and let me know if he gets anywhere," Cath said, "if you're allowed to, of course."

"Will do," said Fabia.

For a long time after Cath had left she sat thinking about her friend. Maybe she'd try her hand at a bit of matchmaking, Fabia thought, then she laughed softly to herself. No, that probably wouldn't be a good idea.

CHAPTER 9

Matt managed to get a search warrant sorted out faster than he'd expected and, later that afternoon, he, along with Dilys, Dave Parry and Sara Gupta, made their way to Gladwin & Shaw Car Sales and Rentals in Cwmbran, just off St David's Road and not far from the railway station. It was on the edge of an industrial estate, quite a prosperous-looking dealership with gleaming cars of various makes in the forecourt, each with a prominent price displayed. Down one side were parked several Mercedes vans with a big notice saying they were for hire.

The showroom was modern, and glass-fronted, with several more cars inside. When they walked in, there was a young woman sitting at the reception desk to one side of the main doors. She got up when she saw them, looking rather flustered, a gleam of recognition in her eyes when she saw Dave Parry.

"Good afternoon, I'm Chief Inspector Lambert, Newport Police," Matt said, holding out his identification. "Could I have a word with Mr Hywel Shaw please?"

"I'll see if he's available," she said, and wove her way quickly between the cars, rather like a nervous rabbit trying to find a bolthole, to a frosted glass door at the back. She opened it and, with a quick glance back at them, stepped into the room and closed the door behind her. Through the frosted glass they could see her talking to someone and could hear an animated murmur of voices, but they weren't close enough to distinguish any words. A moment later she returned, followed by a balding, middle-aged man with a rather lugubrious expression on his egg-shaped face.

"Chief Inspector Lambert, is it? How can I help you?" His eyes flitted from Matt to Dilys, and on to Sara and Dave, whom he too seemed to recognise. "Have you any more information about this awful crime?"

"I'm afraid not, but we are progressing. We need to search Mr Gladwin's office, and possibly the rest of the showroom as part of our investigation." Shaw opened his mouth to protest, but Matt forestalled him, "We do have a warrant." He glanced at Dilys and she held it out for Shaw to see.

The man seemed to sag, then threw his hands up and said, "I suppose I'll have to let you go ahead." He turned to the receptionist and said, "Sheena, show these officers into Ivor's office please."

"We'll need the keys to his desk and to any filing cabinets," Matt said.

"But I haven't got them," Shaw protested. "Haven't you found them at Ivor's house?"

"Not as yet," Matt said carefully. "Do you have duplicates?"

"To the filing cabinets, possibly," said Shaw, "but not to his desk. Ivor was always very careful about keeping the contents private."

"In that case we may well have to force the locks," Matt said firmly. "Any damage done will be repaired at our expense, of course."

"If you must, you must. I'll get some keys that might work on the filing cabinets," Shaw told them, and he turned and went back to his office. It wasn't long before he returned with a large bunch of keys. "You could try some of these."

Dilys took them from him. "Thank you, sir."

"Show them the way, would you, Sheena."

The four of them followed the receptionist to a door at the far end of the showroom. She bent to unlock it and stood aside to let them through, then she scuttled away, leaving them to it.

The room was plainly furnished, the only obvious decoration a calendar on one wall with a picture of a barely clad woman draped over the bonnet of an E-Type Jaguar, the year was 1978 so it must have been left there as a dubious decoration. On the opposite wall were a couple of large posters of more recent vehicles, a Hyundai 4x4 and a Range Rover Vogue. Opposite the door were two grey filing cabinets, side by side. A dying pot plant, its leaves curled and brown, stood on top of one of them. And in the middle of the room was a large desk containing a computer and keyboard, various wire trays with paperwork in them and a ceramic pot in the shape of a nude woman, full of pens and pencils. Dilys's mouth twisted in distaste. "The more I get to know about Ivor Gladwin, the less I like him," she said.

Matt smiled and shrugged. "Doesn't mean we haven't got to put some effort into finding his killer."

"No, of course not, if only to congratulate him or her."

"Now, now, Sarge," Dave said.

"Sorry."

Matt turned to Sara. "Okay, Sara. Would you stand by the door on the showroom side, have your identification ready and give us a shout if you have any trouble. Make sure we're not interrupted. I'd also like you to make a note of any activity you think needs reporting." Matt put the keys he'd been given down on the desk and he, Dilys and Dave pulled on protective gloves, then he picked up the bunch of keys. "We'd better double-check none of these fit the drawers in the desk."

It didn't take long to discover none of them did, so he handed them to Dilys. "Have a go with the filing cabinets. Some of them look like the right kind. And, Dave, go out to the car and get the kit, we'll have to force these drawers open."

Dave was back in a couple of minutes, but before they started Matt looked around, a puzzled frown on his face. "All this security seems a bit over the top. There's no safe in here, as far as I can see. Okay, in his position I might lock my desk, but why the filing cabinets? Surely other people would be using them, not just Gladwin?"

"It may be because I told them they should secure everything until we came to do a comprehensive search," Dave suggested.

"That could be it," Matt agreed. "Right, let's get going."

Dilys stood in front of the first filing cabinet trying key after key and muttering darkly to herself, then she gave an exclamation of satisfaction. Matt had been watching Dave go through his set of tools, trying to choose a suitable one to jemmy open the desk drawers, but he turned when Dilys said, "Got it! This one fits, sir."

He went over as she pulled out the first drawer and then the second. There was nothing in either that seemed out of place, just sales invoices, advertising material, correspondence. But in the bottom drawer things were different. There were no hanging file containers, just a substantial metal cash box, solidly locked. Dilys picked it up by the handle on its lid. "Interesting, I'll try some of these keys." But none of them fitted so the box remained locked. Dilys put it into a large evidence bag and set it aside just as they heard splintering sounds from the desk.

"Got it," Dave exclaimed as he opened the central drawer, took out the contents and placed them on the desk, but everything he found was pretty predictable: pens, pencils, notepads, blocks of Post-it Notes, and various other innocuous bits and pieces. None of it got them any further. He put the notepads into evidence bags and started to work on the other drawers. It wasn't until he got to the left-hand bottom drawer that he found anything of interest. Dave removed several A4 pads of paper and underneath was a large leather wallet, jammed in so that it had to be levered out. Dave checked the contents, but it was empty. "Sod it, what's the point of that," he muttered. However, underneath the wallet was an Apple iPad.

"Well done, Dave," Matt exclaimed, handing him another evidence bag. "Let's hope that can give us a tidy bit of information about Ivor Gladwin."

Not long after this discovery, having bagged up everything they felt would be useful to them, Matt went in search of Hywel Shaw.

"We've finished our search, Mr Shaw," Matt said, going up to the garage manager where he stood beside the receptionist as she sat at her desk. "Thank you very much for your co-operation. We've had to remove several objects, including Mr Gladwin's iPad, and a cash box." Matt held up the clear plastic evidence bag. "Do you recognise it?"

Shaw frowned. "No, I do not, where on earth did you find that?"

"In the bottom of the right-hand filing cabinet. If there's nothing in it that's relevant to the investigation, we'll obviously return it to you. Here are receipts for everything we're taking away with us. It will all be returned, unless it's kept in evidence for any trial that may result."

"And will you be searching any other parts of the garage?" Shaw asked, his tone resentful. "We do have a business to run, you know, in spite of this tragic event. Ivor would have wanted us to keep going."

"I'm sure he would," Matt assured him. "We may have to return, it depends what we find when we've done a comprehensive search of Ivor Gladwin's iPad, etc. Just before we go, could my sergeant and I have a word with you, sir? It might save us having to come back."

Hywel Shaw's frown deepened. He glanced at his receptionist, who looked up at him, her eyes frightened now. For a moment there was a stand-off, then his shoulders sagged. "If you must," he said, "you must. This way."

He led them to the frosted glass door, ushered them in and closed it behind him. "What is it, then?" he asked without offering them a seat.

"I believe Mr Gladwin hinted that he'd turned up some information on an immigration scam being run locally," Matt said. "You mentioned it to Detective Sergeant Parry, and that Gladwin had spoken to you about it a couple of days before he died."

"He did say something, nothing specific," Shaw said, sounding dismissive. "I didn't really take him seriously. Ivor was a great one for conspiracy theories."

"But you told DS Parry that he implied he knew who was behind this scam, that it was something to do with immigration, and that he was going to go to the police. I'd say that was quite important. Why have you changed your mind about the seriousness of what he said?"

"I haven't," Shaw said sharply. "It's just, well, I've thought about it a bit more since he mentioned it and I really don't think there's anything like that going on round here. I mean, it's ridiculous. That's the sort of thing that goes on in London, the South East, not here surely?"

"It's not impossible," Matt told him.

"And you haven't heard anything about such a scam, sir?" Dilys asked.

"No," he said, glancing at her and then back at Matt. "Look, Chief Inspector, Ivor had a bit of an imagination and he was always coming up with this or that person or situation he was investigating. Sometimes it sounded as if he was on to something, and I'd tell him he should go to the police if he thought someone was involved in criminal activity. But last week he really had let his imagination run away with him."

"In what way?"

Shaw sighed and then said, as if the admission was being forced out of him, "He told me he thought there was a people trafficking gang working in this area and that he could prove it."

"That's a serious matter," Matt said. "Did he tell you any more? Who was involved? How he found out?"

"No. He loved to drop these things into the conversation, usually with a knowing grin, and then when you asked for details, he'd refuse to say anything else." Shaw frowned at Matt. "Do you think, perhaps, he had found something out and mentioned it to the wrong people? It all seems so far-fetched to me. But still, if he was right, perhaps someone took exception to his poking around and decided to take things into their own hands?"

"We'll keep it in mind, sir," Matt told him.

"I'm afraid I know nothing more about it," Shaw said, and Matt got the feeling he was regretting having said as much as he had.

"Thank you for your help, sir. Here's my card," Matt said. "If there is anything at all that occurs to you, please don't hesitate to let me know."

"I doubt very much that I'd be able to give you any further help. Chief Inspector."

"But should you hear anything, after all we are, as you're well aware, sir, investigating a murder here."

The man stared at him for a moment then said, "Yes, yes, of course, a terrible thing to happen. Now, I really must get on, I have work to do."

"Thank you very much for your time, Mr Shaw, and for your co-operation," Matt said, and he and Dilys left him standing there, watching as they wove their way out between the cars to join Dave and Sara. "That," Matt said to Dilys, "is a very worried man. I wonder if he had anything to do with Gladwin's death?"

"But why?" asked Dilys.

"I don't know. Maybe he knows more about the trafficking than he's admitting."

Matt and Dilys got into the car and Dilys started up the engine.

"Did you get anything out of him, sir?" Dave asked from the back.

"He says Gladwin mentioned something about people trafficking but that he didn't believe him, thought he was imagining it all. But he's definitely scared, and that could be useful. There's always the possibility that he knows more than he's telling. Another little talk with him might be productive once we've had a look at this iPad and gone through the cash box and notepads.

CHAPTER 10

Oliver Talbot took out his mobile, then paused. Should he phone Geraldine, or should he leave it? He wanted to see her and reassure himself that she was alright. When he'd bumped into her in the high street earlier in the day, she'd looked really strained. This business with Ivor was enough to get anyone down, but it had felt like more than that. He scrolled slowly down to her number and was about to press call, when his phone sprang into life. He looked at the screen. Great minds, he thought.

"Hi Gerry, I was just about to phone you. How are you?"

"Bearing up." He heard her take a deep breath and wondered what would come next. "Oliver, are you up for a drink at The Oaks? I feel in need of company."

He smiled. "Absolutely." He glanced at his watch. It was just before seven. "Shall I meet you there in half an hour?"

It sounded as if she'd just let out a deep breath. "That'd be perfect. See you there."

They arrived at almost the same time.

Geraldine and Oliver were of an age, in their early sixties, and they didn't look dissimilar, both tall, rather elegant and grey-haired, hers swept up into a French pleat, his receding from a high forehead. He clasped her arm as he pushed open the door of the pub and the noise of raised voices and laughter met them like a wall.

"Busy tonight," Oliver remarked. "Why don't we get drinks and then disappear into the snug. It probably won't be as crowded back there."

"Good idea," Geraldine said as they wove their way through the crowd to the bar.

Maggie Evans, the publican's wife, was busy taking orders. She looked up and saw them struggling to get to her. "Come on, folks," she said to a crowd of men and women clustered in a tight-packed group by the bar. "Spread out a bit, let people through, why don't you?" Some of them stepped aside and Maggie smiled as Geraldine and Oliver finally made it to the bar. "Evening," she said, "sorry about the crush."

"Good for business, though," said Oliver.

"Sure is," she said. "What can I get you?"

They ordered their drinks then, glasses in hand, made their way up a couple of shallow steps to the back of the pub. Through an archway they came to the snug where, much to their relief, only one of the tables was occupied. Oliver looked across at Geraldine as they settled in the comfortable armchairs.

"I won't beat about the bush," he said. "We both want to talk about the situation with Ivor. Have you heard anything from Fabia?"

"Only that Matt has been put in charge of the investigation."

"Good Lord," Oliver said. "That's a bit awkward – for him, I mean."

"I dare say he'll cope. He's pretty professional, is Matt."

"I'm sure, but…" He reached for his glass of red wine, took a sip, then changed the subject. "Has anyone spoken to you yet?"

"Well, we were all interviewed when that woman inspector was in charge. She had a car accident, apparently."

"Awkward for them. But that interview was pretty brief, in my case anyway."

"Fabia says we'll all be given a grilling by one or other of Matt's team."

Oliver raised his eyebrows. "Why do you put it like that?"

Geraldine glanced across at the only other two people in the room, but they were deep in conversation. She looked back at Oliver, who sat waiting for her to reply to his question. "All this activity, the questioning and the police presence, everything, it's taking me back to a time I've tried hard to forget." When he didn't comment, she lowered her voice and went on. "I've never told you about my son, have I?"

Oliver looked surprised. "I didn't know you had a son."

Geraldine gave a sad smile. "I think only Fabia knows, at least in Pontygwyn, but I suspect that Ivor had found out."

"Tell me about him," Oliver said, taking her hand in his.

"I was only married to Frank's father, John, for two years; in my twenties. He didn't want children and when I got pregnant, he wanted me to have an abortion, but I refused, so he walked out."

"What a bastard!" Oliver exclaimed.

Geraldine shrugged. "He was very young, a spoilt little rich boy who'd never learnt to take responsibility for his actions. Don't get me wrong, I loved him at the time, but I should have known how it would be."

"But you were young as well."

"True, but not in the same way that he was. I suppose nowadays he would have been called psychopathic, definitely a narcissist, and he just couldn't see beyond what he wanted or understand why he couldn't have it. He had no empathy at all. Anyway, when I went through with the pregnancy and had Frank, John cut me off completely, although his parents did agree to support Frank and me financially. That was just as well as I really don't know how we would have managed otherwise, because Frank was difficult from the start. As a small child he used to have the most awful temper tantrums, and when he was a bit older, and physically stronger, he'd become violent if he didn't get his own way."

Oliver looked appalled. "How on earth did you manage?"

"His grandmother, John's mother, arranged for him to go to a special school, which seemed to help, and he went through university okay. I thought we'd turned a corner." She smiled sadly. "It was fine for a while, and so good to have a more or less normal relationship with my son. He could be so sweet when he was in a good mood. We lived in London then and, after university, Frank got a job, with his grandfather's help, in the City." She took a shuddering breath. "But then, when Frank was twenty-six, everything changed. We had a neighbour, an elderly man who could be a bit difficult. He used to complain about Frank playing loud music and stuff like that."

"And what happened?" Oliver asked quietly, almost afraid to hear more.

"Frank broke into his house one night, tortured and killed him."

Oliver was too shocked to comment at first, then asked, "How? What did he do? No, no. Don't answer that. I'm sure you'd prefer not to go into details."

Geraldine gave him a smile of gratitude. "Thank you. If you really want to know you can Google it, Frank Beeching. It's all there. He maintained that he had every right to do what he did, was even proud of it, boasted about it. His grandfather employed a hotshot barrister to defend him and, after several psychiatric assessments, he was given a life sentence with a whole life order, which means he'll never be released. He's in Broadmoor."

Oliver put his arm round her shoulders and said, "And that's what you think Ivor had found out?"

"Yes."

For a moment they sat in silence then Geraldine looked up at him and the mixture of desolation and fear in her eyes shocked him.

"What is it?" he asked, and when she didn't answer he said, "Look, Gerry darling, I care about you, you know that." She nodded. "And as far as I'm concerned you can tell me anything you like, and it will make no difference. So, tell me what's worrying you. Maybe I can help."

Matt arrived home at half past eight, looking exhausted. Fabia managed to keep all the questions boiling around in her mind to herself until they were sitting down in front of the fire. As Matt sat on the hearthrug, his back against the sofa, Fabia sat behind him and began to massage the tension out of his neck and shoulders.

"Before I forget," Fabia told him, "Cath says Sally came to the vicarage in a real state earlier today."

"Oh dear. What was all that about?"

"Basically, panicking that Ellis is responsible for Ivor's death and that he'll go for Luke next. She overheard her husband telling someone it was good riddance and the end of Ivor's snooping. Apparently, Ellis is a gambler and she thinks Ivor might have found out about it. He's lost a lot of money and she's had to take more hours at the surgery to make up the shortfall. Sally told Cath about the affair between her and Luke, but we knew about that already. The thing is, she's afraid Ellis knows something. She says he would kill her, or Luke, if he does."

"He really is a nasty piece of work, but I'm not sure he's capable of killing."

"Nor me, but there's always a first time. Cath tried to persuade Sally to come and talk to you, but she refused. But she did say Cath could pass it all on to me. She's afraid he'll take her phone away and she won't have any contact with people."

"If I need to speak to her, officially, he's going to have to put up with it, stupid man."

"Anyway, tell me about your day," Fabia said. But before Matt could say anything, Fabia's mobile sprang into life. "Sometimes I hate the person who invented mobile phones," Fabia muttered as she answered it.

"Hallo, Gerry, how are you feeling? ... Matt? Yes, he is..."

She held the phone out to Matt, frowning. "She wants to speak to you." Then, her voice lowered, she added, "She doesn't sound too good."

"Geraldine," Matt said, "what can I do for you?"

Fabia couldn't hear Geraldine's side of the conversation, but it didn't take long for her to realise that she was asking to come around. Much as she liked her friend, her heart sank. She'd been about to suggest they should get an early night, but when Matt said, "Oliver did? Right ... Of course, come now, we're both here ... We'll see you in a few minutes," she resigned herself to the fact that wouldn't be happening.

Matt handed her phone back. "You're right," he said, "she sounded really stressed. She's coming round. I wonder what's up?"

"She didn't say." Fabia got up. "I'm going to go and get us a whisky each, I think we might need it."

When she got back, carrying two generously filled tumblers, Matt told her, "Apparently Oliver insisted she should come and talk to us."

"That's interesting."

"Why?" Matt asked.

"Well, I suggested she tell him... Look, Matt, there's something you need to know before Gerry arrives."

But Fabia didn't have time to go on, as the doorbell rang at that moment.

When Fabia opened the door to Geraldine, she was shocked to see how pale she was. Her usually neat and elegant appearance was somehow diminished, there were deep shadows under her eyes and her shoulders were hunched with tension.

"Come in, love," she said, drawing her friend into the hall and giving her a hug. "Matt's in the sitting room. Can I get you a drink?"

"No, thank you, Fabia – actually, yes, could I have a glass of water?"

"Of course." When Fabia got back, Geraldine was sitting down by the fire, holding her hands out to its warmth.

Matt looked up as she came in. "We waited for you," he said, smiling.

Fabia settled herself next to him, glanced his way and he gave her a little nod, so she turned to Geraldine and asked, "Do you want to tell us what the trouble is, Gerry?"

Geraldine took a deep, shuddering breath. "The thing is, when I spoke to you yesterday, Fabia, I wanted to tell you, but I couldn't bring myself to do so. You see, I was there, in the theatre, when Ivor was killed."

Fabia gave Matt a startled glance, but neither said anything for a moment, then Matt sat forward in his chair. "Hold on, Geraldine, are you sure you want to speak to us about this now? Wouldn't it be better to make it official?"

"No, no!" There was panic in her voice. "Please let me just tell you what happened, Matt. After that you can do what you have to."

"Okay." Matt said, but he didn't sound happy.

Fabia put a hand on Matt's knee as if she was trying to restrain his reaction. She took over. "Gerry, I haven't had a chance to tell Matt about Frank yet.

Would you like me to tell him now, before you go on?"

Geraldine glanced from Fabia to Matt and back again. "I... yes, if you would."

Quickly Fabia gave Matt an account of Geraldine's marriage, Frank's birth, his difficult behaviour and the final tragedy of the murder and imprisonment. Matt showed little reaction and Geraldine sat silent, her arms hugging her body as she gazed at the flames licking around the logs in the fire. When Fabia came to a halt, Matt turned to Geraldine, sympathy in his eyes.

"I'm sorry to hear what a dreadful time you've had." His voice was gentle, then he added, more firmly, "Perhaps you could tell us, now, how come you were there when Ivor was killed."

"I'd lost a bracelet I'm very fond of. It's one of the few presents Frank ever gave me, when he was going through a good patch, a silver bangle. I thought I might have dropped it in the dressing room, so I went to look for it."

"You had a key?" Matt asked.

"Yes. Jean's, I'd forgotten to give it back to her. I was searching around when I heard someone come in and go on to the stage. They were very quiet, but the stage door has a bit of a creak. I went to the door and opened it a crack, heard whoever it was going up the ladder to the gantry, their shoes made a squeak on some of the metal rungs. I didn't let on that I was there because I thought it might be Ivor, and I really didn't want to face him after the remarks he'd made."

"What remarks?"

Fabia opened her mouth to respond to this, but Matt held up a hand and they both waited for Geraldine to reply to his question.

"He'd been winding me up about Frank. I could tell he'd found out about him. He actually mentioned him by name the other day. I think he was going to suggest that I – oh, I don't know – do something or other for him, as a favour, or he'd tell everyone. This was last Saturday. I'd been avoiding him ever since. So, you can understand why I didn't want to get caught by him when no-one else was around. I just stayed there, waiting, and a few minutes later I heard the stage door open again, this person wasn't so quiet, just strode past, onto the stage, and I heard them go up the ladder as well. A few moments later I heard a murmur of voices, then some shouting and banging noises followed by an enormous crash." Geraldine gazed across at them, tears filling her eyes. She gulped them back. "I'm so, so sorry, Matt. I just panicked and ran for it. I know I shouldn't have. That I should have stayed to find out what had happened, but I – well – I just didn't."

"Can you say exactly what time this was?" Matt asked.

"It must have been about quarter past three, because it was half past when I got home. I remember looking at the kitchen clock and being surprised it wasn't later than that. It felt like ages since I'd gone out."

Matt leant forward in his chair, his elbows on his knees. "Geraldine, I want you to go back in your mind to when you were listening behind that door."

"Okay." She closed her eyes in concentration and put her hands up to her face.

111

"The second person you heard could have been Ivor," Matt suggested. "That person made no effort to conceal their presence."

"None at all," she said. "I thought at the time that it was a man, that's why I stayed where I was."

"The first person you think you heard, was there any indication at all whether it was a man or a woman?"

She didn't respond immediately, simply sat with her eyes closed and her hands cradling her cheeks. Matt and Fabia waited in silence, neither wanting to interrupt her train of thought. The seconds ticked by. Fabia shifted, opened her mouth to speak, then changed her mind. Best to let Geraldine take her time.

At last she spoke. "I can't be sure. Like I said, the first person was very quiet. When it comes to the voices, they were very low, but I have a feeling they were both male." Then she shook her head. "But I can't be sure."

CHAPTER 11

Dilys and Matt met up in his office very early on Friday morning before going to join the rest of the team at the theatre. He wanted to run through a mind map Fabia had made of all the personalities involved. Neither of them had wanted to discuss the map in front of everyone else, particularly not Sharon Pugh who, they were both sure, wouldn't have any time for such activities, particularly as the idea came from Fabia.

"I'm not sure what her problem is with Fabia," Dilys said to Matt, "but she definitely has one. When I happened to mention that you would be running something past Fabia when you got home – can't remember exactly what it was, but it was something pretty innocuous, otherwise I wouldn't have said anything – anyway, she stared at me and said, 'That's not very professional, is it?' I pointed out that Fabia had been a superintendent back in the day, and that she was very discreet, but she still gave me one of those sour looks. She's the only one of the team that I have trouble with."

"Give her time," Matt said. "It's difficult being the newbie in a group that's been working together for a while."

"But Sara's fitted in okay."

"Granted, but we're all different, give Sharon time."

Dilys shrugged and said, "Okay, but I just wish we could have Chloe back."

"But she's so enjoying her family liaison work in Cardiff."

"I know." Dilys was silent for a moment, then said in a rush, "I'm not being funny, sir, but I do find Sharon's attitude disruptive. Would it be okay with you if I had a word? I can try to find out what's bugging her."

"I trust your judgement on that, Dilys. Just keep me posted."

"Will do."

Clearing his desk of its usual clutter, Matt unrolled the A2-sized piece of paper with its colourful lines and scribbled comments in Fabia's distinctive handwriting. He weighted each corner down then they bent to study what she had done.

"Okay. So far, I think we can rule out several of these people," Matt said, "or put them in an improbable list. We've just got to sort out whose motive we think is the strongest, and there could be reasons we don't even know about yet."

"Given that practically every one of them has said he was nosy as hell, and complained about it," Dilys said, unable to keep the distaste out of her voice, "I should think there'll be a tidy number of motives to choose from."

Matt pointed to one name in the pattern. "Geraldine Humphries came around to speak to Fabia and me last night." He told Dilys what Geraldine had told them. "I'm not sure it gives her a strong enough motive to have killed him, but what she told us about hearing someone else, well, it could all be made up. I realise it's unlikely, but there's no real strength needed to stamp on the hands of someone going down a ladder."

"What does Fabia think?"

"It's difficult for her. Geraldine's a close friend. But she did try to look at it objectively and she's pretty sure that what we were told was the truth."

Dilys nodded. "But at least, if she's telling the truth, it gives us a definite time of death. When we get back to the green room, I'll get Sara to trawl through all the interviews so far to check on alibis." She pointed to another name. "If you're thinking in terms of it being a woman, how about her?"

"Sally Cadogan?" Matt looked thoughtful. "She has a stronger motive, I think, than Geraldine."

"Because of the affair with Luke Melville?" asked Dilys.

"Yes. She was absolutely terrified Ivor would tell her husband about it." Or it could be to do with this trafficking Luke's been investigating, Matt thought. If he was going to talk to Dilys about Luke's undercover work, this would be the time to do it, when they wouldn't be interrupted. He came to a decision.

"I know, but there's more" he said, and went on to tell her what Luke had told him and Fabia.

"What a bloody cheek, not telling you what he was up to," she exclaimed.

"My thoughts entirely. Luke knows he's seriously screwed up by starting the affair with Sally, but nothing can be done about that now. This is not the time to end it, what with all this going on around them. And this trafficking he's investigating, if Ivor found out who's behind it – and given his constant snooping and listening at doors, he might have – that's a pretty strong motive for the people behind the trafficking to get rid of him. They'd not be worried about disposing of someone who was likely to blow the whole thing wide open. On the other hand, maybe he was involved – a case of thieves falling out."

"Something just occurred to me," Dilys said, then added, "Nah, maybe not."

"What?"

"Well, you know at the garage there were all those white vans available for hire, they'd be perfect for transporting people from port to hotel, from hotel to wherever they were going to be forced to work. Can't see out, can't see in. If Ivor Gladwin was involved, maybe that's how. What do you think?"

"It's worth investigating," Matt said, but he sounded doubtful. "Maybe send some of the SOCO team to have a good look through them."

She went back to Luke. "What info has he turned up?"

"He's not done as well as he'd hoped," Matt said, "probably because falling for Sally caused him to take his eye off the ball."

"I should say so," Dilys said, not bothering to keep the scorn out of her voice. "Did he mention anyone else he suspects?"

"No, just those two I mentioned before." Matt pointed to the names on the mind map.

"Hum," said Dilys. "I'm not sure about that one. And why this one?"

For a few minutes they discussed the merits of each person Luke Melville had mentioned, and then they widened out the field a little. But by the time they'd been through the whole mind map, neither of them felt they were that much further on.

"So, what next, sir?" Dilys asked, getting up from her chair as she glanced at her watch. "It's half nine."

Matt rolled up the map. "Now we get back to the green room and find out what the others have turned up from their interviews. And let's hope Aidan's going to have some information from Gladwin's phone and iPad. I've got hopes for both devices."

On the way back to Pontygwyn, Matt's mobile rang. It was Tom Watkins. Matt put it on speakerphone.

"Are you at the theatre, Tom?"

"Yes, sir. I've had a message from Mr Aubrey, he wants to speak to you."

"Did he say what about specifically?"

"No," Tom told him. "He came to the stage door first thing asking for you. He seemed quite agitated, says it's important, that he's worried about something he's found out."

"He didn't say what?"

"No, sir."

"Okay. Dilys and I are on our way to Pontygwyn now. Give me his address, we'll go straight there. Could you let him know we're on our way?"

"Will do, sir. I'll text you the address."

* * *

Sebastian and Jean Aubrey lived in a comfortable semi-detached house in Church Road with a view of the allotments which, on their far side, gave on to the back of the gardens in Morwydden Lane, including Fabia's. Matt and Dilys arrived outside the neatly paved front garden, with its rigidly clipped box hedge, just before half past ten. They parked and walked along to knock on the front door.

It was opened by Sebastian Aubrey, as smart and dapper as ever in blazer and cravat, looking like a character from a 1950s comedy. "Thank you so much for coming so promptly," he said as he led them through to a sitting room where the slightly old-fashioned décor was neat and regimented, just like the front garden.

Sebastian's wife, Jean, rose from an armchair as they came in. "Hallo, Matt," she said, "What a terrible business this is. Please, sit down. Would you like some coffee?"

"Don't worry about us," Matt said, "we had some before leaving the station." He introduced Dilys and then decided to get down to business immediately. He had no time to waste. "My colleague said you were worried about something you'd found out. Would you like to tell me about it?"

"It's, um, rather awkward," Aubrey said, with a quick glance at his wife, but she remained silent. "If it wasn't for this dreadful murder, I probably would have decided to deal with it internally, so to speak, but now, with this happening and with the police all over… Obviously I realise why you're so involved now, who wouldn't? But this might be relevant, and I don't think I can just leave it, not now."

Jean Aubrey gave her husband a tight little smile. "Sebastian, darling, you're waffling. Get to the point."

"Sorry, dear." He gave Matt a rueful look. "Ivor's death has got us all a bit off balance."

"That's entirely understandable," Matt said.

"Perhaps it would be best if I gave you a bit of background first. I'm sure you know all about the renovation of the Little Theatre, all the fundraising we had to do, the lottery grant, etc. When it really took off, we had to create an official body to run the place, a committee and trustees, patron, etc. I am chairman of the trustees, and also involved, as you know, in directing some of the performances and, as a committee, we invite other performers, such as male voice choirs from all over Wales, some BBC quiz shows, other individual performers, and we were very pleased to have–"

His wife leant forward and patted his knee. "Darling, get to the point."

"Yes, sorry. Anyway, there are several other people you may know on the committee." He took a deep breath. "Including Ellis Cadogan, who is our treasurer. He trained as an accountant before he got into music, so we thought he would be a suitable choice. When I went down to the theatre on Sunday it was because I wanted to have a look at the accounts, bank statements, etc. Although we do our banking online, I do make sure I have hard copies in my little office at the theatre. I wanted to check everything, so

I took my laptop and was planning to sit down and have a good trawl through."

"Why did you decide to do this?" Matt asked.

Aubrey took a deep breath. "I'm afraid I'd noticed a few unexplained entries in the statements. The first one was about a month ago, a sum of five thousand pounds was deposited. Three weeks later there was another deposit, this time of four thousand. I did get on to Ellis about those two and he told me they were anonymous donations from someone whose family would not approve of their giving money to the theatre, so he'd promised to keep their name out of it. Now, don't get me wrong, I'm not complaining, we could do with the money, and donations do come in occasionally from people who want to support the theatre. The problem is, there were also some unexplained withdrawals, one of three hundred and one of four hundred, but then there was another deposit, this time of eight thousand pounds."

Matt frowned. "Who are the signatories on the bank account?"

"On this particular account, the general one, myself and Ellis Cadogan, and we both have access to the online banking. Another account, which is used solely for repairs and decoration, hasn't shown any such anomalies."

"And the signatories on that one?"

"Ellis and Eve Kemble's husband, Trevor, who used to be a builder before he started his present business. Anyway, he looks after the fabric of the building for us and needs access to an account when he's buying materials. He also buys the paint for the scenery, stuff like that."

"At what point did you tackle your treasurer about the further activity on the account?" Matt asked.

Aubrey reddened a little, obviously embarrassed, and when Matt glanced at Jean Aubrey, he noticed she was frowning and tight-lipped.

"I… er… I'm afraid I haven't done so yet," Aubrey went on. "I only noticed the withdrawals and the latest deposit in the last week. I usually leave the money side to Ellis. I'm sure the withdrawals would have been to pay bills, such as the printers for posters and programmes, and advertising material, that sort of thing. I was going to tackle Ellis but, what with Ivor's death and everything that's been going on, I haven't done so yet."

"Sir, could I?" Dilys said.

Matt nodded.

"Where exactly is the account held?"

"At Lloyds in Pontygwyn," Aubrey told her.

"And have you contacted them about your concerns?" she asked.

"Well," – Aubrey looked slightly embarrassed – "I didn't want to make a fuss, but I did have a private word with the manager, who's a friend of mine. I met him last week at a Rotary Club dinner and spoke to him then, unofficially. I really didn't want any publicity, it would be so bad for the theatre, for all of us. But when he heard about Ivor's death, he phoned me and urged me to speak to you."

Matt leant forward in his seat. "Mr Aubrey, Sebastian," he said, "are you suggesting that the unusual activity on the account could have something to do with Mr Gladwin's death? Maybe that he found out who was making these deposits and tackled them about it?"

"The thing is," Aubrey said, not giving Matt a direct answer to his question, "it worries me that Ellis wouldn't be straight with me. And it had occurred to me that someone might be using the theatre account to launder money made from criminal activity."

"What gave you that idea?" Matt asked, he didn't think this was something that would occur to many people.

"I worked in insurance, Chief Inspector, I used to deal with this sort of thing all the time."

"I understand. And you believe Ivor Gladwin knew about this?"

"No, no, well, maybe. I did wonder if he found out something about it and did what he so often did. Had a go, you know, teased whoever it was, maybe Ellis, and hinted that he was aware of it. That's all I have to tell you, really, but I thought you ought to know."

"If you'd be so kind as to let me have the bank statements, or copies, that would be helpful," Matt said.

"I can print some copies for you now. It won't take long."

* * *

Ten minutes later they left the house in Church Road, with an envelope full of the paperwork Sebastian Aubrey had printed out for them.

"Let's have a careful look at these, then sort out an interview with Ellis Cadogan, sooner rather than later," Matt said. "It's not looking good for him, but I suppose there could be a rational explanation."

Dilys looked sceptical but didn't comment.

CHAPTER 12

Matt and Dilys finally ran Ellis Cadogan to ground late that morning in his office at the music shop in Newport. A young assistant, curiosity oozing from every pore, showed them in, and was briskly dismissed by Ellis. "And close the door behind you," he barked at him. The door was nearly, but not quite, slammed.

Cadogan sat back down at his desk, waved a hand at the couple of chairs opposite, saying coolly, "You may as well sit down," and gazed at them over his steel-rimmed glasses. "So, what do you want from me this time?" he demanded.

"First of all," Matt said, "did you receive a call from Ivor Gladwin asking for the key to the theatre on Saturday afternoon?"

Cadogan frowned, as though he was making an effort to remember, then said, "Yes, I did, I told him it was in the usual place."

"And that would be?"

"On a hook in the electricity metre box by the stage door."

"And did you tell anyone else that he'd asked for it?" Dilys queried.

"No, of course not." The response came a little too quickly, but they let it go.

Matt changed the subject. "Can you confirm that you are treasurer for the committee that runs the Little Theatre?"

"I am."

"And you are one of the two signatories on the main bank account which is held with Lloyds in Pontygwyn."

"I am," he said again, showing no emotion whatever.

"Then perhaps you could assist us with something," Matt said.

Dilys bent to take some papers out of a briefcase she'd placed by her chair. She passed three sheets of paper across the desk to Cadogan.

"These are copies of some of the bank statements from that account. Please look at the entries highlighted on each page," Matt requested and sat waiting while Cadogan pulled the sheets towards him and spent some time studying them. He made no comment and Matt got the impression he was playing for time.

"Can you explain these deposits?" Matt asked after the silence had dragged on for some time. "They are for quite large sums."

"I explained it all to Sebastian when he asked me about them."

"I gather you told him they were anonymous donations. Who is this benefactor?"

"I'm afraid I can't tell you that. A condition of the donations was that they should remain anonymous." He paused, then looked straight at Matt as if trying to convince him of what he said. "It was something to do with not wanting their family to find out where they were putting their money, they're very religious and don't approve of theatres and the like."

Matt decided not to push for the names at the moment. "There are also some unexplained withdrawals, here and here." He pointed to them. "Can you explain those?"

Cadogan seemed to relax. "That's easy. They were expenses incurred in advertising events at the theatre, adverts in the local press, stuff like that."

"They seem very reasonable," Matt pointed out. "I thought advertising in the Western Mail and the Argus could be quite expensive nowadays."

Cadogan shrugged. "They give me a good rate."

"Perhaps you could let me have the paperwork involved, you must have a record of some kind, receipts, that sort of thing."

Matt noticed his face had paled, but he waved an airy hand. "Of course, I can have a look if you insist."

"I do," said Matt firmly.

"Have you asked Sebastian Aubrey about all this?" Cadogan asked, his tone sullen.

"We have." But Matt didn't tell him that it was Aubrey who'd pointed out the transactions.

"And how did you get hold of these statements?" He flicked a contemptuous finger at the papers in front of him.

"They were handed to us by Mr Aubrey as part of the investigation into Ivor Gladwin's death."

Cadogan sat chewing at his bottom lip, still staring across at Matt. "I have no idea why Sebastian has questioned these deposits."

"And withdrawals. He tells us he has no knowledge of them."

"Then he's lying."

"I don't think so, sir." Matt sat forward in his chair. "Look, Mr Cadogan, I can insist that you tell us the source of these donations and, if you refuse, I can arrest you on the grounds that you're obstructing the investigation. If I do so we will be able to get access to your phone and to other devices, such as laptops, that you may use. I do not want to do that at the moment, but I'm willing to if I have to. So, I'll ask you again, is there anything more you can tell me about these deposits?"

Cadogan stared across at him, then he seemed to sag. "Look, I'll be honest with you—"

"That would be a very good idea," said Matt, his voice hard.

"I'm in a very difficult position here. If I tell anyone at all, and that was made very clear by the donor, the theatre loses the lot. Can you give me some time? I'll go back to them and explain the situation, see what I can do."

Dilys sat forward in her seat. "Has it occurred to you, Mr Cadogan, that this person could be making these donations in order to launder money from criminal activities?"

"Absolutely not." The response was a little too quick. "Anyway, the sums are too small for that to be the case."

"Did Ivor Gladwin know about this?" she asked.

"What? Ivor?" There was a note of panic in his voice. "No, of course not."

"Are you sure?"

"Look, what is this?" What little colour that remained in his face had drained away. "Are you accusing me of having something to do with Ivor's death?"

"Not at the moment, no," Matt said. "But we are not ruling it out."

As Cadogan sat as if stupefied, Matt decided it would be a good idea to end the interview there, give the man time to mull over what had been said. He leant forward and gathered up the copies of the bank statements. "We'll leave it at that for now, Mr Cadogan, but we'll be questioning you further. Your attitude could be called withholding evidence, we could also call it impeding the police in the pursuance of their duty. Both are indictable offences. I would like you to think about that. Good day to you."

Cadogan spluttered and protested as they left the room. Just outside, Matt stopped as if to tie his shoelace and glanced back through the still open door. He saw Cadogan bring out his mobile and start tapping away at it and wondered who he was contacting. When he saw Matt watching him, he leapt up and slammed the door shut.

As he and Dilys walked quickly through the shop and out to the street, Matt said, "That's a frightened man. I think we need to pass all this on to Luke Melville."

Dilys gave him a sharp look. "That had occurred to me."

"I'll give him a ring on the way back to the theatre."

Matt was pleased to get through to Luke on his first try. He put it on speakerphone so that Dilys could hear what was said and told him about the deposits in the theatre account and about their interviews with Sebastian Aubrey and Cadogan.

"At the moment I've gone along with his determination to keep the so-called donors anonymous, but I've told him I won't wait long. I just left him to stew for a bit, thought I'd get more information out of him that way," Matt said.

"I suppose," said Luke, not sounding particularly happy with this.

"There is, of course, no reason why you shouldn't have a go at him," Matt pointed out, "but that would blow your cover."

"True," Luke admitted, "but do you remember the people I suggested might be involved? This rather links up with them, doesn't it?"

"It does, doesn't it? Why don't you drop into the station and we can discuss tactics."

"Will do. Would five this afternoon be okay for you?"

"Yes, I should be back from the theatre incident room by then. I'll see you later." Matt cut off the call and glanced at Dilys.

"This is getting interesting," she said.

Matt grinned at her. "You could say that."

* * *

When they got back to the incident room there was news about the cash box found in Ivor Gladwin's office. It had been handed over to one of the SOCO team and, having prized it open, they'd found an interesting collection of items. There were several newspaper reports of court cases, all of which were relevant to people involved in the pantomime. Most of them were from the Western Mail, although some were from one or other of the nationals. There was one about the prosecution of Oliver Talbot's erstwhile partner in the firm of solicitors; several were about Geraldine's son, Frank. There was one particularly interesting report about two Romanian women who had gone to the Cardiff police with a story about being trafficked, ending with an appeal for information. And there was another about someone being prosecuted for shoplifting. There was also a small notebook with dates and two columns marked 'out' and 'in', but this remained a mystery to them.

"Why on earth did he make copies of the actual newspaper reports?" Matt remarked to Dilys. "You'd have thought in this day and age he'd just check online."

"I know, sir. It's all a bit obsessive, isn't it?"

"Gives me the creeps. This one here" – Matt indicated the one about the two women – "that's interesting, we must follow up on it, and the shoplifting. What else have we got?"

"There are some photos," Dilys told him. "Here again, he's printed them out, whereas you would have thought he'd just store them in his phone."

"Maybe he used an actual camera."

"Do you think?" Dilys didn't sound as if she thought this was likely. "Maybe he printed them out because he was going to delete them from his phone."

"Could be," Matt said. He was busy leafing through the photos. "These are all of Luke and Sally.

My God, Luke took risks, stupid man. These are of Peony Smith, mainly on her own. He certainly liked to concentrate on the more curvy aspects of her body. What a nasty piece of work he was. Then there are a few of Oliver and Geraldine, and there are these three. Why on earth would he take them?"

Dilys took them from him. Both were of a car, it looked like a high-end Mercedes, parked in the high street. In one the driver was in the driving seat, although it wasn't easy to make out who it was.

"It looks like a man," Dilys said, "but hard to recognise."

In the other two photos the car was unoccupied. The number plate was obscured in two of them, but in one the first two letters and following two numbers were decipherable.

"Let's get this checked out. It'd be interesting to find out who owns this car. It might explain why he took them."

But when the information came back, they were none the wiser. There didn't seem to be any good reason for Ivor to have kept these photos.

"Never mind," Matt said, "maybe some reason will turn up."

* * *

Ever since Sally had come around on Thursday morning, Cath had been worrying about her. She kept see-sawing between following up on things herself and leaving it to Matt. Fabia had said she'd pass on her concerns to Matt, so Cath thought that she should let him deal with it. But then she came back to the fact she was Sally's vicar. Sally sang in the church choir, and she was a friend as well. Cath felt she had a pastoral duty to keep an eye on her, particularly given Ellis's behaviour, but she didn't want to bump into him should she go round. Back and forth it went, and by the middle of Friday afternoon she'd still not come to any decision.

But surely Ellis would still be at work, he'd not be home until six at the earliest. Cath knew that Sally didn't work on Friday afternoons so she should be at home and on her own. She glanced at her watch. It was four o'clock. This would be the perfect opportunity to go and check up on her? Should she phone first? No, best not as Sally might try to put her off. And if by chance Ellis was at home, she could just make some excuse. She'd take a cookery book Sally had mentioned wanting to borrow a while ago, that'd be a good cover. Cath smiled at herself, what an awful pun.

She went to the kitchen and took the book from the shelf, popped it in a carrier bag and shut her cat, Mungo, inside, just in case people started letting off fireworks yet again. Four days after Firework Night and they were still plaguing his life, poor Mungo.

When she arrived at the Cadogans' front door she was surprised to find it ajar. She pushed it open and called, "Sally?"

The stairs rose up to the next floor to her left, and in a corner by the front door was a curled wooden hat-stand draped with coats. A pair of Wellington boots was stacked neatly under it. She was facing a passageway which led to the back of the house, a closed door at the end, and to her right was another door, also closed. Cath knew that the kitchen was at the end of the passageway and, as she stood there hesitating, she heard a muffled sound, as of an animal in distress, coming from the direction of the kitchen. She frowned and her heart set up a tattoo of alarm.

"Sally?" she called again as she made her way to the kitchen. When she pushed the door open, she nearly tripped over a shopping bag that was spilling its contents on to the floor. Then cold shock hit her at the sight that met her eyes.

Ellis was sprawled across the floor, face down, and protruding from his side was the shaft of a knife. Blood had oozed from the wound and pooled on the floor. In the corner of the room Sally crouched, her hands held out in front of her, almost in a gesture of supplication. One hand was blood stained. She was whimpering and trembling violently.

Cath glanced at her but said nothing. Her nurse's training from long ago asserted itself and she strode forward, searched for a pulse in Ellis's neck. There was none. She hadn't thought there would be.

"Sally, what happened here?" she asked, her voice soft and urgent.

Sally shook her head and continued to whimper, then stuttered out, "I– I– found– I found–" then she began to sob hysterically.

Cath went over and pulled Sally's heaving body against her, then dived in her pocket for her mobile phone and dialled 999. When the calm voice responded she identified herself, gave as quick an explanation as she could, asked for an ambulance and the police, and told the person on the line she would wait until they arrived. Immediately she'd ended the call she scrolled down to another number and punched it in. A wave of relief hit her as the call was answered.

"Matt, thank God, it's Cath. I'm at Sally Cadogan's house and–" She took a shuddering breath, trying to keep calm. "Ellis is dead. He's been stabbed."

"What? Have you phoned the emergency services?"

"They're on their way, ambulance and police."

"Is Sally there with you?"

"Yes, she's very distressed."

"Is there anyone else in the house?"

"No, I don't think so," Cath said, trying to keep her voice steady. "I haven't been upstairs. The front door was open. And, Matt, I'm pretty sure this wasn't self-inflicted."

"Stay where you are, Cath. I'm still at the theatre. I'll be with you in five minutes," he said and cut off the call.

* * *

When Cath's call came through only Tom and Dilys were with Matt in the green room.

"Was that the vicar, sir?" Tom asked.

"What's going on, sir?" Dilys asked, eyes wide.

"Yes, that was the vicar, Cath Temple," he told them. "She's at the Cadogans' and she says Ellis has been stabbed. He's dead."

"Christ!" Tom exclaimed.

"Not suicide then?" Dilys asked.

"Cath says it doesn't look like it."

"Does she know who stabbed him?" Dilys asked as she shrugged on her coat and grabbed the car keys.

"No. She's with Sally but she doesn't think there's anyone else in the house. The ambulance and our lot are on their way. We'll get around there now."

They ran out to the car park and, as she got into the driver's seat, Dilys took out the blue light and slapped it on the car roof. Siren blaring, they drove down the high street at speed as other motorists pulled aside to make way. As they drove, Matt called through to the station and checked what was happening. He asked for a SOCO team to be on-site as soon as possible, and for Dr Curtis, the police surgeon, to be notified. After that he texted Luke and told him he couldn't make their meeting, but he didn't tell him why. The last thing he wanted was Luke pitching up on Sally's doorstep to find out what was going on.

Within five minutes they were turning into Parc Road and drawing up outside the house. Tom opened the boot and took out plastic boots to cover their shoes and all three of them pulled on disposable gloves. When they got to the front door, Matt called, "Cath, are you there?"

The door at the end of the passageway opened and Cath stood there, looking white as a sheet but calm. Matt and Dilys made their way towards her, leaving Tom, at Matt's instruction, to stand guard at the front door.

"Thank God you've come," Cath said, her voice shaking a little. "In here, he's in the kitchen. I've taken Sally into the sitting room. She's very upset, as you can imagine."

She turned to go back into the kitchen, but Matt clasped her arm, stopped her going any further. "Best let us go through, but first, did she give you any idea of what happened here?"

"No. All she's said was that she found him. She keeps repeating it, over and over."

"How long is it since you dialled 999?"

"Just before I phoned you. I actually got here about ten, fifteen minutes ago. It feels like much longer. You see, Sally came round to see me on Thursday, she was very upset about... about Ivor and everything."

Matt was sure she'd changed her mind about what she was going to say at the last minute, but he didn't comment as she went on.

"I decided to pop round and check up on her, and this is what I found."

"I think it'd be best if you go and sit with her," Matt said. "We'll wait for the team to arrive."

Cath went into the sitting room without another word as Matt and Dilys went through to the kitchen to find Ellis Cadogan's body lying face down on the floor. A few feet away from the body was a broken mug, smashed into shards, and just inside the door was a shopping bag that had obviously been dropped where it lay. Without touching anything, Matt crouched down to look more closely at the body. A knife protruded from Ellis's left side, about fifteen centimetres below his armpit. The shaft of the knife was distinctive, hard black plastic with a flat stainless-steel disc at the end and three steel rivets evenly spaced along the length of the handle. Blood had pooled on the floor below the wound, but not as much as Matt would have expected, although there were some marks on the floor as if someone had stepped in the blood. He stood up and looked around. On the work surface, just by the cooker, was a knife block and several knives with similar handles protruded from it. There was one empty space.

Dilys followed his gaze. "Ah," she said, but made no other comment.

Into the silence came the wailing of sirens getting closer. The first vehicle to arrive was an ambulance and, a moment later, two green-uniformed paramedics strode into the room.

Matt introduced himself. "I'm afraid there's no chance of survival. The person who found him used to be an A&E nurse and she's checked, so have I. But you'd better do what you have to do anyway."

They nodded and crouched down to inspect the body, making sure they didn't touch the knife while doing so. It wasn't long before the kitchen was full of people in white overalls. Matt and Dilys, meanwhile, had retreated to the sitting room where Cath was sitting with Sally.

Matt sat down opposite them and leant forward in his chair. "Sally." She didn't react at first. "Sally," he said again, and this time she looked up at him and recognition dawned slowly in her face.

"Oh, it's you," she said.

"Can you tell us what happened?" he asked gently.

She didn't respond. Cath intervened. "Sally, tell Matt what you've told me."

"I– I got back from work. I don't know what time it was. I think – yes – the front door was open. I thought Ellis had just forgotten – oh my God, Ellis!" She began to shake uncontrollably. Cath put an arm round her and pulled her close to her body. Matt knew he ought to stop her but couldn't bring himself to do so.

"Sally, Sally. You're safe. I'm here," Cath said quietly, then turned to Matt. "Can we get her a glass of water?"

Dilys said, "Leave it to me," and disappeared into the hall.

Cath turned back to Sally. "It's best if you try to answer Matt's questions, Sally," she said.

Gradually the shaking diminished. Dilys returned with a small glass filled with water. "I found this in the bathroom," she said, and handed it to Sally who gulped down half of the contents.

"You found the front door open?" Matt prompted.

"Yes, which isn't like him. He's always going on about security. I heard something as I came in, footsteps or something."

"Footsteps?" Matt said. "Where?"

"I think it was out the back, like someone running. It could have been anyone, I don't know. I was scared, because of the door being open, so I crept along the hall to the kitchen, and when I got there, Ellis was lying..."

She sat shaking her head as if denying what she'd seen.

After a moment, Matt asked, "What did you do then?"

"I think I knelt down and touched him. I must have, because then I realised – realised I had blood – oh God – it was horrible." She began to cry in great, heaving sobs.

Cath, still with her arm round Sally's shoulders, gave Matt a glance of appeal, as if asking him to stop. He nodded, got up and indicated to Dilys that she should follow him. They both went out into the hall.

"If she's telling the truth and she didn't kill him," he said, keeping his voice very low, "when she says she heard someone running, it could have been the murderer. Sorry, statement of the obvious. Get Tom and ask him to investigate ways out of the garden from the back. This house is semi-detached and I think there's a gate through to a narrow area at the side, and there's an alleyway which goes all the way round to the church end of Morwydden Lane, so far as I can remember. Obviously, the SOCOs will be going over the garden as well as the house. They'll need to get a move on because it's going to be dark soon."

"And what do we do about Mrs Cadogan?" Dilys asked.

"I'm going to ask Cath to take her back to the vicarage. We can go on with our questioning later, but I don't think she's in any fit state to make much sense at the moment."

Dilys went out to speak to Tom, and Matt went back into the sitting room. In a few minutes he'd arranged for Dilys to drive Cath and Sally to the vicarage, then he went back into the house.

CHAPTER 13

On Saturday afternoon Matt sat with his team in the green room at the theatre and brought them up to date.

"Okay, folks, this is what we've got so far on Ellis Cadogan. The victim's wife, Sally Cadogan, is adamant she did not stab him. Obviously, we can't take her word for it, but for now we can't push her too hard. She's been sedated by her doctor and I don't think questioning her will produce much that makes sense for the next twenty-four hours. We're aware that her husband was a demanding person, into controlling her every move, which could be called a motive."

"A pretty strong one, I'd say," Dilys pointed out.

"I don't know, she could have tried standing up for herself," Sharon said.

Dilys glanced at her. "Have you not done the domestic violence training yet, Sharon?" she said, her voice cool.

Sharon reddened, but made no comment.

Matt glanced from one to the other of them, then went on. "It wouldn't be the first time an abusive man has been killed by his partner, as you all know."

There were murmurs of agreement round the table. "One thing I do know is that Ellis Cadogan never did anything in the kitchen, no cooking, washing up, whatever. He insisted that the kitchen was not a man's place apparently." He didn't tell them Fabia had told him that. "This means he never used the utensils in the kitchen, so, if anyone's fingerprints would have been on the shaft of the knife that killed him, they would most likely have been his wife's. In spite of this there were no fingerprints on it at all, which seems strange unless she wore gloves or held it with a cloth of some sort, or had the presence of mind to wipe it clean after she had killed him, which I doubt she would have been capable of doing."

Dilys glanced at the screen of her laptop. "It says here there were no fibres of any kind on the shaft and no gloves or cloth containing bloodstains has yet been found. Of course, something might still turn up."

"If she did kill him," Matt said, thoughtfully, "I think it would have been unpremeditated, an action born of desperation."

"But it still would have been murder, sir," Sharon said.

"But, given the circumstances, it would almost certainly be manslaughter, not murder," Dilys said firmly.

"But–"

Matt held up a hand. "We're getting ahead of ourselves," he said, and Sharon subsided, chewing at a nail and looking a little resentful.

Matt went on. "The SOCO team found spots of blood on the floor by the back door, which seemed to have been smeared by something, possibly the sole of a shoe, but they say they can't be sure. They also found a similar smear of blood in the hall, just outside the kitchen door. There were also some very small traces of fresh blood on the paving stones of the terrace. And there was evidence that someone with largish feet, probably size ten or eleven, had run across the lawn very recently. The grass hadn't been cut for quite a while and the ground is pretty waterlogged out there. The depth and shape of the impressions made by the shoes, boots, whatever, were quite deep and easy to see. They had a distinctive pattern and they were all pointing away from the house. Those two photos up there" – he indicated a whiteboard with several photographs pinned to it – "show you those footprints. The deep impressions made in the grass make it clear they were pretty heavy, possibly mountain boots but I think more likely heavy-duty Wellingtons, and that the person was running. They're very clear so definitely recent, otherwise the rain would have washed them away. Now, we can't be certain that they were made by an intruder, but it seems likely. We're pretty sure they were not made by the victim since they were going away from the house."

"Is there easy access out of the back garden?" Sara asked.

"Yes, there is," Matt said. "There's a gate in the fence at the end that gives on to the alleyway, the other side of which borders the industrial units between Parc Road and the back of the high street shops. A bit further on it curves up behind the houses on the eastern side of Morwydden Lane. There are only five other houses that back on to the alleyway and, as you all know, we've interviewed the owners of four of them, but no-one saw anyone running, or even walking, away from the back of the Cadogan house. We still have to get hold of the people in" – Matt glanced at his notes – "number three, which is next door to the Cadogans'. A Dr and Mrs Nelson. Their other neighbour says they're away for the weekend."

"Lucky buggers," muttered Tom, and Matt gave him a quick grin.

"When Dilys and I interviewed Ellis Cadogan yesterday morning, he admitted that he knew the identity of the person who made the deposits into the Little Theatre account that Sebastian Aubrey picked up on. We have no idea, as yet," Matt went on, "if these have any relevance to his murder. Any ideas from you lot would be welcome, but first we have to start the round of interviews again."

"And we don't really know, as yet, if there's any connection between the two murders," Dilys pointed out, "but it would seem unlikely that they aren't connected. That has to be borne in mind when we interview people."

"It does change the emphasis somewhat, doesn't it?" Tom Watkins said.

"Yes, Tom," said Matt, "it does."

* * *

Before they closed up shop, as Dilys called it, she asked for a word with Matt. Once again, they found themselves sitting in the gloom of the auditorium, the lighting coming from the strip of bulbs along the front of the stage. Matt leant back and stretched his legs out into the aisle. He was desperate to get home, but he knew he must find out what was troubling Dilys before leaving.

"I wanted to have a quick word with you about Sharon, sir," Dilys said.

"I thought that might be it," he said wearily. "She's a bit chippy, isn't she? What do you think her problem is?"

"I'm not sure, but I don't think we should put up with her behaviour for much longer, it's undermining the team. It's usually difficult to wind Tom up, but he's getting a bit pissed off with her as well, and I've overheard her making mildly racist remarks to Sara. Put it like this, I doubt that Sharon will be going on a Black Lives Matter march."

"What sort of remarks?" Matt snapped, sitting upright. Now she had his full attention.

"I don't know what the context was, but I heard her asking Sara how she would feel if she had to arrest a Muslim. Sara dealt with it quite well, said that since she was from a Hindu background, she didn't think it'd be a problem, and asked why Sharon thought it would be anyway. Tom was there too, and he asked Sharon if she'd have trouble arresting a Roman Catholic, so I left them to it, thought that made the point quite well."

"Why Roman Catholic particularly?"

"Sharon's got an uncle who's a Catholic priest."

"Ah," said Matt. "But I really won't have this sort of behaviour in our team," he insisted. "Sara's a tidy sort, she's got great potential."

"I agree. And there's something else, sir."

Matt wondered what the 'sir' was about. "You're beginning to worry me, Dilys," he said, smiling round at her, but she didn't return the smile.

"She's been asking around about Fabia, her background and how come you two are" – Dilys paused, sounding a little embarrassed – "are together. It's all been sort of casual and gossipy, but I think it needs to be dealt with. We don't want another Gerry Foulweather situation."

Matt gave her a quick grin. He hadn't realised that Dilys had cottoned on to his and Fabia's adaptation of the name. Gerry Fairweather had been an officer who had caused problems for Fabia in the past, when she was an inspector at the Newport station, and more recently for both Matt and Fabia. Earlier in the year he'd tripped up, blotted his copybook one time too many, and ended up leaving the force, but it had been unpleasant at the time.

"She has, has she?" Matt said. He came to a decision. "I tell you what, I'm going to leave this in your capable hands, Dilys."

Dilys groaned, but Matt took no notice.

"You're the same rank, but she's only just been made sergeant so, to all intents and purposes, you out-rank her. If she doesn't accept what you say, I'll have a go."

"Have you ever heard of the term 'passing the buck', sir?" Dilys asked sweetly.

Matt gave a bark of laughter. "Are you being insubordinate, Sergeant?"

"Never to God!" Dilys said, giving him a bland, innocent look, then she sighed. "Okay. I'll do my best."

"You always do," Matt said, levering himself up from the seat. It snapped back into the upright position and the sound echoed through the auditorium. "Now let's get going." He stretched and looked around. "One of these days I'm going to come to this theatre and watch a performance of something that makes me laugh."

"But not a pantomime," Dilys said sardonically.

"No, not a pantomime," Matt agreed.

* * *

Fabia had been waiting for Matt to call all afternoon. When at last her mobile rang, she grabbed it, but it wasn't Matt.

"Fabia? It's Luke. I've just heard about Ellis." He didn't wait for her to respond. "What the hell's going on? I've been trying to see Sally, but Cath won't let me near her. She said Matt has told her to keep Sally isolated, no-one to come near but the police and Cath."

And me, thought Fabia, but she didn't tell him that. She sighed. This was not what she wanted to be dealing with. "I'm afraid that's going to be the situation for a bit, until this is resolved. Come on, Luke, you should know that."

"I do, but I can't – oh shit, what am I going to do?"

"You're going to calm down," she said briskly, as if he was some young constable overstepping the mark. "You're going to be patient, and wait, like the rest of us. I haven't heard from Matt since he left this morning, but I'll try to keep you informed, once I know what's going on, and if I'm allowed to."

"Thank you. Look, I'm sorry to bother you, but I couldn't think of anyone else to call."

"I do understand, but I suggest you keep on with the job you were sent here to do. Anything you can turn up that'd help Matt could, possibly, help Sally if it takes the spotlight off her."

"Do you think so?"

"Yes," said Fabia firmly, "I do."

She heard Luke take a deep breath, then he said, "Fabia, you're a star. Thanks for listening."

"No problem," she said.

She put the phone back in her pocket and stood thinking, then went into the dining room to get out her copy of the mind map she'd made. She wanted to check something. But a few minutes later there was another interruption, this time from the landline.

"Fabia? It's Jean Aubrey. I've just heard the terrible news about Sally."

"What exactly have you heard?" Fabia asked, her voice a little cool.

"That she's been arrested for killing Ellis. Oh, it's so dreadful."

"But she hasn't – been arrested, that is."

"Hasn't she? But Morgan told us–"

"Jean, Ellis was stabbed, that is true, and Sally, poor girl, found his body. That's as much as I know. Matt will be interviewing everyone again and we should all know more after that."

"It's so dreadful," Jean said, but Fabia couldn't get away from the idea that Jean was enjoying the drama of it all. "Do you think, then, that the same person was responsible for both terrible murders?"

"I have no idea, Jean. I'm not privy to inside information."

"But surely, Matt tells you…"

"No, he's not allowed to," Fabia said firmly, crossing her fingers as she did so. "And, even if he did, I wouldn't be able to pass it on."

"I suppose not." She sounded disappointed. "Oh dear. I'll have to give Cath a ring, see if there's anything I can do."

Fabia didn't comment. She was sure Cath was perfectly capable of dealing with anyone trying to get information, or access to Sally.

But Fabia wasn't to be left in peace. The next person to call, ten minutes later, was Oliver Talbot.

"I heard about Ellis this morning, from my neighbour. Is it true he was stabbed?"

"Yes, I'm afraid so."

"Oh hell! This will really get to Geraldine."

"Yes, I know," Fabia said. "I wish she could get away while all this is going on, but Matt needs to do more interviews, and–"

"She's not a suspect, is she?" There was panic in his voice.

This is my day for dealing with panicky men, Fabia thought.

"I doubt it," she said, "but everyone's in the frame until the investigation is done."

"Yes, I know, but–"

"I'm sure you realise we may all know things or have information that we may not even realise is important," Fabia said patiently. "With a group like the cast, and everyone else involved in the pantomime, people notice things and then they slip to the back of the mind. All of us need to think back and see if there's something that struck us at the time but, given recent events, has a whole different meaning now."

Fabia heard Oliver sigh. "The trouble is I've been trying to persuade Geraldine not to think about it all. It brings back far too many dreadful memories for her."

"Would you like me to have a word with her?" Fabia asked with sympathy.

"Would you? After all you've known her longer than I have."

"Leave it with me," Fabia said. "I'll give it a try."

* * *

It was often the way, when Matt was in the middle of a complex case, that he didn't get home until late in the evening, and today was no different. Fabia put off asking him anything about his day until he'd eaten, but then she couldn't resist. But instead of asking questions, she began by telling him about the phone calls she'd had.

"First it was Luke in a panic about Sally."

"Yes, I had him on this afternoon. His information could be useful. I must check up on things with him. Who else called?"

"Just after Luke, it was Jean," Fabia told him. "She'd heard a rumour that Sally had been arrested. I managed to disabuse her, but there's going to be a lot of that kind of gossip in the next few days."

"That's one of the reasons I asked Cath to keep her isolated. Where did she get the rumour from?"

"Morgan, which seems a bit odd. I wouldn't have put him down as a gossip, but he was the one who told Jean."

Matt shrugged. "I expect the whole of Pontygwyn is gossiping and nattering away, bloody parasites."

"Probably. And after that it was Oliver worrying about Geraldine and how all this will get to her."

"It's upsetting for everyone," Matt pointed out.

"I know, Matt, but it'll remind her about what Frank did. Did you know that he knifed his victim? Well, in the end, he did."

"Don't dwell on it, darling," Matt told her, putting an arm round her. "You could always just leave the answerphone to pick up landline calls and not respond if you don't want to talk to whoever is calling your mobile, check before picking up."

"That's the theory, Matt, but you know me, I can't bring myself to do that."

He grinned. "True. You're far too keen to know everything that's going on around you. Nosy, that's what you are," he said, dropping a kiss on the end of her nose.

CHAPTER 14

Matt had been hoping that Sunday evening would be quiet but a call from Dilys destroyed any prospect of this at half past five.

"A Dr Stewart Nelson phoned the office, sir. He lives in number three, Parc Road, and he and his wife got back from their weekend away late this afternoon. One of their neighbours told them about Ellis Cadogan, and he says they might have some information for us. He said they're home this evening if we wanted to go and have a word."

Matt sighed. "I suppose we'd better. Are you in the office or at the theatre?"

"In the office. I was just finishing up some paperwork when the call came in."

"Do you never go home, Dilys?"

"You sound like Susan," she said.

"We should introduce Susan to Fabia, they'd have a lot in common."

Dilys laughed. "True."

"You'd better come straight round here, and we'll go to speak to the Nelsons together."

* * *

Dr Nelson was a tall, distinguished-looking black man whose short-cropped hair and beard were beginning to go grey. His wife, in contrast, was a slight, fair-haired woman who barely reached her husband's shoulder.

"I'm Stewart Nelson, this is my wife, Mary."

Matt noticed a slight accent and placed it either in South Africa or Zimbabwe.

Dr Nelson went on. "I'm sorry we weren't here when you called round before," he said as he ushered them into a comfortably furnished sitting room full of African artwork, carvings and paintings, and a stunning tapestry of a market scene above the fireplace.

Matt couldn't resist going up to have a closer look. "What a marvellous piece. My partner, Fabia Havard, is an artist. She would truly appreciate this."

"I've met her a couple of times, and we bought a watercolour from her when she had that exhibition last year, it's in the dining room," Mary Nelson said. "She's very talented. We must invite her round, Stewart."

"Sure. But now we must get down to the reason the chief inspector is here. I'm sorry we weren't at home when you called. We've just been up to see our daughter, she's at university in Birmingham."

"We heard about this awful business from our neighbours when we got home," Mary Nelson told them. "How is Sally? Is she coping okay?"

"She's at the vicarage, the Reverend Temple is looking after her," Matt told her.

They settled themselves around the open log fire glowing in the grate. Dr Nelson leant forward with his hands clasped, his elbows on his knees. "Let me give you a bit of background. I'm a lecturer in forensics at the Pontypridd campus and I know how important it is for you to gather as much information as you can as early as possible."

This is the kind of witness I like, thought Matt.

"My wife and I were just about to get going on Friday afternoon," Dr Nelson went on, "when she noticed someone hurrying away across the Cadogans' garden."

"What time was this, sir?" Matt asked.

"It must have been about half past three," Dr Nelson told them. "We were aiming to get to Birmingham about five thirty to check in at our hotel before meeting up with Emily. I was packing up the car, my wife always insists on taking boxes of food to—"

"The thing is," she interrupted him, looking a little embarrassed, "I'm sure she doesn't eat properly, and anyway, her housemates love what I take up."

"I know," he said, smiling at her. "Anyway, Mary was in the kitchen and – well, you tell them, darling."

"I looked out of the kitchen window and saw someone running across the lawn to the gate at the back."

"Did you recognise the person?" Matt asked.

"No, but they did look, well, furtive. I don't know, that was just the impression I got."

"Was it a man or a woman?" Dilys asked.

"I couldn't tell. They were moving very quickly but, sort of stumbling. I wondered why, then I realised they were wearing Wellington boots, I think that must have made moving fast a bit difficult."

Eyebrows raised, Matt glanced at Dilys and quickly away again. "You're sure about the boots?" he asked.

"Yes, I think so. Other than that, they had a long, mac-like sort of coat on with a hood, which was up over the head. I couldn't swear to it, I think they were quite slim, but I didn't see their face."

"And you're sure you couldn't tell if it was a man or a woman?" her husband asked her. "That's very important."

"I realise that," she said, sounding a little irritated. "My instinct was that it was a woman, but I've no idea why. As to their height, quite tall I think but not as much of a beanpole as you, darling."

They asked a few more questions but there wasn't really anything more she could tell them and, after a few more minutes, Matt and Dilys got up to go.

"Thank you very much for your help, Mrs Nelson," Matt said. "If anything else occurs to you, please get in touch. Here's my card."

Dr Nelson escorted them to the door. As he did so he asked Matt, "Is Pat Curtis on this case?"

"She is." There must have been something in Matt's short comment that got through to Nelson.

"A serious young woman," he grinned. "She attended some of my lectures years ago. I thought she'd go far, but she does have quite a scary manner, somewhat grumpy. I think it's down to shyness."

Matt smiled. "That could well be the case. Grumpy puts it in a nutshell, but she's very good at her job."

"I'm glad to hear it. Give her my regards when you see her."

"I will," Matt said.

Nelson shook hands with them both. "I do hope you manage to find out who's responsible for this awful murder, and it follows on the other one at the theatre, doesn't it? I wonder if they're connected."

"We're still trying to decide on that, sir," Matt told him.

* * *

As they drove away Dilys said, "Now there's a useful witness."

"That's exactly what I was thinking, but I do so wish that it had been Dr Nelson who saw the person in the garden. I think he might have noticed more specifics than his wife."

"But I think that business about the size of the person was useful," Dilys said. "I, for one, hadn't thought that the killer might be a woman. Do you think it could be? It takes quite a lot of force to shove a knife in someone's back. But if we concede that it could be, that puts Sally Cadogan in the frame again."

"That had occurred to me. But if Sally is responsible, who on earth was the person in the garden?"

"That's what I'd like to know." They walked on in silence for a bit. Dilys had left her car outside Fabia's house. When they got there, Fabia flung open the front door.

"Thank goodness you two are back, I've been dying of curiosity. Can you stay for dinner, Dilys, it's a Moroccan lamb tagine and I know you like that."

Dilys smiled. "How can I resist? Susan's out this evening so I was just going to go home and bung a ready meal in the micro."

They were soon settled round the table with bowls of rice topped with the fragrant tagine.

Fabia wasn't willing to wait any longer for them to report back on their interview with the Nelsons. "So, what did you find out? Please tell me what they had to say before I go doolally!"

Matt grinned, said, "Lovely tagine," and went on eating.

Dilys took pity on her. "Did you know Dr Nelson is a lecturer in forensics at Pontypridd?"

"No, I didn't. I've only met them a couple of times and we talked more about art than anything else."

"They were getting ready to go up to Birmingham on Friday," Dilys told her, "and just before they left, his wife, who was in the kitchen, noticed someone crossing the Cadogans' garden." She described what Mary Nelson had told them. "It looks as if, in Ellis Cadogan's case, we're looking for someone tallish and they could be slim, either a man or a woman."

"That could be absolutely any of them," Fabia said, "if you take into account how wrong people can be when they describe what they thought they saw."

"I realise that, but she did say quite tall. That could be, say, Geraldine."

"Oh, come on, Matt. I know she's nearly six foot, but are you really suggesting Geraldine could be responsible?"

"No. I think it's highly unlikely, but no-one has been completely crossed off the list yet."

"And Luke's over six foot."

"I wouldn't think he's a suspect," Matt protested.

"What? Just because he's a fellow police officer doesn't mean a thing," Fabia said firmly. "He's obsessed with Sally Cadogan and might well have wanted to get shot of her husband, but I can't think of any reason he'd go for Ivor. The Aubreys are both pretty tall but, not to put too fine a point on it, they're rather large as well. Oliver Talbot is tall as well, but I can't really think of a reason he'd go for either of them. So that leaves us with Jason Phillips, unlikely; Morgan Conway, he's only about five foot five; Eve Kemble" – Fabia grimaced – "unlikely I'd say; and the two youngsters, Peony and Lewys, who're both smallish."

"You've missed out Ivor's partner, Hywel Shaw," Matt told her.

"Is he short?"

"He's not tall, but he's overweight. Mrs Nelson said something about the person appearing thin, but she wasn't entirely sure about that either. Like you said, we all know how faulty people's impressions can be."

"And there is, of course, one other person," Fabia said.

"Who's that?" Matt asked.

Fabia told him. "I thought of it when I was looking at my mind map and I remembered Ellis making a comment or two that made me think they didn't get on one little bit."

Matt looked taken aback. "Now that hadn't occurred to me, but I'd say it's unlikely. After all, what motive?"

"I don't know, but that doesn't mean there isn't one."

"Other than Hywel Shaw," Matt said, "I'd been concentrating on the pantomime cast and crew, but maybe we should widen the field."

"Maybe we should," Dilys said.

At that moment Fabia's mobile phone rang. She glanced at the screen. "It's Cath," she said to Matt, and answered the call.

"Hallo, love, how's it going? … Poor girl, she really has been through the mill … Oh? What did she say? … That's interesting … She has? That'll be useful … Okay, I'll pass that on to Matt."

"What was that about?" Matt asked.

"Sally has remembered something she noticed when she got home. She hung up her coat, I suppose that's automatic really, and she saw that there was only one pair of Wellingtons under the coat stand where there should have been two. She says hers were where they should be, but Ellis's were missing. She noticed particularly as he'd been grumbling to her that they were too big and she – she, mark you – should have made sure he'd bought the right size. They were brand new and she thought he might have taken them back to the shop to change them, and it surprised her because, normally – if there is anything normal about that relationship – he would have made her go and do it."

Matt frowned across the table at Fabia, but he didn't comment for a moment and both Fabia and Dilys waited for him to speak.

"What are you thinking?" Fabia asked, impatient.

"Did she remember which shop they were bought from?" Matt asked.

"Cath didn't say. Hold on, I'll ask her." Fabia scrolled down to the right number and was soon asking Cath the question. Matt could hear Cath's voice but couldn't distinguish the words.

Fabia put the phone back in her pocket. "They were bought at that outdoor clothing and camping shop in Cwmbran, the one on the precinct."

"Wouldn't it be great if she had the receipt," Dilys said.

"Cath says she has. She always had to keep receipts so that Ellis could check through everything they bought."

Matt laughed. "The gods are on our side at last. We'll have to find out where all these receipts are kept and then go and search the right one out. I'll get Tom to go and have a word tomorrow."

CHAPTER 15

First thing the following morning, Matt got a message from Aidan Rogers asking to speak to him about what he'd turned up on the iPad found in Ivor Gladwin's desk. Matt went into the station before going to the incident room. Aidan had also had a trawl through the phone that had fallen under the floorboards of the stage and discovered that it had indeed belonged to Gladwin. Matt had great hopes of both.

Aidan, his round face as keen as usual, sat down in a chair beside Matt. The chair creaked in protest. "I must lose weight," he muttered. Matt was tactful enough not to comment.

"I haven't finished yet, but I thought it'd be useful for you to go through what I've retrieved so far," Aidan told him. "I've made notes in hard copy. I thought it'd be easier to show you what I've got that way."

"You know me too well," Matt said, smiling.

"I went through all the information we have about those involved so that I had the background information fixed in my mind. When I went through what I'd retrieved, it made what I found easier to understand," Aidan told him. "Some of his comments I could understand pretty easily, some I couldn't. He put all this in a notes section of his iPad and he was certainly interested in his pals, if you can call them that. I've managed to salvage a tidy bit of data and I've charted it according to the person who is, or could be, the target of his notes. I tell you, sir, if I thought someone was making notes like this about me, I'd be tamping, I would. Maybe he deserved what he got—"

Matt interrupted him. "It seems he wasn't a likeable person, but that's no reason to bump him off."

"Of course not, sorry, sir," Aidan said apologetically. "What he's done is made a list of names, not in full, just initials, sometimes with a description, sort of, like this one, he calls her Marilyn Monroe."

"I think that could be Peony Smith, she plays one of the female leads in the pantomime and she looks just like her."

"That follows. It's all rather odd, like. I can't imagine why he did it, maybe just for his own satisfaction, you know, to make him feel he was in control of them. It comes across some sort of game. Anyway, the notes he's made about Peony Smith are, *tasty bit of totty, young and juicy, wouldn't mind getting into her knickers.*" Aidan's round cheeks went a little pink as he read out the description. "This is followed by *Idiot Boy LB fancies her, I'll soon cut him out.*"

Matt frowned. "That'd be Lewys Bennion, he's of an age with Peony and, according to Fabia, is inclined to be a bit naïve, but I certainly wouldn't call him an idiot. He's doing an MSc in computer sciences at Pontypridd campus."

"Good on him," Aidan said. This was right up his street.

"This one here," Aidan went on, "male I think, he calls him The Ex-Con. The note is, *changed his name, used to be Eddie Martinez, stupid fucker thinks no-one knows.* That rather confirms the identification doesn't it?"

"It does. We're aware of him, but some more research must be done."

"I was planning to start on that once we'd finished here."

"Good, but give me the rest first," Matt said.

"There are a few more, three of which I think might be interesting. This one called *Music Man*, it's pretty obvious that's Ellis Cadogan as he refers to him later as EC, and isn't he the musical director for the panto?"

"Yes," said Matt.

"Well the note following his name is, *up to his ears in it, needs the money, accountant?* with a question mark. The next one is called Snooty Cow*, thinks she actually* *is* *bloody royalty, I'll enjoy bringing her down*, couldn't work out who that was, unless he's connected it up to the fact that Geraldine Humphries is playing the Empress of China in the panto."

"I suppose she can be haughty at times. I think it's a defence mechanism. It's not in the notes, but her son is in Broadmoor, and she thinks that Ivor might have found that out."

"Ah, poor dab."

"That's not quite how I'd describe her, but I understand what you mean."

Aidan gave him a self-conscious grin then went back to his transcript. "Next there's LM and SC, they're grouped together, the note is, *more and more interesting, she shouldn't have brushed me off, definitely going to hint to Music Man that he's not what he seems.*"

"Well that's pretty clear, really, given that he used initials and mentions Music Man. That'll be Luke Melville and Sally Cadogan." Matt wondered why Ivor Gladwin had suggested Luke wasn't what he seemed and decided he'd better have a word with Luke about it. It seems he'd slipped up there, yet again, or maybe it was just Ivor's imagination.

"I thought it was them," said Aidan. "Then there's one I can't identify but I think it's a woman, the name is Rules the Roost and the note says *definitely in charge, worth investigating, he's scared of her, what a cow.*"

"I'll think about that one, but I do have an inkling. Are there any more?"

"Just two entries, one of a pair and" – Aidan looked a little embarrassed – "one of a woman. The first two are called Lord and Lady Muck, and it says *always on his high horse, she's as bad, would love to prick that pompous bubble.*"

"That could be the Aubreys. In a way I see what he means."

Aidan nodded then paused and Matt prompted him, "And the last one?"

"Sir, I'm not sure this one is relevant to the present case."

"Never mind, let's have it."

"It says, *Corrupt Cop, artist my arse, bet she thinks she got away with it, going to do some digging, watch out FH.*"

"Ah, I see what you mean," Matt said, trying to keep his face impassive in spite of the lurch of anger he'd felt. "Well, that's clear enough isn't it? I wonder what the hell he thought he was going to find out?"

"I can't imagine," said Aidan tactfully.

"Thank you for all that, Aidan, and did you find anything on his mobile?"

"Yes, I did. Apart from several texts and calls that seem pretty innocuous, some of them winding people up, the ones in his notes that is, like Sebastian Aubrey and Sally Cadogan. But the last series of texts was interesting. I've noted it down here." He pointed to a sheet of paper. "That's the other party and Ivor was definitely trying to wind them up. The first one says, *Heard about your money-making scheme, how's it going? You could let me in on it. In my business I could be useful.* The response is a straight denial, *Don't know what yr talking about.* Gladwin comes back with, *Come on, I know you're involved, if I don't get a cut cd go to the cops.* And the reply is, *I think that would be a very bad idea, watch yourself,* which sounds like a threat to me."

"It does indeed. So, I'd better go and have a word. When were these texts sent, by the way?"

"The day before he was killed."

Matt nodded. "All this matches up with the contents of the cash box we found in his office. You've done a good job, Aidan, thanks."

* * *

A few minutes after Aidan had gone back to his desk, Dilys came into Matt's office. "I've got Mr Shaw on the phone, sir. He says he's remembered something you should know."

Matt grinned. "I thought that might happen, put him through." The phone on his desk gave one single

163

ring. He picked it up. "Mr Shaw, how can I help you?"

"I think it's more how I can help you, Chief Inspector," Shaw said firmly, then paused for a moment. "I'm not being funny, see, but it wasn't until yesterday that I remembered a conversation I had with Ivor, and it struck me it might be useful – you know – revealing."

"Go on," said Matt.

Shaw's tone became more assertive. "I don't want you thinking I've been withholding information, Chief Inspector, but the thing is, I mentioned it to my wife at the time and she reminded me of it when we were talking about this terrible business last night. Like I told you on Thursday, Ivor was always going on about conspiracy theories and criminal activity he imagined was happening all around. Obsessed by it, he was. He said he could do a better job than the police... Of course, fair play, I didn't agree with him on that."

"I'm sure you didn't, Mr Shaw," Matt said, trying to keep the smile out of his voice.

"When he went on about that scam he said was going on, he said he supposed it was a good way of finding cheap labour. I'm not sure what he meant, but he refused to go into details."

Matt wasn't sure he believed that Shaw didn't know what Gladwin had been referring to, but he let it go. When Shaw went on, he became even more certain that he knew more than he was admitting.

"And, of course, I pay my staff well, the going rate. Don't get me wrong, I know these things happen, but my business has always been as clean as a whistle, that I can say. Ask anyone in Cwmbran and beyond. I would never have had anything to do with such criminal activity."

"So, what was this conversation that you've remembered?" Matt asked, trying to stem the flow.

"We were in my office and he mentioned it again and said something like 'they think I don't know what they're up to, but I do, and I'm going to tell them so'. I assumed he meant the criminals, not the police. I'm afraid I told him he was a fool and brushed it off. I thought it was empty boasting, yet another of his stories, but now it comes back to me it does sound as if he knew exactly who was involved, doesn't it?"

"That's the implication," said Matt. "Did he ever mention any particular name or names, or indicate who he was talking about?"

"No." But Shaw didn't sound too certain, then he rallied. "No, I'm sure he didn't. If he had, I would certainly have mentioned it to you or your sergeant. But, the thing is, if he did tell whoever it was of his suspicions, maybe that was why he was... was killed."

"It's always a possibility."

"Well, Chief Inspector, I must get on, but I thought you should know."

"Thank you, Mr Shaw, and if you should remember anything else, please let us know."

"Of course, of course," Shaw said, sounding relieved to have got it all off his chest.

Matt put the receiver down and sat in thoughtful silence for a moment, then went to the door of his office and called to Dilys. "Can you come through? I want to run something past you," he said.

* * *

It was as Tony Vaughan was coming out of the Legionnaire Arms in Caerleon that he bumped into Morgan Conway. Tony, who worked at the Roman Fortress and Baths museum in Caerleon, had popped out for a quick sandwich and a pint and needed to get back to work, but Morgan grasped his arm and stopped him in his tracks.

"Tony, can I have a word?"

"What are you doing round here?" he asked Morgan. "Not your usual stomping ground is it?"

"My sister sent me to pick something up from a dress shop round the corner; a friend of hers runs it." He held up a smart-looking paper carrier with a logo scrawled on its side in gold lettering. "She orders me around like a bloody lackey," he complained, then gave Tony a grin that didn't quite come off. "Have you heard any more about Ellis?"

"No, I haven't. I think Sally is still staying at the vicarage. Best place for her, I'd say. I doubt that any of the press pack will get past the Reverend Temple."

"She's a scary woman, that vicar. Has Fabia said anything more?"

"No, Morgan, and I doubt very much that she'd gossip to me about it. After all, she used to be in the police force, she knows the rules, and she's hardly going to pass on anything Matt tells her either."

"I suppose so. But it's really getting to me, all this," Morgan said. There was exasperation tinged with panic in his voice. "First Ivor, then Ellis. I mean, who the hell's going to be next?"

"I don't think we're dealing with a serial killer, here, Morgan," Tony said, trying to calm him down.

"Then what's it all about?" He lowered his voice a little. "You know something, I think Luke Melville might have something to do with it. Carmen says she's sure he and Sally were more than just friends. She says she saw them in Hywel's cafe and she could have sworn they were holding hands."

"I don't think that's any of our business, is it?" Tony said. "Look, I've got to get back to work so–"

But Morgan took no notice. "You know what, I think Ivor may have had a go at Luke, maybe threatened to hint to Ellis or something. Ivor did that sort of thing, didn't he? I'll tell you for why – I think Luke might have been trying to protect her. And he could have been responsible for getting rid of Ellis as well. Ellis was a right bully, I should know, he's had enough goes at me over my singing. And he was always criticising Sally and telling everyone how hopeless she was. Once I heard him say that, before he met her, she used to spread it around a bit, with the men I mean, what Carmen calls all red shoes and no knickers."

"I really think it's useless to speculate, and best not to spread any more rumours about the poor woman, or about Luke for that matter," Tony said repressively. "If you have any legitimate" – he stressed the word – "information, you really should pass it on to Matt."

"Well, since he's your next-door neighbour, maybe you could pass on what I've told you?"

"No way, Morgan," Tony said briskly. "It's up to you, and if you've got anything that'll help them find the killer, or killers, you have to tell the police. Withholding information is never a good idea."

"I know that. I'm not stupid."

Tony gave him a look that expressed doubt about this, but all he said was, "I must get going. Work to do. Shouldn't you be getting that dress back to your sister?"

Morgan stood glaring after Tony as he walked away towards the Roman baths, but slowly his expression changed. Shrugging, he started off in the opposite direction.

CHAPTER 16

Matt and Dilys spent some time going through Aidan's information and discussing each of Ivor's notes, the texts, the contents of the cash box and all the possible implications. They mapped out what they needed to do next. It was obvious to both of them that they were getting close, and Matt was now pretty sure that Luke's investigation overlapped with theirs.

"But I don't want to move too early, I want to bring in those responsible for the two deaths as well as break open this trafficking racket."

"Didn't you say you wanted to go and speak to Sally Cadogan again?" Dilys asked.

"Yes. I want to be able to cross her off the list if we possibly can, but I'm still not sure about her involvement, or whether or not she knew what Ellis was up to."

Sally had been kept sedated over the weekend but, when Matt phoned Cath, she told him that on Saturday evening Sally had refused to take the pills. She'd told Cath she couldn't think straight, and she felt she needed to have a clear head. Matt was surprised. He hadn't expected Sally to be that strong-minded.

They arrived at the vicarage in the middle of the afternoon. Cath answered the door to them.

"Come in," she said, stepping aside to let them in. "Before I go and fetch Sally, can I ask – would it be alright if I stay while you talk to her? I feel she needs the support."

"It's not exactly usual practice, not with an adult, but since you're a vicar," Matt said reluctantly, considering Cath's determined expression, "okay. But I need you to sit on the sidelines and let us do what we have to do." He hoped he wasn't agreeing simply because Cath was a friend, but he did have a feeling that might be the case. This was what he'd been afraid of when he took over from Jess Foyle. He wondered how long it would be before she got back to work, or he seriously screwed up. He'd have to rely on Dilys and Fabia to stop him doing that.

A few moments later Cath ushered Sally into the room. Used to interviewing people who had been through trauma of some kind, Matt wasn't really surprised by Sally's appearance. Her auburn hair was a mass of tangled curls, she was very pale and there were deep shadows like bruises under her eyes. Cath settled her solicitously in a comfortable armchair then went to sit a little behind her on an upright chair. Matt and Dilys sat down. Quietly Dilys took out her notebook and pen.

"Sally – may I call you Sally?" Matt asked.

"Of course," she said. Her voice was hoarse when she spoke.

"I need to go through the events of Friday afternoon with you, in detail. Can you start off by telling me where you were immediately before you arrived home?"

Sally put a hand up to her forehead as if to help her remember. "I was at work until about one o'clock, which is my usual time for leaving on Fridays. I went to Matalan in Cwmbran, Ellis needed some new socks. After that I went to Sainsbury's, then I came home. I suppose I got back about four."

"Just about the time I decided to come round and see you," Cath said. Matt gave her a warning glance and she mouthed, "Sorry."

"Can you tell me exactly what you did when you arrived back?"

"I was worried that I was a bit late. Ellis always gets" – she paused and swallowed, then went on – "got home earlier on Fridays and he'd told me I must cook a leg of lamb for supper. I was worried I wouldn't be able to prepare it all in time. He was very particular about the vegetables and things and would have been angry if it wasn't just right, and he liked to eat at exactly seven thirty."

Matt heard Dilys shift in her chair beside him, but he didn't look at her. He knew what she'd be thinking.

"Was the front door open when you arrived?" Matt asked.

"I'm not sure." She frowned and chewed at her lower lip. "Yes, I think it was ajar, because when I tried to put my key in the door it just opened. I got into a bit of a panic because I thought Ellis had got home before me, but then, when I got into the hallway, I realised he probably wasn't."

"How did you realise that?" Matt asked.

"Because, when I was hanging up my coat, I saw that his new Wellingtons weren't by the coat stand, so I thought he'd gone out to the shop to change them, or was in the garden. I think I heard the back door close, then I heard what I thought were footsteps, in the garden. I thought it was Ellis, so I called out, but there was no response."

"Did it occur to you that it was odd, the front door being open?" said Matt.

"I sort of forgot about it. I was so relieved that he wasn't back – well, that's what I thought. And afterwards I didn't think about it again."

"And what did you do next?"

"I think I went and got the rest of the shopping out of the car – no, I didn't. I went straight through to the kitchen with what I was already carrying."

"Matt? Could I say something?" Cath asked.

He looked at her, then said curtly, "Go ahead."

"When I got to Sally's kitchen on Friday, I nearly tripped over some shopping bags on the floor just inside the door."

"Thank you. That's useful," he said, remembering that the bag had still been there when they arrived on the scene. He turned back to Sally. "Did you notice Ellis's body immediately?"

"Of course I did!" The words were sobbed out and she pressed a hand to her mouth while her eyes filled with tears. Quietly Cath reached for a tissue from the box on her desk and handed it to Sally.

Matt waited a moment for her to recover. He glanced at Dilys to check if there was anything she wanted to ask, but she gave a slight shake of the head, so he went on. "I'm sorry to upset you, but I do have to ask these questions, Sally, so that I can get a clear picture of what happened."

"I know. I'm sorry."

"Can you tell me what you did from the moment you got into the kitchen?"

"I– I went over. I thought he must have passed out, or something, and I bent down. It was then I saw the knife." She put a hand up to her mouth again. Her eyes were wide and staring above her fingers. "Oh God! It was awful, so awful. I think I put out a hand because, when I looked down at it, there was blood on my... on my fingers."

"Now I want you to think really hard about what you did next. Did you touch the knife?"

She shook her head and went on shaking it as if she couldn't stop.

"Are you absolutely sure about that?"

She nodded. "I think I crawled away across the floor," she told him, then whispered, "I couldn't bear to look at him. It– I've never seen a dead body before."

"You knew he was dead?" Matt asked.

Sally gave a hysterical bark of laughter. "It was pretty bloody obvious. He had that... that knife sticking out of his side!" she exclaimed. Tears filled her eyes and she scrubbed at them with the tissue which was still clutched in her hand. "Then I saw the blood on my hand. It made me feel sick, but I couldn't get up to wash it off, I just couldn't, and then Cath arrived." She glanced round at Cath, and gave her a watery smile.

There was a pause in the questioning. Cath handed Sally another handful of tissues and asked her if she'd like a glass of water.

"Oh, yes, please," Sally said.

As Cath left the room, she gave Matt a stern look as if to say, don't upset her while I'm gone. Matt didn't react. He had to do this his own way and he couldn't afford to take any notice of what Cath thought.

He turned back to Sally, leant forward with his elbows on his knees, and asked, "Can I take you back a little further? From what you've told us so far it appears to me that Ellis was quite controlling, is that right?"

Sally nodded wordlessly.

"Have you heard of the term, coercive control?"

Yet again she nodded.

"Would you say that is what your husband imposed on you?" Matt asked, choosing his words carefully.

For a long moment Sally stared back at him, her eyes full of fear. Cath came quietly back into the room and handed her a glass of water while Matt waited for Sally's answer, hoping Cath would not intervene. Sally took a gulp of the water. Matt glanced at Dilys, who had done some concentrated training in dealing with victims of domestic abuse. She got the message.

"There's absolutely no shame in being the victim of that kind of behaviour, Sally," she said firmly. "Mental and physical abuse are the responsibility of the perpetrator, not the victim. Do you feel that your husband had a desire to control you?"

"He... he liked things done his way, and yes, he did get angry if I didn't do what he wanted. He used to say that I was hopeless and if he hadn't been around to make sure I did things the way they should be done, our lives would have been completely unmanageable. I never seemed to be able to get things right though. I'm so scatty."

"Did you feel his demands on you were unreasonable?" Dilys asked.

"I suppose. Well, yes, but not until recently, then it came home to me."

Matt took over once again. "Why do you say that it came home to you recently?"

Matt saw a flush slowly rise up Sally's pale cheeks. "A friend of mine pointed it out. He told me Ellis was being unreasonable and I shouldn't let him bully me."

"And who was this friend?" Matt asked, aware that he probably knew already.

Sally glanced round at Cath and said, "Do I have to…?"

"I think it's best," said Cath gently.

"But what if…"

"Sally, I think I know who you're referring to," Matt said. "It's Luke Melville isn't it?"

"But he didn't do it!" she burst out.

Matt was taken aback, then realised what she was implying. "Didn't do what, Sally?"

She was looking at him as if she was the mouse and he the cat. For a long moment she didn't speak, then she whispered, "He didn't kill Ellis."

"I hadn't suggested he did. Why would you think I'd suspect him?"

"Because he– because we–" she stuttered to a halt, put her head in her hands and began to sob.

Cath got up and put her arm round her, looked pleadingly at Matt.

"Shall I go and make some tea?" Cath asked.

"Yes, that'd be a good idea," Matt told her.

175

Cath got up and left the room with a worried glance back at them as she did so.

Gradually Sally calmed down, whispered an apology and scrubbed at her face with the tissues. Matt sat waiting quietly until Cath returned with the tea tray, handed the mugs around, then sat back down.

"Are you able to go on, Sally?"

"Yes, sorry."

"Don't worry," Matt said. "I know how difficult this must be for you."

"Thank you."

"Just a few more questions, and then we'll leave you in peace," Matt said. "Why would you think that we'd suspect Luke of being responsible for Ellis's death?"

"Because he cares about me, he's a good friend."

"Is that all he is?"

She didn't respond.

"Sally, are you and Luke having an affair?"

"Fabia told you!" Her tone was accusing.

Matt said nothing, just waited for her to go on.

"Yes," Sally said defiantly, "we love each other, and if Ellis had found out he might well have attacked Luke, but there was no reason at all for Luke to attack Ellis, none whatsoever. I'd already told Luke I was going to leave Ellis."

Matt nodded, as if in agreement, then he said, "I'd like to go back to something you said earlier. You mentioned hearing footsteps going through the garden. Is that right?"

"Yes."

"I want you to think very hard about this. Could you tell whether the footsteps were those of a man or a woman?"

Sally frowned then slowly shook her head. "I don't know. I'm not even sure if what I heard was actually footsteps, but no, I did hear them, I did. But I've no idea who it was." A look of horror slowly dawned on her face. "Do you think it was the person who killed Ellis? Oh my God. It must have been. Is that what you think?"

Matt didn't respond to this and, soon after, he decided there was no point in continuing the interview. As Sally sat there, her head resting on the back of the armchair, he could see that she was finding it hard to keep her eyes open. Although there was more that he wanted to ask her, she was looking so exhausted that he felt it might be counterproductive to persist now.

Cath saw them out and as they got to the door, she put a hand on his arm. "Thank you for being so gentle with her, Matt."

"Just doing my job, Cath," he said, a little stiffly. "I will need to speak to her again."

"I understand."

As they drove away, Dilys turned to Matt and asked, "Sir, why didn't you ask her direct if she killed him?"

"I might have to at some point, but I noticed something about her which makes me think she probably wasn't responsible."

"What was that?"

"She wears her watch on her left wrist; when she was wiping her eyes, she used her right hand; and when Cath handed her the glass of water and the tea, she used her right hand. What's more, there was an ink stain on the index finger of her right hand, which could indicate that a pen she was writing with leaked. The person who killed her husband was almost certainly left-handed. I don't think she is."

"You said you wanted to cross her off the list," Dilys said.

"I know, and I think this means we can."

CHAPTER 17

There were several developments to address when Matt and Dilys got back. Pat Curtis's report from the post-mortem on Ellis Cadogan had come through and they sat down to go through it together.

"This confirms what I thought. She says he was stabbed by someone who held the knife in their left hand. The killer was standing behind him," Matt said. "The knife went in at an upward angle and pierced the heart. She thinks he must have been stretching up to get something." Matt frowned. "Maybe a coffee mug. Remember, there was a broken mug on the floor. It must have taken quite some force, which indicates someone physically strong and, given the angle, probably taller than him. Exactly how tall was he? Have we got a record of that?"

Dilys scrolled down her screen to some notes. "Yes, small for a man, five foot five. It's all pretty clear, isn't it?"

"She's good, is Pat," Matt said, grinning. "One of the first things to do is find out who the left-handers are."

A moment later a call came through from Aidan. "I've got a bit more about that Martinez bloke," he said. "It looks like he changed his name after he came out of prison. He'd been dealing in drugs, cannabis, amphetamines and such like. He finally got caught. This was in 2008. He came out in 2010 and then, as Eddie Martinez that is, dropped off the map."

"But why should he go to such lengths? Most people who come out of prison don't change their name."

"I'll do some checking with the prison service, find out who he was in with," Aidan said. "Maybe he was being threatened."

"Could be," Matt said, but he wasn't convinced. "Any idea where his wife lives now? It might be useful to have a word."

"No, but I can try to find out."

"Thanks, Aidan, good work."

Matt went over to Dilys. "Can you get someone to check up how long each of the people involved in this business has been living locally?" He told her what Aidan had said. "Go back as far as, say, 2003."

"I'll get Tom on to it," Dilys said, grinning, "he's going to love me."

"Sir," Dave Parry called from across the room. "I've got something interesting here."

Matt walked over to him.

"A Mrs Rodgerson says she's found a pair of what she says are brand new Wellington boots at the end of her garden. She insists she heard some kids in the alley at the back, she says they threw them over her garden fence."

"Did she phone it through to the station?"

"Yes. Apparently, she's a bit of a regular caller, always reporting kids playing around in the alleyway and suspicious behaviour by her neighbours."

"What made them call it through to you?" asked Matt.

"I was talking to Claire Gooding about the case yesterday. When she mentioned Wellies, it rang a bell with her, so instead of going herself she got through to me."

Claire Gooding was an officer they'd all worked with in the past. She was sharp as a tack.

"What's Mrs Rodgerson's address?" asked Matt.

"Seventeen, Parc Road."

"Interesting. Get round there and pick them up, would you? And get a few more details from this Mrs Rodgerson, then give the boots to the SOCOs to have a look at."

"Will do, sir."

Half an hour later Matt looked up and said to Dilys, "I think it's about time I had another word with Luke Melville, a private word. I'm surprised he hasn't been on to me about Sally, to be honest."

"Has he tried to see her at the vicarage?"

"Cath hasn't said so."

"She's soft-hearted, that vicar," Dilys pointed out. "She might not choose to tell you."

"You're not wrong," Matt said ruefully. "As to Luke, I'm not sure he's given me all the information he's gathered."

"But surely, sir–?"

"You know what it's like, Dilys. Quite apart from his personal involvement, each department is inclined to be possessive about their own territory and not share information, it happens all the time, even when it isn't complicated by a love affair."

"I s'pose so, but it shouldn't," Dilys said emphatically.

"Not everyone has your common sense," Matt said, smiling at her tone.

* * *

It was as Fabia came out of the River's Edge restaurant in Newport with her agent, Sheena Morley, that she heard her name called out. She turned to see Eryn Jackson, small, dark and stylish, who was a dance teacher in Pontygwyn. She was also the choreographer for the dances in the pantomime.

"I'll leave you to it," Sheena said, "I've got to get a move on if I'm going to catch the next Cardiff train."

"Okay. I'll get those illustrations to you soon as I can."

"Do that," Sheena said, brisk as always, and she strode off in the direction of the station.

Fabia turned to Eryn. "Hi, what's brought you into town?"

"I've just been to Molly's Dancewear to have a look at some kit for my pupils." She paused, giving Fabia a sideways glance. "Look, I'm rather glad I've bumped into you, actually. Have you got time for a coffee?"

"Well, I've just had some, actually."

"Please, I really need to talk to you." She gave Fabia a pleading look and put a hand on her arm.

Fabia looked down at her earnest, serious eyes. "Okay, another won't go amiss, let's go around to the cafe in the arcade."

They walked the short distance without exchanging more than a few words but, once settled, and having ordered their coffee, Fabia looked up at Eryn and said, "You seem to have something on your mind. How can I help?"

Eryn didn't respond immediately. She stirred at her coffee far longer than it needed, gazing down at the swirling liquid as she did so. Fabia waited and, at last, Eryn looked up, her eyes troubled.

"First of all, can you tell me exactly when Ivor was killed?"

This was not what Fabia had expected, but she responded to the question readily enough. "From what I've gathered, it was in the middle of the afternoon on Saturday last week, the third."

"That's what I thought."

"Why do you ask?"

"It's difficult," Eryn said. "I'm sure you know I was no great fan of Ellis Cadogan."

"I had got that impression in the past." Fabia thought back to several confrontations during rehearsals for the dance sequences in the pantomime. "But Eryn, that doesn't mean you'd be suspected of either–"

Eryn made a dismissive gesture with her hand. "No, I know, but what I was thinking is that he might have been suspected of being responsible for Ivor's death. Much as he irritated me, I wouldn't want the poor man to be accused now he's been a victim as well. And I do feel that Sally might have had reason – well, you know what I mean."

Into Fabia's mind came an image of Sally and Luke standing very close together talking in low tones. It had been at a rehearsal and she'd been on the sidelines, making sketches for potential scenery. She'd looked up and caught sight of Eryn watching them, an intent expression on her face that spoke volumes. Fabia had thought at the time, oh dear, she fancies him too, what a mess. He'd better be careful, and not only of Ellis. But now she homed in on what Eryn had said.

"Why do you think that he couldn't have been responsible?"

"It's not that I think he couldn't have," Eryn said, not meeting Fabia's eye. "I just think it's far more likely to have been – well – to have been Sally or Luke, or both of them."

"And what makes you say that?" Fabia asked.

"It's difficult. I feel as if I'm telling tales."

"But if you have information, Eryn – and you did ask to speak to me."

"I know," said Eryn, sounding agonised. "The thing is, I saw her near the theatre on Saturday afternoon, and that was when Ivor was killed wasn't it?"

"What do you mean, you saw her near the theatre?" Fabia asked sharply. "Where exactly?"

"Walking past, towards the high street."

"Have you said anything to Matt about this?"

"N-no. You see, I hadn't thought it through until I heard about Ellis being killed. We were talking about it yesterday evening."

"Who's we?"

"Peony, Lewys and me. We were–" She paused, looking slightly embarrassed. "Well, I'll be honest with you, we were at the pub and we were discussing whether or not Sally was responsible for killing Ellis, and that's when I remembered seeing her on Saturday."

Fabia was finding all this hard to believe, but she made sure her doubts weren't obvious as Eryn went on. "I'm confused. Why should she kill Ivor?" she asked.

"Because he might have threatened to tell Ellis about her and Luke. Everyone knows how Ellis bullied and abused her, verbally that is, but he could have been violent as well, and everyone was aware of the way Ivor snooped. The three of us thought that it would be understandable if she just, like, snapped. You hear of it happening time and time again when a woman is abused, don't you?"

Fabia didn't comment, and Eryn went on. "And Lewys said something about having seen Ellis have a go at Sally several times, and Peony said the same. Like I said, we all knew that he gave her a hard time. It seems to me" – Eryn leant forward and lowered her voice a little – "that the most likely person to have killed them would be Sally, or maybe Luke, to sort of protect her. And who could blame either of them is what I say. I wouldn't want anyone to be arrested for doing something they were sort of forced into."

Fabia very much doubted Eryn's motives. She didn't think this outpouring of confidences was quite as innocent as Eryn was implying. She gave her a straight look. "You really shouldn't go around making that kind of accusation."

"I wasn't accusing them!" Eryn said indignantly. "It was just thinking sort of along logical lines. And I thought the police wanted as much information as they could get."

"They do, but not when it's just speculation and gossip, which can be very damaging. The facts, time and place, etc., is what they need, but guesswork, not so much."

A sulky look came into Eryn's face. Fabia could tell she wasn't getting the reaction she wanted. "And there's really no point in talking to me," she told Eryn firmly. "You should be talking to Matt or someone on his team."

"But I was wondering, could you tell him what I've told you?"

"No, no," Fabia said, shaking her head. "That's not how it works. I'm no longer a police officer."

Eryn didn't seem convinced, so Fabia insisted, "Eryn, I mean it. I will tell Matt you've spoken to me, and he'll almost certainly make contact, but that's as far as I can go."

CHAPTER 18

Matt arranged to meet up with Luke away from the bustle in the green room. Since Fabia was in Newport having lunch with her agent, he suggested they meet back at the house. He was pretty sure Fabia would be annoyed with him for choosing a time when she wasn't at home, but needs must.

He was just getting out of the car when Luke arrived, looking haggard. Matt had the good sense not to remark on this and neither of them spoke as he let them in and made straight for the kitchen. He was pretty sure strong black coffee was going to be needed.

While Matt busied himself with the coffee, Luke slumped into a chair, leant back and thrust his hands into his pockets. "This is a fucking nightmare."

"You could say that. Have you made contact with your gaffer?"

"Yes, and she is, understandably, pissed off."

"I'm not surprised, butt," Matt said, not without sympathy. "If you look at it straight, she has every right to be."

"I know, I know."

"Did she recall you?"

"No. She said, given the murder – murders now of course – I'm to sit tight and wait for developments."

"Have you been to see Sally?" Matt asked, eyebrows raised.

Luke didn't look up. "I have, but only fleetingly, and Cath was there all the time."

"Well, at least she has that much sense. Please don't make contact again, not until we've cleared up a few odds and ends."

"Like what?" Luke said sharply.

Matt debated whether or not to tell him about the fact that Ellis had been killed by someone who was left-handed, but before he could say anything Luke looked up and asked, "Can you tell me how Ellis was killed? Sally just said he was stabbed, but she didn't tell me anything about the scene, and I obviously wasn't going to ask her for details."

"You know I can't do that, Luke."

"Why? Because I'm a suspect?"

"Come on, man, with your training you should realise that."

"I know, but I swear I didn't kill him," Luke said passionately. "I had no need to. Sally had decided she was going to leave him and come to me. It was just a matter of timing, that was all."

"And when did she make that decision?"

"We managed to meet up at lunch time on Thursday, went to a pub in Monmouth so that we wouldn't bump into anyone we knew."

"Luke!"

"I know, sir, but I had to see her. And she finally agreed that she'd leave, but she was going to do it without telling him beforehand. I didn't want her to do that, but she insisted it was the only way. She was so scared of him. But I still know she couldn't have killed him."

"You can't know it, Luke."

"But I do. It takes some force to knife a person in the back and Sally isn't strong, physically."

"He was knifed in his left side," Matt said, then could have bitten his tongue out for doing so. "I shouldn't have told you that."

Luke looked up at him sharply, his police training taking over. "From behind?"

In for a penny, in for a pound, Matt thought ruefully. "Yes." Fabia was never going to let him forget this lapse if he told her about it.

"But Sally's right-handed," Luke said, and it was as if the sun had come out.

"That's what I suspected when I was interviewing her."

"Thank God for that," Luke said and, elbows on the table, buried his head in his hands.

"She's not free and clear yet, Luke," Matt warned. "There's still a way to go."

Luke looked up and nodded. "I know, but that's good news, for her I mean, isn't it?"

"We'll see." Matt got up to make more coffee. "Now, for a bit of light relief, let's have your news. How's your investigation going?"

Luke straightened and took a deep breath. "Well, I feel as if I'm getting close. Our jailbird definitely had some useful contacts in prison, but I'm not sure he's the main mover. There's something that makes me think the person in charge is more intelligent, sharper than he is, but don't quote me on that, it's just a gut feeling. That's not to say he isn't up to his neck in it, of course. And I think the whole organisation is wider than we first thought, I wouldn't be surprised if several of the people we've both been investigating are involved in one way or another. Let's face it, the drama group is such a delightful cover, I've used it for the same purpose. You know, meeting up at rehearsals, going to the pub afterwards, a lot of information and arranging could be passed back and forth under the cloak of socialising within a group with a common purpose. And right there, on your doorstep, there's the Little Theatre, a registered charity to clean up all your lovely lolly."

Matt suddenly remembered one of the notes from Gladwin's iPad. He must ask Luke about that. He explained about what Aidan had turned up and then asked, "Did you ever mention your real job to anyone other than me and Fabia?"

"No, I–"

Matt held up a hand to stop him in his tracks. "Ivor had put yours and Sally's initials into his notes, which identifies the two of you pretty clearly. He said something was 'more and more interesting' which makes me think he'd managed to ferret out information of some kind, maybe overheard a conversation. That fits in with his habit of sneaking around listening to people. And he said he might mention to Ellis Cadogan that someone, presumably you, since it followed in the same note, were not what you seemed."

"But that could have meant anything," Luke protested. "That I wasn't simply a friend of Sally's, that I wasn't just another member of the cast, something like that."

"Granted, but it could also mean that he suspected you weren't being up front about your job and your reasons for being in Pontygwyn. And, if that's the case, I'd say you're in even more trouble."

Luke scowled but didn't comment, so Matt went on. "I want you to think back, really concentrate. First, did you ever say anything, anything at all, to Sally about your actual job?"

"No, not really." But there was uncertainty in his voice.

"What do you mean, not really?"

"I did tell her that I couldn't tell her, if you see what I mean, what exactly my job was." He wasn't looking Matt in the eye as he spoke. "I asked her to be patient and that I would tell her as soon as I could."

"Luke," Matt said, not bothering to keep the exasperation out of his voice. "If you were one of my officers, I'd have you up on a disciplinary before your feet could touch the ground. You seem to have broken every bloody rule in the book. What on earth did you think you were up to?"

"Look, I know I've screwed up," Luke protested, "but I didn't tell her any more than that, and she said she trusted me."

"More fool her."

"Thanks!"

Matt sighed and shook his head, but added more calmly, "Okay, let's get back to the trafficking itself. In one of the other notes found, Ivor mentioned someone he called the Ex-Con. This person changed their name from Eddie Martinez. Do you think that's the same chap?"

"I do," said Luke, and gave him the name. "It's rumoured he got on the wrong side of some seriously nasty types inside. The change of name might have been in an effort to disappear, in case they came after him."

"And you didn't think to pass this bit of information on to me, in spite of the fact it's so close to home?"

"I'm sorry, I should have done. Look, one of my problems has been–" Luke paused, biting at his bottom lip. "My boss is a difficult woman. She's a Londoner through and through, deeply metrocentric. She thinks everything should be centred on the capital, and she's a control freak as well. When I was sent on this job, she told me to keep everything, but everything, to myself. All information was on a strictly need to know basis, which is one of the reasons you weren't told. She had to allow me to inform the NCA personnel down here, but insisted on the minimum of information, and I had to inform Rees-Jones, couldn't avoid that, but she said no-one else. I'm sorry to repeat this, but her words were 'these provincial forces are notoriously leaky'."

"What the–?"

"I know, I know." Luke threw his hands up in an apologetic gesture.

"God, give me strength!" Matt exclaimed. "I know this attitude used to be a problem, but I didn't think it was still so... so, well, prevalent, and arrogant, quite apart from anything else."

"She's old school and coming up to early retirement. I don't think the newer intake is as bad, at least I hope not, and I'm certainly not of that mind."

"I'm glad to hear it," said Matt sarcastically. "I think…" But at that moment they heard the front door open and decisive footsteps coming down the hall. Fabia pushed the kitchen door open.

"Hallo, you two," she said, eyebrows raised in Matt's direction.

Luke got up. "Fabia," he said, "good to see you, but I think I must get going."

"Don't let me chase you away."

"No, no, but I think Matt and I have done all we can."

"For now," said Matt, and Fabia, noting his tone, gave him a curious look.

When Luke had left, she turned to Matt. "What was all that about?"

"Ugh! How long have you got?" grunted Matt.

"That bad?"

He shrugged. "Some of what Luke and I discussed has meant progress, but the politics… how I hate internal politics." He ran a hand through his hair, then his mobile set up a clamour for attention and he pulled it out of his pocket, glanced at the screen. "That's Dilys. I've got to get back. I'll have to bring you up to date later."

"But, Matt, I've got some info for you."

"Who from?"

"Eryn Jackson, I bumped into her in Newport." As quickly as she could she told Matt what Eryn had said. "I'm not sure I believe her about Sally being near the theatre on Saturday. I think she's got the hots for

Luke and she's trying to make trouble for Sally – a case of a woman scorned."

"Not another one! Look, I'll have to go, love. I promise I'll tell all when I get home, and thanks for that info, you should be on the payroll."

Fabia gave a bark of derisive laughter, and Matt looked at her apologetically. "Sorry, not a tactful thing to say." He gave her a quick kiss, whispered "I love you," and strode off down the hall and out of the front door. Fabia stood watching him go.

* * *

As Matt drove back to the theatre, he could have kicked himself. What a stupid thing to say to Fabia. To talk to her about being put on the police payroll, that was just about the most tactless thing he could say after all that she'd been through when she left the force. He'd have to make it up to her when he got home. Flowers? No, not Fabia's sort of thing. She always said flowers should be in the garden not in a vase. It would have to be wine, maybe a bottle of that Austrian white she liked, or better still, a bottle of Penderyn malt whisky.

Directly he walked into the green room, he was bombarded from several sides.

"Oh good, you got my text," Dilys said, "could I have a word?"

But they were interrupted by Dave Parry. "I handed those wellies over to the SOCOs, sir," he told Matt. "Mrs Rodgerson is positive it was the kids that threw them over, so I've got the local community chap on to that. He knows most of the toerags round here. He says he'll find out where they found them, if it was them. Anyway, I told the SOCOs we need the info back yesterday, they've promised to make it a priority."

"Well done, how did you manage that?"

Dave grinned. "Fluttered my eyelashes at the teenager who's going to be working on them."

"You're showing your age, Dave," Matt said, grinning, "but well done."

"Sir?" Matt looked round to see Sara making her way across the room towards him. "I've turned up some more information on Morgan Conway, well, on his ex-wife."

"Good work, Sara, let's have a look." He read through the information that Sara had put together. "Divorced ten years ago. Has she remarried?"

"No," said Sara, "look at that bit." She pointed to a part of her notes.

"Ah, I see. You've done well. Can you contact the Chepstow force and fix up to have a word with her, soon as possible?"

"Will do, sir."

Matt turned to Dilys. "Okay, I'm all yours."

They both sat down at the desk Dilys had been using and she brought some documents up on her screen. "I've been doing some research into the Aubreys, sir, well him, specifically, and I came up with something quite interesting. This goes back twenty years, maybe more. See, here we have an article from a magazine that covers the insurance and mortgage broker businesses."

Matt leant forward to look more closely at the screen.

"He was a freelance broker who used his contacts in the insurance and banking community to introduce people to high loan-to-value, what's called LTV, mortgages," Dilys told him. "Some of them were between ninety-five and a hundred and ten per cent. Hard to believe nowadays." She scowled at the screen. "You know my sister and her husband, they're both senior nurses, but they're still being refused a mortgage. It makes me sick. Sorry, sir. Anyway, back to Sebastian Aubrey. Most of the people he targeted were inexperienced first-time buyers. He received a commission from the mortgage provider, bolted on to a PPI policy, and got commission for that as well. Apparently, they used to roll up the costs under a nebulous 'service charges' term, no details given."

"It beggars belief, doesn't it?" Matt said. "Where's the morality? It may have been legal, but it wasn't bloody ethical."

"I know. The risk to the buyer, of course, was negative equity when the finance industry went tits up in 2008, and they'd have an ongoing PPI policy that nobody wanted, as we now know. But he'd got out by then and moved to Pontygwyn."

"Where were they living when this was going on?" asked Matt.

"In Bristol, I think. Why?"

"Just curious," Matt said. "All this doesn't really go with the image he puts across, does it? Pillar of the community, chairman of the trustees of a charity. Seems to me he's got as many faces as the town clock."

Dilys grinned at the expression. "My mam often says that."

"So does Fabia." But they were soon back to the matter in hand. "I wonder whether Ivor Gladwin had stumbled across this information."

"I wouldn't be surprised. But why kill Ellis as well?"

"I've been wondering whether Ellis was killed because he knew, or had found out, who was responsible for Ivor's death."

"That's always possible," Matt said wearily. "And we also have to consider the fact that they could have been killed by two different people, but that would throw the whole thing wide open again."

"I'm afraid so, and there's more."

"Oh Lord, what now, Dilys?"

"Don't worry, sir, this should be helpful," she assured him. "I've made a bullet point list of what we have so far and what is on-going, other than further interviews that is. Do you want to look at it now?"

"Absolutely."

She selected a document on her laptop and turned the screen towards Matt. At the top was a list of the people involved in the pantomime and below that another list, of those involved in the case but not part of the cast and crew of the pantomime, like Hywel Shaw, Morgan Conway's ex-wife, and others. Below that was a timeline for both murders and a list of those who had alibis and those who did not. At the end was a list of what Dilys called pointers, which included the information retrieved from Ivor's devices, the smear of blood on the Cadogans' kitchen floor and also, they'd discovered, in the hallway, the footprints across their lawn and the fact that Ellis's murderer was probably left-handed. And right at the end there was a note about the information given to them by Dr Nelson and his wife, and the Wellington boots found in Mrs Rodgerson's garden.

"Those boots," Matt said, having run his eyes down Dilys's succinct list. "I wonder if the SOCOs have finished with them." He looked up and called across the room. "Dave, can I have a moment?"

"Yessir," said Dave, coming across to stand beside him.

"Have you heard from your SOCO girlfriend yet?"

"No, but I can give her a call."

"Do that will you?"

It took Dave a while to get through but, half an hour later, he came over to Matt. "Good news, sir, she'd just finished when I got through. She says there were traces of blood on the inside of the boots, same type as Ellis Cadogan, and there were also some shreds of a black material, cotton, she thinks, or lace of some kind, but she's still checking on it. Maybe the socks of the person who was wearing them. The imprints on the grass are a little more difficult to pin down, but she's pretty sure they match the pattern on the sole of the boots. It looks like whoever killed him could have used those boots when they legged it."

"But didn't arrive wearing them," Matt said.

"Probably not, given the blood inside."

"But if the murderer used the boots," Matt went on, "what did they do with their own shoes? Mrs Nelson didn't say anything about the person she saw carrying anything." He turned to Dilys. "Can you get on to Mrs Nelson and double-check that?"

"Will do, sir," she said, taking out her mobile.

"Tom picked up the receipt from the Cadogan house this morning and went to the sports shop in Cwmbran," Dave told him. "They were definitely bought there, and the assistant remembers the couple who came in. She said the man was giving his poor wife a hard time, really rude to her, he was. She identified them both from the photos Tom had with him."

"I still want to know how they ended up in that garden," Matt said. "Do you think the kids found them?"

"Possibly. If they were worn by the murderer, whoever it was would have wanted to get rid of them asap."

"Get someone down to that alleyway, I want it combed down to the last bramble, and see if the community chap has found those kids yet."

"Will do, sir," said Dave.

"And let me know when your girlfriend comes back to you about the fabric inside the boots."

"Rightio, sir."

CHAPTER 19

It wasn't long before Aidan sent through an e-mail with the rest of the information he'd found on Ivor Gladwin's devices, and some research he'd done as a result. Aidan had found two points that stood out.

Prompted by notes Gladwin had made, he'd researched a news story from some years ago about a woman who had been had up for shoplifting. She'd protested her innocence, told the court that it was just a case of being absent-minded, but she hadn't been believed. She had been fined and given a community service order. The woman was Eve Kemble. Matt wondered why Fabia hadn't mentioned this. Surely, she'd have known about it. He checked if there was any date mentioned. Yes, there it was, 20th June 2009. That could explain it. Fabia may not know. He frowned. Surely Eve was a rather unlikely murderer. Granted, she could have pushed Ivor off the gantry, but killing Ellis Cadogan? Surely not. She was in her mid-sixties, maybe older, and didn't look as if she was the sort that worked out. Matt doubted that she would have had the strength to knife someone in that way.

The second thing he'd turned up was a series of texts on Gladwin's phone, these between him and Eryn Jackson. They appeared to imply that she'd known Luke many years before, when they were both teenagers, and that they had been very close. Matt found it hard to believe that Luke would not have realised this – Eryn was an attractive woman. Matt couldn't believe he wouldn't have recognised her. There was no indication in the texts of where, or exactly when, she was suggesting they knew each other, but she was insistent about their past association. After what Fabia had told him earlier in the afternoon, Matt was particularly interested in these exchanges.

Lastly, there was an interesting report about a drugs ring who'd managed, so far, to evade the police. It was all rumour and circumstantial evidence, no real substance, but the one thing that seemed to be clear was that it was a local outfit, based in the Pontygwyn area. Drugs were a serious problem in Newport and Cwmbran, in the Gwent area generally, but in Pontygwyn? That didn't seem so likely. He decided it'd be a good idea to contact someone he'd worked with in the past, Glyn Evans, who'd gone from community police work to the drugs squad. He put that on his mental list of things to do.

Who to tackle first? For a few minutes Matt sat frowning at the screen of his laptop. He glanced at his watch, it was half past three. He picked up his mobile and scrolled down to Luke's number. Apart from anything else, he wanted to ask him about Eryn.

When Luke picked up, Matt suggested he walk down to the drovers' bridge and they meet there, it would afford privacy without looking unusual, people often stopped on the bridge to admire the view up and down stream. He could do with stretching his legs and there was a while yet before it would begin to get dark.

* * *

Ten minutes later he was standing on the bridge looking down towards Gwyddon Park, the soft brown of the water running fast and tumbling over rocks beneath him. The pond where witches used to be ducked, innocent if drowned, guilty if not, was round the bend of the river and out of sight behind the trees, and along the north-west bank ran the park with its rugby playing field and cricket pitch. Matt turned and leant his back on the ancient stones and looked to his right, up the high street, to see Luke, in the distance, striding towards him.

As he waited, a memory from two years ago returned to him so vividly that, for a moment, he thought he saw Fabia coming towards him too. He had been on his way back from a meeting in Abergavenny when he'd stopped in Pontygwyn to get a sandwich and a drink and, for the first time in several years, he'd bumped into Fabia. He had been completely taken aback by the overwhelming emotion that had swept over him at the sight of her. Back then they'd been estranged and had had no contact for some time, something for which he now blamed himself. He smiled now, what a long way they'd come in two short years.

"What are you smiling about? Made some progress?" Luke asked, joining him at that moment.

"Nothing much, just thinking of Fabia."

"Ah. You're a lucky man."

"I know, very lucky." But Matt was soon getting down to business.

"There are several things I need to run through with you. First of all, we've come up with some information. Well, Aidan Rogers has, our techy expert. He's gone through Gladwin's phone, and found a couple of e-mails on his iPad. There were texts between him and Eryn Jackson implying that the two of you knew each other way back—"

"What? Eryn and me?" Luke said, frowning.

"According to her you knew each other as kids, well in your mid-teens to be more precise, and she implies you were pretty friendly. You don't half spread it around, Luke," Matt said with a sideways look at his companion.

"Thank you, sir!" Luke exclaimed, only half joking.

"Then, in an e-mail to Gladwin, she went into more detail," Matt told him. "This was in response to one from him asking all about you. According to her, it was when you lived with your parents at Nant Fach, when it was still a working farm."

"But that's ridiculous. She's a pretty distinctive-looking woman with those high cheekbones and that dark skin, more South American than Welsh I'd say. And I've got a bloody good eye for faces, I'd have recognised her."

"Are you sure? It's what? Twenty-five odd years ago?"

Luke stood frowning out over the river. "No, not possible. I was away at school, Clifton College in

Bristol, to be precise, and most of my holidays were spent working on the farm. My father was a hard taskmaster, said I had to repay them for the money they were ploughing into my education." There was resentment in his voice. "I didn't have time for chasing after women – well, girls. No. She's either lying or she's got me mixed up with someone else."

Matt was inclined to believe him. He wondered what would come out when he questioned Eryn about it. And if she was lying, why?

"There's another thing. She also suggested that it wouldn't be surprising if Sally had snapped and killed Ellis because he was abusing her, and that you might have been involved."

Luke turned to look at him, a mixture of fear and anger in his eyes. "But what about the fact he was killed by someone left-handed?"

"That has to be borne in mind, I grant you."

"What do you mean, borne in mind?" Luke said, sounding anguished. "She just couldn't have done it, for so many reasons. Please, sir, Matt, I don't–"

"Calm down. I think it's highly unlikely she was responsible for either death, but we must keep as open a mind as possible."

Luke drew in a deep breath in an effort to calm down. "Are you going to tackle Eryn? I'd like to be there when you do."

"Sorry, that's not possible. It'd blow your cover, and I don't want that to happen yet. It's useful that very few people know what you're up to, and I want to keep it that way for as long as I can."

Luke shrugged but agreed, obviously reluctant.

Matt glanced at his watch. "I must get going. I'll let you know, if I can, what happens with Eryn, and Morgan for that matter."

* * *

Half an hour later Matt and Dilys were making their way to a small cottage right down the end of Sycamore Road, opposite the main gate of St Madoc's School. Although the cottage was pretty, painted white with green window frames and a neat front garden, attached to the side was a rather ugly, one storey extension. Above its double front doors, a plaque announced, rather ostentatiously, 'Eryn Jackson Academy of Dance' and below that, 'Dance will set you free'.

Dilys gave Matt a sardonic look. "I wonder how she got planning permission for all that?" she remarked. Matt wasn't sure whether she was referring to the building or the wording on the plaque.

"Friends in the right places, perhaps," Matt said.

"You mean, give me my planning permission, Mr Councillor, and I'll teach your snotty little brat to point her toes?"

"You, Dilys, are a cynic," Matt said, grinning.

They walked up the short path to the front door of the cottage. They had not rung ahead, preferring to surprise their quarry without giving her time to prepare herself. There was no sound of music or shouted instructions coming from the extension, so they assumed there was no lesson in progress. All to the good, thought Matt.

It wasn't long before a response came to their knock and Eryn appeared in the doorway. Her eyes widened in a mixture of fear and excitement, then were quickly veiled as she glanced at Dilys then smiled in recognition at Matt.

"Oh," she said, putting a hand up to her neck, "it's you. Did Fabia send you?"

"No, that's not how it works," Matt told her, unconsciously echoing what Fabia had said. "Could we come in and have a word?"

"Of course," she said, gracefully stepping aside, her feet moving as if she was practising dance steps. She had herself well in hand, although Matt could sense the tension in her.

"Come through," she said, leading them into a living room to one side that spanned the cottage from front to back. There was a comfortable sofa and two armchairs, all covered in colourful throws, and photos everywhere, on the walls, on an upright piano opposite the fireplace and on bookshelves either side of it. Most of the photos were of dancers in one pose or another, many of them of a younger Eryn in various ballet costumes. Matt noticed that she had changed very little.

"Please, sit," she said, sweeping her hand out in a graceful gesture. Matt felt as if they were being received by royalty.

Once they were settled, Dilys took out her notebook.

"Fabia did mention what you suggested earlier today," Matt began, "but I was planning to come round and speak to you anyway. It just speeded things up a bit. I gather you believe that Sally, and maybe Luke, could be responsible for the two deaths."

"Well, it does seem quite likely," she said, drawing herself up. "Ivor was particularly nosy about Sally's activities."

"And when exactly do you think it happened, Ivor's murder I mean?"

"Wasn't it on Saturday afternoon?"

"It was. What time?"

"I– I don't know." She didn't sound quite so sure of herself now. "When was it?"

Matt ignored this question. "I gather you saw Sally near the theatre on Saturday afternoon. What time would you say that was?"

She frowned at Matt and chewed at her lip. "Well, let me see. I'd had my lunch, and I'd put things away, so, I suppose it must have been about half past one, maybe a bit earlier. I always try to eat at half past twelve precisely. Always vegetables, pulses, seeds, that sort of thing. Meat never passes my lips. A vegetarian diet and strict timing for meals is best for the metabolism and builds up my strength, in my core, you know." She pressed her hands either side, just above her waist. "And I always take a walk after my meal, it energises me to work through the afternoon."

Matt heard Dilys give a little sigh. He could sense her impatience and didn't risk looking at her.

"And that is when you saw Sally?" Matt asked, trying to bring Eryn back on track.

"Ye-es." She sounded rather hesitant. "Does that coincide with the time Ivor was killed?"

"It might," Matt said smoothly.

"But why won't you tell me the exact time?" Eryn protested, pushing aside any pretence at calmness.

Dilys intervened, "Because we don't know yet." Her impatience had obviously got the better of her. "These things take time."

Eryn glanced at her, then back at Matt. "Yes, yes, of course." Then she added, in a rush, "Oh, this is all so upsetting. I just can't bear the thought that one of us could have done such terrible things. Of course, one would understand that Sally could become desperate, what with being so put down and disparaged by her husband, and I dare say he might have been *violent* as well, but why would she kill Ivor?"

"Do you think she killed either of them?" Matt watched her closely.

"Well, yes," she said, clasping her hands tight in her lap. "That's what we were talking about."

"Who is 'we'?" Matt asked, his voice cool.

A flush rose up her cheeks. "Didn't Fabia tell you?" she asked, a little huffy.

Matt didn't give her a direct answer. "You tell me," he suggested.

"Lewys and Peony and me, in the pub. We weren't gossiping," she assured them, "but we were talking about it all. Who wouldn't? Everybody is. And we could completely understand if she, just, lost it, you know, with Ellis. Particularly as she has other interests now."

"Which are?" Matt asked.

"Well, she and Luke, you know, are very friendly." Her lips pursed into a thin line and there was malice in her eyes.

"Luke Melville?"

"Is there another one?"

"Not so far as I know," said Matt, sitting back in his chair. "I wanted to ask you about him."

Her eyes narrowed but she didn't comment. Matt paused, considering how to phrase his next question. It really was time to be more assertive. If he wasn't, they'd be here all day.

"We have searched through Ivor's mobile phone and found records of a series of texts between the two of you. These imply that you and Luke had a relationship when the two of you were teenagers. Is that true?"

Eyes wide, she put up both hands to her mouth.

The seconds ticked by, then Matt repeated, "Is that true?"

"I– I– Yes." The word was defiant. "Yes. It is. We were at school together. But why do you want to know?"

Matt ignored the question. "Can you tell me exactly how old you were at the time?"

"It was years ago."

He waited.

"Maybe fourteen, fifteen," she said.

"And where was he living then?"

"Where he lives now." There was a note of triumph in her voice. "He bought his parents' farmhouse when he came back to Pontygwyn."

"But that's common knowledge, isn't it, Eryn?" Matt pointed out. "And what school were you both at?"

Matt waited. Other than the whispering sound of Dilys's pencil, the silence was profound. Then Eryn said, "Caerleon," but it was almost a question.

"But Luke was at Clifton College in Bristol."

"Yes, I know, and I went into the sixth form there. They only took girls in the sixth form back then, and I was one of–"

"In the sixth form, at fifteen?" Matt asked. "No, no. This won't do, Eryn. Your first reply was Caerleon. Now, I want you to tell me the truth. Why did you make all this up and tell Ivor about it?"

"How dare you suggest I made it up," she exclaimed, her face flushing up even more now. "It's true! It is!" she said, thumping her fists on the arms of her chair as she spoke.

"Then why would Luke deny ever having met you before he came back to Pontygwyn six months ago? Your looks are distinctive, and you haven't changed much at all, I can tell from the photographs around this room, yet he says he definitely didn't recognise you."

"That's his problem. Maybe it's because of Sally, he doesn't want her to know I came first," she insisted.

Matt glanced at Dilys. This was getting them nowhere. He decided to change tack. "Let me take you back to the Saturday afternoon Ivor was killed. You've already told me that you went for a walk. I want you to think very hard about how long you were out and what time you got back."

The flush had receded now, and she gave Matt a wan smile. "I'll do my best. Let me see, lunch at twelve thirty, as I told you, then I tidied things away, put on my coat and boots and got going." As she spoke, she ticked the points off on her fingers. "I suppose I was out for half an hour, so I probably got back about half one. Are you happy with that?"

"It's not a case of our being happy," Matt said patiently. "It's a case of getting exact timings so that we can establish alibis for the various people involved, including you."

"I don't need an alibi!" Eryn protested, panic in her voice. "I could never, ever kill anyone. What are you suggesting?"

"Exactly what I said," Matt pointed out. "We need to establish alibis for everyone."

Matt decided this would be the right time to end the interview, but before doing so there was something he wanted to find out.

"Could you give me your mobile number? It would be useful to have if we need to contact you again." He took out his phone, prepared to key it in, then said, "Damn. I forgot to charge it. Dilys, can I have your pen and notebook?"

Dilys glanced at him, curious, but then handed them over without comment. He gave them to Erin.

"Perhaps you could jot them down for me."

She almost snatched the notebook and pen from him and wrote rapidly then handed them back without a word.

"Thank you," Matt said, "and thank you for your co-operation, Eryn. We must get going now. If you think of anything else that you think would be useful to us, please contact me immediately. We'll probably want to talk to you again at some point. Don't worry, we'll see ourselves out."

Eryn made no protest. Matt was sure she'd be delighted to see the back of them.

As she started up the car, Dilys asked, "What was all that about?"

"I wanted to find out if she was left-handed."

"Ah, and she is, isn't she?"

"She is," Matt said, with satisfaction.

"That's a frightened woman," Dilys said.

"You're not wrong," Matt said. "And had you noticed, if her timing is right, it means she has no alibi for Ivor Gladwin's murder. How strong do you think you have to be to be a ballet dancer?"

"Pretty strong, I'd say. I heard a story once about a bunch of footballers being put through the same training and workouts that the corps de ballet go through and being completely wiped out by it all."

Matt gave a snort of laughter, but he was soon serious again. "And she was talking about strengthening her core, wasn't she?"

"She was," Dilys said. "Morgan Conway next?"

"Yes, but that'll have to wait until first thing tomorrow. It's half past eight, Dilys, and I'm going to check back at the theatre then go home. Drop me off and I'll walk from there."

CHAPTER 20

Just as he was about to leave the incident room Matt had an unexpected call from Glyn Evans.

"Great minds, I was about to phone you, Glyn," Matt told him. "How's it going with the drug squad?"

"Busy, sir, but I'm enjoying it. Managed to put away a couple of toerags last week. We've been after them for a whole twelve months and finally collared them, which was satisfying, but getting our hands on the big boys, that's another story." He paused. "But that wasn't what I was phoning about. I had a pint with Tom Watkins earlier, sir, and he gave me the griff on this murder case of yours. Seems like the Pontygwyn loonies are at it again!"

"Tell me about it! And I've ended up as CIO, which is somewhat awkward."

"How did that happen? Tom didn't say."

"Inspector Foyle was in charge, but she's out of commission, she was injured in a traffic accident, so Rees-Jones handed it to me. Bit of a poisoned chalice, I can tell you."

"I suppose, given that Fabia lives there," Glyn said, sounding a little embarrassed.

Matt realised that Glyn might not know he'd moved. "And so do I, now." There was a soft whistle from Glyn. "I... er... moved in with Fabia a few weeks ago, so Pontygwyn is part of my patch in more ways than one, if you see what I mean."

"Awkward, but at least you're on the spot."

"There is that. Anyway, what can I do for you?"

"Tom told me about the current case and who the two victims are. He also said you've got a pretty wide field of suspects, most of them involved in some pantomime or other, which will make for a few drama queens, I should imagine."

"Tell me about it," Matt said with a rueful grin.

"And he said that it seems neither victim was well liked."

"That's about the sum of it – one a wind-up merchant, the other a bully."

"Nice. I wish you joy of them," Glyn said. "But why I'm calling, sir, is that I know a couple, well, one of the people involved. Bloke called Morgan Conway, he's a taxi driver."

"You know him professionally or personally?"

"Professionally. He's got a bit of a past, has Morgan."

"So I gather. We've got some info on that. He was inside for a stretch, on a drugs charge, and changed his name when he came out, used to be called Eddie Martinez. We're not sure why he did that. His ex-wife lives in Chepstow and we're hoping to interview her tomorrow, maybe get some of the background."

"Yep, that's our Morgan. We believe the name change could have been down to getting on the wrong side of the Michaelson gang while he was inside."

"Ah," said Matt, understanding.

"You can see why, can't you?"

Matt could hear that Glyn was smiling.

"Anyway, he's been on our radar for a bit now, but we haven't been able to pin anything on him. I mean, as a dealer, being a taxi driver must make meeting up with your clients a piece of piss, but we still haven't got enough on him to move in. I'd really like to have a good clean through of his taxi. We've found out where he goes to have it serviced, so we may be able to have a look at it the next time he takes it in, I'm working on that. And, obviously, if we find traces of any drugs, he could just say it was one of his clients and insist he knew nothing about it."

"What are you suggesting, then?" Matt asked. "In relation to the case I'm working on, I mean?"

"Several things. Were either of the victims clients of his? If he is a pusher, I mean. Did the snoopy one–"

"Ivor Gladwin."

"–pick up on his activities and let it be known he'd done so? Did the bully, Cadogan isn't it?"

"Yes."

"Was he a druggie and failed to pay for what was supplied?"

"Now that's a thought," Matt said. "I gather Ellis Cadogan was a moody type. He certainly had a gambling habit and, what's more, there's been some dubious activity on the Little Theatre accounts, and he was their treasurer."

"Aha!" Glyn exclaimed. "If he got chopsy, either refused to pay or questioned the price or supply in some way, maybe he needed to be got rid of."

"This is all very useful, Glyn, I owe you. I'll get Aidan to do another trawl through the devices belonging to both victims, see if we can turn anything up about drugs."

"No problem. I'll keep my ear to the ground and let you know if I pick up anything more, sir."

"Thanks again."

"And, sir, give my regards to Fabia. She's a great loss to the force."

Matt grinned. Praise of Fabia always pleased him. "You're right there, I'll tell her you said so."

* * *

When Matt got home, he relayed all this information to Fabia, including Glyn's last comments.

"Bless him," she said, looking pleased. "Wasn't he the lad who was brought up on a farm, did such a good job of searching the stables at White Monk Abbey?"

"He's the one. An asset to the drug squad, I'd say. What do you think of Morgan Conway as a drug pusher?"

Fabia screwed up her face in doubt. "I'm not sure, he's a strange one. He's not stupid, but he's sort of innocent, as if his mind doesn't quite work along the same lines as others. If it was a case of passing over a few Es or amphetamines in his taxi, possibly, but I'm not sure I see him as someone who'd be dealing in the heavy stuff, or organising distribution without taking clear instructions from someone else. I wouldn't put him down as someone who'd be in charge of a drugs ring but, of course, I could be wrong."

"You rarely are."

"Why, thank you, kind sir. But there is someone of whom I'd say being in charge fits like a glove."

"Who?"

Fabia told him and Matt's eyes widened, he hadn't thought of that. "And that would also be a good cover."

"It would, wouldn't it?"

For a moment Matt stared thoughtfully into space, then he turned to Fabia and asked, "What have you got planned for tomorrow?"

"Tomorrow morning, nothing much. Tomorrow afternoon I was going to drive to Tintern Abbey. John Meredith has asked me to do a watercolour of it for him to give Anjali for her birthday. I want to do some preliminary sketches, get some idea of what angle to paint it from. Why?"

"Fabia, I've had an idea."

"Oh Lord, what do you want me to do now?"

Matt described what he wanted of her and, at first, she resisted, but, as he knew she would, she gave in in the end.

"You're a slave driver, you are," she protested.

"Why? What's so bad about—"

"Okay, okay, I'll do it."

* * *

Matt found out the following morning that Sara Gupta's interview of Morgan Conway's ex-wife had produced a few useful odds and ends.

"They separated before he went to prison," she told Matt. "She found out he'd been dealing in drugs. She confirmed that she actually reported him to the police. She told me she wouldn't have someone who'd do a thing like that anywhere near her children, so she chucked him out."

"How did she find out?"

"He left some packets of Es in his trouser pocket and when she emptied them so she could put them in the wash, she found them."

"Not the brightest penny in the bunch, our Morgan."

"No. She seemed to imply that," Sara said. "What was it she said? That he had trouble understanding what the consequences of his actions would be, didn't think ahead."

"I don't suppose he's unique in that."

Sara grinned. "True, sir. Anyway, she says she has little to do with him now, except on his very occasional visits to see their two children. Both girls, fourteen and sixteen now. She says they see very little of him by choice," Sara told him. "There was, however, one thing that may be useful. Apparently, he and Ellis Cadogan knew each other as children. Conway comes from round here, and they were big butties, both heavily into gambling. His gambling was also a bone of contention in their marriage, and so was the fact that his sister was always interfering, trying to tell her how to bring up the kids and saying she neglected Morgan."

"A managing woman, it seems," Matt said.

"Looks like it." Then Sara went on, "One thing she mentioned was that his sister was responsible for his change of name. She told him she'd set him up with his taxi business if he changed it, as she didn't want anyone to make any connection between him and his prison record and her very successful hairdressing business. Apparently the Pontygwyn salon isn't the only one she owns."

"At least that explains it," Matt said. "So it wasn't to do with the Michaelson gang as we thought."

"Seems not. As to his going back to dealing, it occurred to me that if he's still into the gambling, he could well have debts that he has to pay off. That may mean he's desperate for cash and the dealing solved the problem for him."

"Could you keep digging, Sara? And well done so far. Once you've typed up your notes, Dilys and I can go and have a word with him."

But Morgan Conway proved difficult to contact. Dilys tried his mobile several times but he wasn't picking up. Matt considered contacting his sister to find out where he was, but decided against it, he didn't want Conway to be forewarned.

"How the hell does he manage to work if he never picks up?" Dilys complained. "He's an independent taxi driver, doesn't work from an office, so you'd have thought he'd answer his bloody phone in case it was a client."

"Agreed," Matt said, "just keep trying."

In the end her patience was rewarded, but Conway refused to meet them at his home. "I'll come to the station. I don't want my sister bothered. And I've got bookings this afternoon that take me into Newport, so it'd be convenient for me."

"That will be fine, sir," Dilys told him.

"I should be finished about four thirty. I could come in after that."

She wondered at his attitude. He seemed to be implying that he was doing them a favour. Ah well, they'd be able to disabuse him of that should the need arise. "Just ask for Sergeant Dilys Bevan when you get to the desk."

"Okay. I'll do my best."

"That would be a good idea, sir," Dilys said, trying to keep the irritation out of her voice. She cut off the call and frowned across at Matt. "I wouldn't have put him down as someone who'd want to be visiting police stations. He said something about not wanting his sister to be worried, what's all that about?"

"No idea, Dilys, but let's try to find out."

* * *

Fabia hadn't woken when Matt had gone off to work at half past six that morning. She woke two hours later and dragged herself out of bed, mornings were not her best time as a rule, and she'd been feeling even worse the last couple of weeks. But she couldn't laze around, she had work to do. Having finally finished the illustrations for the children's book, she needed to pack them up and send them off to the publisher for approval. She printed off copies as she never trusted the originals to the vagaries of the post. After going to the post office, she dropped off a couple of small watercolours to an arts and crafts gallery in the high street. They'd taken some of her work before and she hoped they'd sell these two, one of Gwyddon pond and one of the drovers' bridge. Having been to the post office and delivered the pictures, she decided she'd go to Hywel's for a coffee as she'd not bothered with breakfast.

The cafe wasn't very busy mid-morning on a Tuesday, but the window tables, which Fabia liked best, as they provided an opportunity for people watching, were occupied. Instead she found a small table not far from the counter and ordered a latte and an almond croissant, then got out a copy of the Western Mail that she'd bought and flattened it out on the table. Vaguely, in the background, she could hear a conversation between the woman at the counter and another customer.

"Do you really enjoy it? Kickboxing?" the assistant asked, sounding dubious. "Sounds a bit, well, violent to me."

"Not at all," said the customer. "It's great exercise, keeps you really fit."

"I don't know. Isn't it, sort of, a bit unladylike?"

"Come on, a young woman like you shouldn't think like that. We can do everything a man can do nowadays, and more. You should try it. There's a great club in Cwmbran. I've been going there for years. Really builds up your muscles and keeps you fit."

Fabia glanced round and recognised the customer. It was Carmen Lloyd, Morgan Conway's sister who owned the hairdressing and nail salon a few doors along from the cafe. She was leaning her arms on the counter as she waited for her order. Kickboxing? thought Fabia. It was not something she would associate with such a sleek woman. What about those gorgeous scarlet nails?

"I'll think about it." The assistant placed a cup of coffee in front of Carmen. "Was it shortbread you wanted with that?"

"Please."

"Jack's just bringing it up. Sorry to keep you."

"No problem," Carmen said.

Fabia went back to her newspaper, but a moment later she was distracted again by the on-going conversation.

"A dreadful business, that poor girl," the assistant said, lowering her voice a little.

"Yes, terrible," came the reply from Carmen. "They're saying he was quite a bully, so maybe it was self-defence."

"And then there was that awful business at the theatre. I just don't know what the world is coming to."

"I know, dreadful. I was in the salon all day Saturday, so I heard all the police cars going past, but I didn't find out what had happened until the evening. With this second one, my brother is sure it was the wife, poor dab."

"Your brother?" she said. "He's a taxi driver, isn't he?"

"He is. Let me give you his card, you might need a lift at some time, and he's local, see, which is always better don't you think."

Fabia turned to get a better look at her. She was a thin-faced woman with sleek fair hair, neatly cropped longer on one side than the other. She had strong features and a pleasant smile. With her artist's eye, Fabia studied her and could see the likeness to her brother.

"It's the usual story, really, a woman pushed beyond her limit," Fabia heard her say, then she leant towards the young woman behind the counter and Fabia could only just catch the words. "Apparently that Ivor Gladwin, the one who fell from the metal bridge above the stage in the theatre."

"Is that how he died?"

"Yes. He was giving her grief as well. It's possible she pushed him, that's what I've heard."

"Never to God!" said the counter assistant, but she didn't have the chance to continue the conversation as, a moment later, the owner of the cafe came up behind her, a plate of shortbread in his hand. "I'll take over here, Charlotte. Could you pop round the back and get some more Earl Grey tea bags, we've run out."

From the expression on his face, Fabia got the impression he'd overheard the conversation and wanted to put a stop to it. She could sympathise. This kind of gossip did nobody any good.

She watched as Carmen picked up her tray and made her way to a table at the back of the cafe where someone else was already sitting.

Seeing Carmen Lloyd had reminded Fabia that she should be making a hair appointment, and now was as good a time as any. Once she'd done her bit of shopping, she'd go to the salon and fix that up.

* * *

Half an hour later she walked into the humid warmth of the salon. There was an overwhelming smell of shampoo and other hair products which Fabia found a little hard to cope with. The murmur of gossipy voices was accompanied by quiet music, and Fabia was relieved it wasn't too loud, she'd never been a great fan of anonymous muzak rumbling away in the background. The décor was smart, minimalist cream and black with touches of stainless steel, and there were posters of various models on the walls, their hair advertising the latest styles. The salon was busy. Several women were having their hair done, a

223

woman was sitting with her fingers dipped into a bowl of water and another was having her nails painted a bright green.

She went up to the reception desk where a young girl with purple hair sat tapping away at her phone. She put it down immediately Fabia approached. "Good morning," she said, giving Fabia a professional welcoming smile. "Can I help you?"

"I was wondering if I could make an appointment for a trim and blow-dry," Fabia said, pushing a hand through her hair. "This mop is really getting to me."

"Ah, don't call it that. You have beautiful hair, such lovely curls, and a good colour."

"Thank you," said Fabia, "but it's a bit difficult to control."

Fabia heard the door open and turned to look at the newcomer. It was Carmen Lloyd again. She came up to the desk, gave Fabia a smile, and asked, "Is Leanne looking after you?"

"She is, I was just wanting to make an appointment. My usual hairdresser in Usk has just closed down and I need to find someone else to deal with this mop of mine."

Carmen gave her an enquiring look, her head on one side. "Surely, we know each other, don't we?"

"We have met." Holding out her hand, Fabia said, "Fabia Havard. I'm involved in the pantomime, painting the sets. I believe you're in charge of all the props, is that right?"

"Yes. My brother, Morgan, is playing Wishee Washee, although I suppose we should say was, really. It'll be cancelled now, don't you think? They can hardly go on with it, now, after all this–"

"No, I suppose not," Fabia said.

Carmen Lloyd turned to the receptionist. "I've got a space until lunch time, haven't I, Leanne? Wasn't there a cancellation?"

"Yes, your next is Mrs Fullerton, at one."

"I could look after you now, if you have time," she said to Fabia.

"That's very kind, thank you."

"Come this way," Carmen said.

Fabia followed her, glancing at the people in the other chairs, a woman with what looked like silver ribbons attached to her hair lifted a magazine to her face, and another was telling the person cutting her hair about her son's success at university. The rumble of conversation competed with the music.

At the back of the salon Carmen helped her into a gown and settled her in the chair. Little more was said until Carmen led Fabia back to a seat at the front of the salon. Once they'd discussed what Fabia wanted her to do, Carmen pulled a trolley towards her and searched around on it.

"Hey," she called to the others in the salon, "who's pinched my scissors again? You know I can't use these ones."

"Sorry, Carmen," said one of the other girls, "here you are." She handed Carmen a pair of scissors and she started snipping away.

"That's an interesting name for a Welsh woman," Fabia remarked. "Have you got Spanish ancestry?"

"As a matter of fact, I have. My father was Spanish, and my grandparents still live in Seville. My brother and I try to visit them as often as possible."

"How lovely, that's a beautiful city."

"It is. So much history. But we were both born in Wales, so Spain is more like a holiday place for us rather than home."

For a while there was silence between them, then Carmen asked, "Am I right in thinking that your partner is a policeman? Matt Lambert, is it?"

"Yes, he is." But Fabia said nothing about his being in charge of the current investigation. She suspected that would generate far too much interest all around the salon.

"And you're an artist," Carmen said. "I'm sure I saw some of your paintings in the arts and crafts shop next door to Spar, some lovely watercolours."

"I did take some to them."

"Lovely, they were. You're very talented."

"Thank you," Fabia said smiling at her in the mirror.

"Have you got any particular project on the go?" Carmen asked, then added, with a rueful look, "Other than the scenery for the pantomime. Do you think they'll cancel it now?"

"I gather it's on hold, but from what I hear, the Aubreys are still hoping to go ahead."

"Surely not. Oh dear, an unpleasant subject," Carmen said, shaking her head. "Tell me, what other work have you got on the go?"

"I'm doing some illustrations for some children's books, and I'm planning to go and have a look at Tintern Abbey this afternoon – a friend wants me to do a watercolour of it for his wife."

"Now there's a place that's got atmosphere." She turned to the receptionist. "Didn't you have your wedding photos taken at Tintern Abbey, Leanne?"

"I did. Lovely, they were."

"There's years since I've been there," Carmen said. "I must visit it again."

The woman in the chair next to them turned and said, "I always take my grandchildren there when they visit, they love it. Beautiful, it is."

"It is, isn't it?" Fabia agreed. "The trouble is you're inclined not to go to places like that unless you have a specific reason, like when you're showing visitors around. I was really pleased when John, my friend, asked me to do the painting. Apart from anything else, it's the perfect excuse for a wander around those incredible ruins."

At this moment there was an interruption. Someone had just come into the salon and Carmen turned to see who it was. "Ah, would you excuse me a moment," she said to Fabia.

Fabia watched her in the mirror as she made her way across to the reception desk. "I'll deal with this," she heard Carmen say to the receptionist, then she turned to the woman who had just come in. "Thank you for coming back, Paula, it was my fault entirely. I took the wrong shampoo off the shelf. Leanne, hand me down the Shea Butter formula, yes please, that one."

Leanne turned to reach up to the shelf behind the desk, then handed Carmen a box. "Let me just check this is correct," Carmen said to the customer. She opened the box, pulled the bottle out then nodded, and carefully replaced it. "Yes, that should really help the dryness," she said and handed it to the customer. "No, no extra charge, I should have got it right in the first place."

With a murmur of thanks, the customer scuttled away. As Carmen turned back to Fabia and picked up the scissors again, their eyes met in the mirror. "Sorry to desert you," Carmen said. "Tintern, yes, you should enjoy that."

CHAPTER 21

Fabia returned home and grabbed a quick lunch. She'd tried to get hold of Matt to tell him about the conversation in the cafe and her hair appointment, but he wasn't picking up. An hour later she packed her painting gear into her car and begun the forty-minute drive to Tintern Abbey. Still puzzling over what she'd seen and heard, she tried Matt again, but there was still no response. "Bugger it, Matt," she muttered, "where the hell are you?"

It was as she was driving along the stretch of road that ran along just above the Anghidi River that she noticed the car behind her. It was a Land Rover, battered and muddy and travelling very fast. She slowed and kept to the side of the road, thinking that at that speed it would go on past her, but it didn't. It stayed on her tail, getting closer and closer. She increased her speed, but so did the Land Rover. What on earth was he up to? The next moment there was an almighty crash as he hit the back of her car.

Fabia hit her forehead on the sun visor and felt the jar of the seat belt across her chest. "Christ! What the hell?" She swerved and sped up, but he kept coming. Again, he hit the back of her car. The noise was horrendous. Really scared now, Fabia tried to get away, but her little Skoda wasn't nearly as powerful as the Land Rover. She tried to think clearly. She checked his number plate, but it was obscured by mud except for one letter, she thought it was a B. It was hard to identify the driver. Whoever it was wore a baseball cap and all-enveloping dark glasses, but she thought it might be a man. The next moment he came at her again and this time pushed her towards the dip into the river. She felt and heard the bottom of her car grating and scraping across the rough ground, then it teetered over the edge and continued down.

There was a cacophony of noise, a car horn blaring, the crunching and tearing at her car, snapping branches, the sound of small stones ricocheting off the Skoda's bodywork. All this happened in a matter of seconds, then Fabia's car came to a jarring halt against a tree trunk.

Slowly the noise subsided as twigs, small tree branches and stones settled around her. Fabia sat there, dazed and bruised, until she heard someone banging on her car window. "Hallo! Hallo! Are you alright?"

She turned her head and saw that someone was gazing through the window at her. For a moment she was afraid that it was the driver of the Land Rover, but then realised it wasn't. This was a young brown-faced man dressed in a neat suit and tie, his curling hair cropped short to his head. He wore wire-framed glasses which magnified the size of his anxious eyes.

"I can't open the door," he said. "It's wedged against this tree, but you must get out, the petrol might be leaking and…"

Fabia pressed the window button. It went down, then jammed halfway. But relief flooded through her. At least that was working, sort of.

"You weren't the driver of that car, were you?" she said, and found her voice was shaking.

"No! Of course not. I was coming in the opposite direction and saw him trying to push you off the road. I thumped my horn and the bastard swerved round me and just drove off."

"Thank God! Thank you so much."

"Who the hell was he?"

"I don't know," Fabia said. She felt anger rising up inside her and was glad of it. It cancelled out the fear. "But I'm planning to find out."

"You must try to get out," her rescuer said urgently. "Just in case – I'll go round the other side and check the door."

He did so, found he could open it and, with his help, Fabia managed to clamber over and slither out of her car. She grabbed her handbag from the passenger seat and, with his help, stumbled up the bank to the side of the road.

"My name's Brett Morris," he told her.

"Fabia Havard," said Fabia, holding out her hand and, in the circumstances, feeling a little spurt of amusement at the formality of the gesture.

He took a mobile out of his pocket. "By the way, I got the whole thing on my dash cam, only installed it last week." He grinned. "I'm a bit of a geek when it comes to that sort of thing, and anyway, the insurance is cheaper if you have one."

"Well done you," Fabia said, giving him a slightly shaky smile.

"I'm going to call 999," Brett said. "I think you should be checked over, and I think the police should be informed. That idiot was crashing into you deliberately. I could see that he was."

"I know. But I can get hold of the police. I have contacts."

He gave her a sharp look but didn't comment.

"But I think you're right about the ambulance, I do feel a bit shaken up."

"Sit in my car." He turned and opened the door of a dark red Jaguar parked by the side of the road. Fabia hadn't noticed it until now. She subsided into the passenger seat as he tapped at his phone. "Did you get his number?" Fabia asked.

"It'll be on the dash cam but I think it was covered in mud... Ah, ambulance please."

While he spoke to the ambulance service and gave directions as to where they were, Fabia took out her mobile phone and keyed in Matt's number, but it went to voicemail. She felt tears threatening. Where the hell was he? She told herself not to be a wimp, wiped the back of her hand across her eyes and chose Dilys's number instead. It was answered after two rings.

"Dilys?"

"Hiya, Fabia, have you been trying to get hold of Matt?"

"Yes. Has he let his bloody phone run out again?"

"This time he left it on charge in his office. Do you want to speak to him, he's right by here."

"Thanks, Dilys."

When she heard Matt's voice Fabia found it hard to keep the tears at bay. Her voice shook as she described what had happened as briefly as she could manage.

"Christ, Fabia! Are you okay?"

"A bit battered and bruised, and I think there's a cut on my forehead." She put fingers up and then looked at them. They were stained with spots of blood. "But I don't think there's anything serious."

"And this Brett Morris chap has phoned the ambulance?"

"Yes, he's been very kind, and he thinks he's got some of what happened on his dash cam."

"Good man. What about the police? This is a hit and run."

"I know that," Fabia snapped, "I was there!"

"Sorry, darling. Shit. I wish I was with you. Look, I'll come–"

"No, Matt, you've got far too much on your plate. Just get on with the job and send someone, preferably someone I know. If they blue-light it, they might get here before the ambulance arrives."

"Just give me a quick description of the car, as much detail as you can remember, I'll get the team on to it in case it's connected, you know, to the investigation."

Fabia did as he asked. "Okay? And, Matt, send someone soon, would you?"

"I'll do that now. And I'll get someone to go and pick up my bloody phone. This'll teach me to be such an idiot with it." She could hear him take a shuddering breath. "And, Fabia, my love, if this is to do with the present case, I'll never forgive myself for involving you."

"Don't be stupid. Go. I'll keep you posted. If I can't get you, I'll phone Dilys."

* * *

In the green room at the theatre everyone was standing around listening but trying to pretend they weren't. Matt handed the phone back to Dilys.

"Fabia's been in an RTA," he told her.

"What? Is she alright?" Dilys asked anxiously.

Now they were all unashamedly listening and there were murmurs of concern all around the room.

"Whereabouts?" asked Tom.

"On the road to Tintern, some bastard tried to run her off the road."

There were exclamations from several people at once.

"She sounded pretty shaken up," Matt said, "but she says she's okay. Another driver stopped and the car that rammed her buggered off. She says there's an ambulance on the way."

"I expect they'll take her to Chepstow," Dilys said.

"Probably. Can I borrow your phone again? I want to get hold of Alun Richards."

"Of course," Dilys said, and scrolled down to a number then handed the phone to Matt.

It wasn't long before Matt had described the situation to Inspector Alun Richards, head of the local Traffic Division and a close friend of Fabia's from back when she was in the force. He promised to send someone to the scene.

"Don't you worry, butt, I'll have them there in no time. Hang on a moment." Matt could hear a muttered conversation in the background, then Alun came back to him. "All sorted. I might even go myself." Alun was a law unto himself, he'd never been one for rules and regulations. "Have you been involving Fabia in your investigations again?"

"I... er... well, you know Fabia, it's hard to keep her out."

"True. So, you think this might be something to do with the case you're working on?"

"It's possible."

"Right, you'd better get out an attempt to locate bulletin on this one," Alun said. "Do you want me to fix that up?"

"No thanks," Matt said. "One of my team can do that, we've got a pretty clear description of the vehicle from Fabia and the chap who rescued her has got a dash cam."

"Well done him," Alun said, then added, "And, Matt, don't start worrying yourself to shreds. You'll have to put me in the picture about what you're up to, all the gory details mind, and sooner rather than later, but now I'm off to rescue your lovely lady."

Matt handed the phone back to Dilys. "Right, listen up folks." Matt raised his voice so that he could be heard across the room. "You all heard what happened. Fabia said the car that rammed her was a battered Land Rover. The number plate was covered in mud, but she thinks the last letter was B, the car was a dull green and the passenger side mirror was hanging by its wires. She also thinks there was a dent in the passenger side wheel arch and the front bumper was strapped on one side with what looked like gaffer tape."

"I'd say that's a damn good description, given that he was trying to ram her at the time," said Tom, "but that's Fabia for you."

Matt smiled at him but noticed Sharon frown as he did so. He nearly asked if she had a problem, but then decided against it. He couldn't trust himself if she started being chippy. "I want an ATL put out on this. I want that bloody car."

"I'll get on to that, sir," Dave Parry said. "Did I hear a dash cam mentioned?"

"Yes, but I don't want to wait until the info on it is downloaded. I want you to get on to this right now."

"Will do," said Dave.

"The rest of you, concentrate on what you were doing." He looked directly at Sharon as he went on. "We can't take our eye off the ball just because Fabia's been in an accident that may have no connection to the case."

He noticed her redden. Yes, he'd been right, that was exactly what she'd been thinking he'd done.

He sat down and put his head in his hands, tried to control the images in his mind. A moment later Sara came up and put a mug of strong black coffee down beside him. "I thought you could do with this, sir," she said, giving him a sympathetic smile.

"You're a star, Sara, thank you."

Work, that's what he needed, anything to distract him from thoughts of what might have happened if the man who'd rescued Fabia hadn't come along at just the right moment.

* * *

Two police cars arrived almost at the same time. As they'd waited for them – Brett Lewis Morris having insisted on staying with her – Fabia had found out that he was an estate agent from Chepstow who'd been returning from a viewing. She'd told him she

236

was an artist on her way to do some sketches of Tintern, but she hadn't given him any other information. She could tell he was curious about the incident, and about her access to the police. He was obviously wondering why she'd been targeted, but he was tactful enough not to press it after a couple of careful questions.

But it was obvious his curiosity increased when Alun Richards, in full uniform, jumped from one of the police cars and strode over to greet Fabia, saying, "My darling girl, what has happened to you? Matt phoned and I said I'd come along myself, couldn't have you languishing on the side of the road without a friend, could I?"

As he wrapped her in his arms, she gave a shaky laugh. "Alun! Bless you. But I haven't been on my own, Brett here has been looking after me." She turned to Brett with a smile. "This is an old friend of mine, Inspector Alun Richards, we used to work together."

Alun shook Brett firmly by the hand. "Well done, sir. I'll be wanting to hear all about this incident from you. Do you mind if I take your details?"

"No problem," Brett said, and gave Alun his full name, address and phone number, and told him about the record that would be on his dash cam.

"That'll be really useful, sir," Alun told him. "Perhaps you could let me have the SD memory card, I'll give you a receipt for it and get it back to you directly we've downloaded the information."

When all this had been organised, Brett glanced at Fabia and asked, "You used to be a police officer?"

"Yes, I did, up until two years ago."

"Do you think that idiot was someone who had it in for you?" His curiosity got the better of his desire to be tactful. "Maybe you arrested him or something and he's got a long memory?"

"It's always possible," Fabia said.

Alun intervened. "Perhaps you could go with my colleague here," Alun said, indicating one of the other police officers who'd been standing on the sidelines, "and tell him exactly what you saw, sir. Then later we'll get your statement typed up and maybe ask you to come to the station, in Newport, and sign it. We can return your SD card then."

"Of course," Brett said.

It occurred to Fabia that this young man was one of the most co-operative witnesses she'd ever had to deal with. She turned to him and reached up to kiss his cheek. "Thank you so much for all you've done, I owe you."

"No problem." He gave her a slightly embarrassed grin. "It's not often I have such an exciting afternoon." He lifted a hand as he walked away and Fabia determined to get his details from Alun, maybe write him a note to thank him properly.

At that moment an ambulance, blue light flashing, also arrived on the scene. Alun led her towards the paramedics as they jumped from the vehicle and he stayed with her until she was settled on the stretcher. They'd insisted she put her legs up while they checked her over, in spite of Fabia saying she'd be fine just sitting on the seat, and in truth she was glad of it. Reaction was setting in and she felt much less in control than she tried to pretend.

CHAPTER 22

Early in the afternoon Matt and Dilys were making their way back to the station. They both had work to do before their interview with Morgan Conway. As she drove, Dilys glanced at Matt occasionally, but he sat there in brooding silence, clutching his newly charged mobile and glancing at it occasionally. Luckily someone from the station had been on their way home and dropped it in to him.

He kept glancing at it as if willing it to ring, and when it finally did, he fumbled, dropped it by his feet, grabbed it up and barked, "Hallo? Fabia? … Ah, thank God for that." Dilys glanced at him and noticed his shoulders sag and relax. He put his hand up to his mouth and dragged it down over his face, closing his eyes for a moment, then he went on. "That's good news. So … Okay. We're on our way to interview Morgan Conway. Do you want me to organise a car to come and pick you up? … Of course, I can … Don't be silly. I'll get on to Tom right away … And Fabia, love…" He glanced across at Dilys, gave her a slightly embarrassed smile. "When you get home rest, okay, and I'll see you later."

He scrolled down to Tom Watkins' number and briefly explained what he needed, then looked across at Dilys. "The doctor says there's no lasting damage, a bit of whiplash, some bruising and a small cut on her forehead, otherwise she's fine. Oh God, Dilys, it brings back all that shit from two years ago."

"She survived that," Dilys said briskly, "she'll survive this. She's tough is Fabia."

"I know, but I'll never forget walking into that hospital and seeing her looking so– so small, all bandaged up and battered."

"You can't blame yourself every time she gets into a pickle."

"Pickle is putting it mildly."

"But you know what I mean. She's her own woman, Fabia, and I doubt anyone would be able to persuade her to take a back seat on anything."

"Don't I know it!" Matt said with a rueful grin. "The trouble is, it's probably my fault, this time. I actually asked her to become involved."

"Involved in the case, generally, but that was the boss's idea."

"I know, but it's more specific than that." And he told her about the conversation he and Fabia had had on Monday evening and what he'd asked her to do.

"Ah," said Dilys, then gave Matt a quick glance before negotiating the two roundabouts as they came into Newport town centre. "So, you think something she saw, or something she said, is the reason she was targeted?"

"It seems logical, doesn't it? Otherwise how would that bastard have known she'd be on that road?"

"But it could all be a coincidence." Dilys was always one for concrete proof and no speculation. So was Matt – most of the time. "It'll be well worth keeping in mind, though," went on Dilys, "when we're doing the interviews, and best to mention all this to the team."

"Absolutely," agreed Matt, "except, perhaps Sharon…?"

"I don't think we can exclude her, sir."

Matt grimaced. "Maybe you're right. But I'm pretty sure she thought I was over-stepping the mark when I asked for an ATL. I think she thinks I'm letting my personal feelings affect my job. Do you think I am?"

"No, sir," Dilys said quickly, then added more firmly, "No, I don't."

"Dilys, you're one of the few whose opinion I feel I can trust completely, and one of the few who'll tell it to me straight. I want you to think about it. I realise Fabia could have been targeted by someone involved, but it could have been some random lunatic who – say – has a thing about red Skodas or female drivers, or both, and I could have left it up to Alun to sort out."

They had parked at the station now and, as they got out of the car, Dilys turned to Matt. "Look, sir. I think that hit and run was far too convenient to be a random event. I think Fabia might have heard or seen something that worried them, and they were trying to scare her off. You're always saying she takes ages to do the shopping because she stops to talk to so many people. It could have been anywhere. We'll need to ask her exactly where she went this morning and who she spoke to. Anyway, we may be able to get some useful info out of Morgan Conway." Her voice hardened. "I'd enjoy putting the frighteners on him. I haven't taken to him right from the start."

Matt laughed. "You're putting the wind up me, Dilys, let alone him. And you're right, best to wait until we've got all the details from Fabia. Okay, let's go and tackle Conway. He should be here by now, it's already a quarter to five."

As they were walking into the station, Matt's mobile rang again. He glanced at the screen. It was Cath. He answered it as they went up the echoing stairs.

"Have you got a moment?" she asked when he picked up.

"If you can make it quick, Cath, it's been a bit of an afternoon."

"Anything wrong?" she asked.

"Fabia's had an accident." He could hear her quick, indrawn breath. "Someone drove into her when she was on her way to Tintern." He didn't go into more details.

"Oh, Matt, is she alright?"

"Yes, no lasting damage. They took her to Chepstow and she just phoned to say she's okay. I've sent someone to pick her up."

"I'll give her a ring."

"Cath," Matt said, as they got to his office. "I've got to get going. Can I phone you back?"

"Would you, please. It's just that, well, Sally's been talking about some things she's remembered."

"What sort of things?"

"Conversations she remembers overhearing, between Ellis and others, particularly Morgan Conway."

Matt's eyes widened. "Anything specific?"

"Not that she's told me. She's very agitated about it, but she says she doesn't want to worry me, that she should speak to you. I haven't pushed her. But I think there's more to it than that. She seems very afraid, but I don't think it's for herself. Understandably she's still in something of a state, but– no, you'd better speak to her rather than listen to me speculating."

"Right. I'll get back to you, to Sally that is, as soon as I possibly can." He didn't mention that he was about to interview Conway. He turned to Dilys and told her what Cath had said.

"That might be useful, sir."

"Yes, but let's get on with this interview for now."

But they didn't have the chance to do so as Morgan Conway didn't turn up at the arranged time and, although Dilys called him several times, yet again there was no response. By the end of the day Matt had put out a call for him to be stopped if seen, but he seemed to have completely disappeared off the radar. Hopefully they'd be able to trace him through the CCTV system.

* * *

When Morgan Conway didn't turn up at the station, Matt asked Dave Parry to go around to the flat he shared with his sister. The smart block of modern flats didn't seem to fit in with the rest of Pontygwyn's surroundings, but each to this own, Dave thought. He knocked but there was no response. He knocked again. No-one called out and he could hear no footsteps inside the flat. After one more attempt, he gave up and phoned Matt who told him to leave it for now.

Sharon was despatched to the salon to speak to Carmen Lloyd, but she denied any knowledge of her brother's whereabouts, told them he was hopelessly absent-minded and insisted he was probably working. She promised to tell him to contact them when he returned.

"It's a serious matter, not to keep an appointment with the police," Sharon told her. "We would like to check whether or not he's taken his taxi. Where does he keep it when it's not in use?"

"In a garage behind the flat."

"Could you please check whether or not it's there?"

"What, now?"

"Yes."

"Absolutely not," Carmen said. "I stay open until seven on Tuesday evenings and I have three clients lined up."

"Do you have a key to the garage?" Sharon asked her. "We could always make this official and get a warrant, but it would be much simpler if you could provide us with a key."

"There was a bit of a standoff at this point, sir," Sharon told Matt when she phoned in, "but I managed to persuade her. I think she was getting worried that the clients were all earwigging our conversation. Anyway, she gave me the key which she says she keeps because Morgan is always losing his."

Sharon sent Dave round to open up the garage, but there was no sign of the car, and no sign of Morgan Conway either. He decided to have a quick look around.

It was quite a spacious garage with plenty of room to move around even if the car had been there. There were shelves down one side, but he discovered nothing unusual on these, boxes of odds and ends, some tools, a pile of rather lurid pornographic magazines and another pile of motoring magazines. At the back of the garage was a small, sturdy cupboard fixed to the wall, but it was locked. He wondered what was in it, decided it'd be a good idea to come back and have another look, but that would entail a search warrant. He was about to leave when he noticed a hook on the edge of the cupboard with a key hanging from it. Smiling to himself, he lifted it down. It fitted perfectly. He opened the door, took out his phone and used it to light up the recesses of the cupboard.

There were two shelves. On the bottom one was a collection of jump leads in a box and a small tool kit. On the top one was a shoebox with an elastic band round it. He lifted this out and placed it on a nearby shelf, opened it up and then gave a low whistle. Inside the box were two rolls of small, self-seal plastic bags, a pair of sophisticated scales and something wrapped in wax paper. When Dave opened this up, he wasn't surprised at what he saw. He recognised it immediately – a block of cannabis resin. Now this is more like it, he thought. He took out his mobile and took several photographs of what he'd found, then replaced everything as it had been and closed the door of the cupboard.

He called in to tell Sharon what he'd found. "I need to seal Morgan Conway's garage. I've found some useful evidence."

"What have you found?" she asked.

Dave explained about the contents of the cupboard.

"Interesting," said Sharon, sounding more enthusiastic about the investigation than she had so far in Dave's experience. "Stay where you are. I'll contact the chief inspector and get him to organise a warrant. I got the impression Conway's sister wasn't at all keen for us to check his garage, maybe she knows something about her brother's activities."

Half an hour later, having got the all-clear from Matt, there was a shiny new padlock and a police seal on the garage door and Dave had the drugs paraphernalia safely stashed in evidence bags.

* * *

Although he was desperate to get home to Fabia, Matt knew there was one thing more they'd have to do before he could consider going home. He and Dilys would have to speak to Carmen Lloyd, find out if she knew where her brother was. They made their way to the salon and arrived just as Carmen was closing the door on the last client and turning off the lights.

"Miss Lloyd?" Matt asked.

She gave him a professional smile which didn't quite reach her eyes. "Yes?"

"I'm Chief Inspector Lambert, this is Detective Sergeant Bevan. Could we have a word please?"

"Well, it's not really convenient at the moment."

"But I'm afraid it's important that we speak to you," Matt said firmly. "It's about your brother, Morgan Conway."

"Oh dear," she smiled again, ruefully this time. "What's he done now? Has he still not turned up? You'd best come in." Once they were inside, she closed the door and locked it, then flicked a couple of lights on in the reception area.

"We had arranged to interview your brother this afternoon."

"So I gather. Your colleague told me when she came and asked for the garage keys."

"His car was not in the garage," Matt told her.

"Well it wouldn't be if he's working," she said dismissively. "He said he had a full schedule this afternoon."

"I don't think you realise how serious this is," Dilys said, a little impatient. "We're hoping your brother will be able to help us with our enquiries into the deaths of Ivor Gladwin and Ellis Cadogan."

This didn't generate the reaction they were expecting. "Morgan?" she laughed derisively. "You have to be joking. He can't swat a fly, let alone kill someone."

"But he may have information that will help us," Matt said. "What's more, the officer who went to check the garage found some evidence that he's been dealing in drugs."

This wiped the smile off her face. "Oh no! Not again."

"What do you mean, not again?"

She turned and sat down in one of the chairs in the reception area, then looked up at them. "I'm sure you know that Morgan has been inside," she said wearily.

"We are aware of that, yes," Matt said. He and Dilys took seats opposite her as she went on.

"When he came out, and his stupid wife wouldn't have him back, I told him he could come and live with me on condition he changed his name." She shrugged. "I had a good business going and I didn't want my clients knowing that my brother had been in prison. I told him I'd set him up as a taxi driver on condition he kept his nose clean, and he promised me, swore to me, that he'd not go back to his old ways." She gave them a sharp look. "What is this evidence? Maybe somebody planted it on him."

"Who would do that?" Dilys asked.

"Oh, I don't know, someone he'd got on the wrong side of."

"I don't think that's likely," Matt said, "but we'll be doing the usual tests to find out who's been handling what we've found."

"Have you any idea where he might have gone?" Dilys asked. "Does he have particular friends he might be with?"

"Not really. He's a bit of a loner, my brother. And he may simply be on a job."

"There is always that possibility, but he told us he'd be free by half past four."

"For goodness sake," Carmen said, exasperated by their questioning. "I'm not his keeper."

"But you do live together, don't you?" Dilys pointed out.

"Yes, but we don't live in each other's pockets," Carmen snapped.

They didn't seem to be getting anywhere, so Matt decided to wind up the interview. He got up. "If you hear from him please let us know, and point out to him that the longer he stays away, the worse it's going to look for him."

"Do you think I don't know that?" She took a deep breath. "Sorry, sorry. Yes, I'll do as you ask."

"Thank you, Miss Lloyd," Matt said.

They left and made their way back to the green room, none the wiser when it came to Morgan Conway's whereabouts.

* * *

At eight o'clock Dilys virtually ordered Matt to go home. She'd assured him that the rest of the team would be able to manage without him, and that, if anything came in on Morgan Conway, or anything else for that matter, she would let him know immediately.

As he got out of the car and opened the gate, a beam of light stretched out across next door's garden as Tony Vaughan came out of his front door. "Matt. I've been keeping an eye out for you. Could I have a quick word?"

This was the last thing Matt wanted, but he didn't feel able to refuse. "A quick one, yes, I need to check on Fabia."

"Check on her? What's up?"

"Some bastard forced her off the road when she was on her way to Tintern."

"Good God! Is she alright?"

"A bit shaken up, obviously." Matt was finding it hard to contain his impatience. "Anyway, what did you want me for?"

"It's about Morgan."

Matt made an effort to keep his face expressionless. No need to give away how interested they were in Morgan.

"I'm not sure it means anything." Tony was sounding a bit unsure of himself now. "And I might be over-reacting, but he's been on at me to find out what's going on with the investigation, keeps stopping me in the street or phoning, he's just called again."

This was even more interesting, but Matt just asked, "Why do you think he keeps getting on to you?"

"Well, I suppose I could say he's a friend, we're in the same darts team. But I think there's more to it than that."

"Did he say where he was when he phoned just now?" Matt asked, trying not to sound as if he really needed to know.

"No." Tony's eyebrows rose in query, but Matt didn't say anything else. "I think he's getting on to me because he thinks I have some kind of direct line to information from you and Fabia as I live next door."

"I suppose everyone involved is a bit anxious," Matt said.

"But this seems a bit over the top, he's very jittery."

"This sort of situation takes people in different ways, Tony. Are you implying he's got something to hide?"

"I'm not sure." Tony was looking a bit embarrassed now, as if he was regretting bringing the subject up. "It could mean nothing. I shouldn't interfere, should I?"

"Every bit of information is useful. I'll have another word with Morgan." When I can track the bloody man down, Matt thought.

"Best not tell him I spoke to you."

"Don't worry." Matt's tone was cool now. "I'll keep you out of it. Now, I must go and find out how Fabia is."

"Give her my best, and if there's anything I can do to help, let me know."

Matt nodded and opened his front door. He wasn't sure he'd be calling on Tony for help any time soon, but he told himself not to be disagreeable.

* * *

Fabia was curled up on the settee in the sitting room, half asleep. The television was muttering away, but she wasn't really taking any notice of it. On hearing the closing of the front door, she looked up and called, "I'm in here."

Matt strode into the room, an anxious frown on his lean face. He sat down beside her and gently gathered her into his arms, kissed the top of her head. "All I could think of was that time you ended up in the Heath with all those bruises and bandages."

"You worry too much," Fabia told him, putting her arms round him.

He sat back a little. "How long do you have to wear this collar thing?"

"Only a few days. It's just a precaution, and the cut on my forehead's nothing much. I've got some lovely bruises developing across my front, though."

"I've got virtually the whole team on to this one, and Alun's pulling out all the stops. I've very little doubt it's got something to do with the present investigation, particularly as Morgan Conway didn't turn up for his interview this afternoon and seems to have disappeared. Tony stopped me on my way in, told me Morgan's been on to him several times trying to find out what's going on."

"Why Tony?"

"Because he lives next door to us, he thinks."

"But– ah well, I suppose that might follow if Morgan's desperate."

"Desperate?"

"If he killed them," Fabia said.

"But why, Fabia? What's his motive?"

"In my experience motive always comes last."

"You've said that before. Anyway, we couldn't get any information out of his sister who just says he's a hopeless prat and probably forgot. I find that very hard to believe, but neither Sharon nor Dilys and I could shift her on it. Sharon did manage to persuade her to hand over a spare key to his garage and Dave went to have a look, which turned out to be a very good idea."

"Why was that?"

"Dave found a whole pile of drugs paraphernalia in a cupboard at the back, and a wodge of cannabis resin, so we got the garage sealed up and asked the CCTV chaps to trawl through for sight of his taxi."

"Did you get the impression his sister knows where he is?"

"No, not really. We're leaving her to stew. Of course, she may have no idea what her brother is up to."

"That's possible, I suppose," Fabia said. "She's got a reputation to keep up and a good business going. She probably wouldn't want to take any risks."

Fabia sighed and went back to what was uppermost in her mind. "I wish I could have got a better look at the driver of the Land Rover, but he had the peak of his cap pulled down low and was wearing enormous dark glasses, and I felt as if he was sitting as far back in his seat as he could, sort of leaning back. But I've got a feeling it was a man, and anyway, it'll probably show up on Brett's dash cam."

"He was the man that rescued you?"

"Yes, bless him."

"I'm going to get us a whisky each," Matt said. "I certainly need one, and then I want you to tell me every detail about what happened, this morning as well as this afternoon." Then he frowned and paused. "If you're feeling up to it, that is."

"Of course, I am," she told him, but he wasn't sure she was telling the truth.

"We don't have to go through it, darling. We can pretend nothing happened and just have a quiet evening if you like."

"No. I'll tell you. And I've got some bits and pieces to pass on as well. Quite a lot has happened today, quite apart from being driven off the road." She got up, rather carefully.

"Stay where you are," Matt said. "I can get the drinks."

"No. I'll just get stiff if I don't move around a bit. Anyway, I'm hungry, seem to be permanently hungry these days, so I want to check what there is to eat."

Matt put an arm round her waist as they went through to the kitchen. "You're an amazing woman, you do know that don't you?"

"Well, thank you, kind sir," Fabia said, never good at receiving compliments.

As they were sitting down to a supper of cold meat and cheese, Fabia looked up at Matt.

"I know that expression," he said. "Something has just occurred to you."

"It has. You said that Ellis was killed by someone who was left-handed."

"He was."

She told him what had popped into her mind and Matt's eyes widened. "Yet another little bit to add to the rest," he said.

They ate in silence for a while then Matt pushed his empty plate away and looked across the table at Fabia. "There's one more thing I want to know now, and then I think I should run you a hot bath and get you to bed."

"That sounds like a good plan," Fabia said, smiling across at him. "What is the one more thing?"

"Where exactly did you go this morning? What did you do?"

"Other than what you asked me to do?"

"Yes. Start from when you left home," Matt said.

"I'd printed off copies of the illustrations to post, so I went first to the post office. After that I took a couple of paintings into the gallery–"

"Did you mention to anyone in there that you were planning to go to Tintern Abbey?"

"Yes, I did as a matter of fact," Fabia told him, her eyes widening.

"And were there many people in the gallery?"

"Quite a few."

"Any that you recognised?"

"Not that I can remember."

"Then what did you do?" Matt asked.

"I went to have a coffee at Hywel's, and I saw Carmen in there. She was talking to the girl at the counter about kickboxing, of all things. I remember wondering how she does that with those nails of hers. And I was interested to see she was having coffee with Trevor Kemble, but I suppose there's no law against it."

"Not that I know of," Matt said.

"I can't say I'd want to have much to do with him. The way his eyes always seem half-shut, that scraggy beard and the sort of half-smile he always seems to have on his face. Distinctly unattractive in my opinion."

"Your artist's eye for detail again. And what next?"

"I went to Spar, and yes, I did mention Tintern in there because I bumped into Geraldine and told her what I was planning. Several people could have overheard me. And I talked about it in the salon as well, when Carmen was doing my hair – she had a cancellation, so she was able to give me an appointment immediately. So, most of the people in there would have heard, and it was pretty busy."

"You see what I'm getting at?" Matt asked.

"Absolutely," Fabia said ruefully. "Half of Pontygwyn knew I was planning to go to Tintern Abbey this afternoon."

"That's about the sum of it," Matt said, with a shrug. "But at least it gives us an idea of how that bastard knew you'd be on that road. Come on now, let's go and run that bath."

CHAPTER 23

Matt and Fabia were woken early the next morning by his phone. He rolled over and grabbed it from the bedside table, grunted, "Lambert ... What?" He pushed himself up. "Now that's great news. Well done them ... Where have you got him? ... Okay, I'll be there soon as I can."

He turned and kissed Fabia. "Good news. That was Tom Watkins, they've got the driver of the Land Rover."

"Who is he?"

"Not sure yet. He's refusing to co-operate at the moment. I must get going. I'm going to enjoy this."

"Keep me up to date, won't you?"

"Of course."

Fabia gave him a sleepy smile. "I might stay in bed for a while. I feel a bit sick."

"Are you sure you're going to be okay?" Matt said, smoothing her hair back from her forehead.

"I'll be fine."

"You must rest today, my darling, understand?"

"For once I think I'm going to do as you say."

"Good Lord," Matt said as he got out of bed and padded towards the bathroom, "that has to be a first."

* * *

An hour later Matt got into his office and was joined by Dilys. "Okay," he said, "bring me up to date on what happened."

"A couple of off-duty officers were at a pub in Cwmbran last night and, when they came out, they noticed this Land Rover in the car park. One of them was aware of the description from the bulletin and had a look at it, saw that the mirror was hanging off then checked for the gaffer tape on the bumper, also in place, as was the mud over the registration numbers. He went round to the back and cleared the mud, bright lad not to interfere with the front number plate, then he called in the info. The car is registered to a Cledwyn Hughes, petty criminal, been up in front of the magistrate for speeding, affray, drunk in charge, done a few months inside a couple of times, and there's a suspended sentence hanging over him."

"Sounds like a good bloke," Matt commented.

Dilys grinned, then went on with her account. "They had the wit to park one of their cars in front of the Land Rover and then sat and waited for the driver to come out, which he did quite soon after, and they nabbed him. He tried to resist so they brought him in. He's been shouting the odds down in the cells, police brutality and all the rest, usual crap."

"And has there been any news on Morgan Conway?"

"No," Dilys told him. "We had someone go and speak to his ex-wife, but she's not seen him, nor has his sister. I think we need to go and have another word with her. There's been nothing from the CCTV yet."

"And talking of another word," Matt said. "Cath says Sally has some further information she's very anxious to give us. I must fix that up. Now let's get down there and see what this boyo has to say for himself."

They made their way downstairs to an interview room on the ground floor. It was a bare room with grey-painted walls and one window, the lower half of frosted glass, which looked out onto the station car park. On the opposite wall was a large map of Newport and in the middle was a Formica-topped table with two plastic chairs either side. At the end of the table was the usual recording equipment. Matt and Dilys sat down one side of the table and waited for Tom to bring Hughes in.

The man that entered the room, his wrists dangling in front of him encased in handcuffs, was an unattractive individual. His grubby T-shirt barely covered the large stomach it housed, and his tracksuit bottoms were sagging. He was wearing a baseball cap which had seen better days and one side of his neck was covered in intricate tattoos, including a swastika. As he sat down in one of the chairs opposite, his small eyes, full of defiance, stared across at Matt and Dilys. He said nothing. Given his unruly behaviour in the cell, Tom went to stand by the closed door in case reinforcements were needed.

Dilys switched on the recording equipment as Matt said, "This interview will be recorded and may be given in evidence if you are brought to trial."

Hughes sat back in his chair and crossed his arms, still saying nothing.

Matt said where they were and the date and time, then went on, "I am Chief Inspector Lambert, this is Sergeant Dilys Bevan. Detective Constable Watkins is also present. Please state your full name and date of birth."

There was silence as Hughes stared across at them, his mouth twisted in an insolent half-smile.

"It's a simple request. We are aware of the name of the owner of the Land Rover you were driving and assume that the car is yours. Of course, if it isn't we can find this" – he took out a notebook, checked through it – "Cledwyn Hughes and ask him to identify you."

Matt and Dilys sat and waited. It was a battle of wills, but Matt knew he had the upper hand. After about a minute, Hughes sat forward in his chair and rested his folded arms on the table. "Okay, Mr Chief Inspector, yes, that's my name, and the car belongs to me. What of it?"

"Can you tell me where you were yesterday afternoon between two and three o'clock?"

"Shagging my woman, if you must know," he said, grinning across at Dilys.

"Her name?" Dilys asked, unperturbed.

"You have to be fucking joking. I'm not going to tell you that."

"Never mind," Matt said. "It'll be easy enough to find out. But we know that you're lying, that you were nowhere near your woman, as you call her."

"Prove it."

Matt ignored this question.

"You have a long list of previous convictions," Matt said calmly, "and, I notice, a suspended sentence which could be activated if you don't co-operate."

"That was a stitch-up," he said defiantly, but he sounded less sure of himself.

"Now you're the one that's joking." Matt leant back in his chair, a slight smile on his face, and looked at the man opposite him. "I'll ask you again, tell us where you were yesterday afternoon? We know where you were, we just need you to confirm it."

No reply was forthcoming.

"Why make this difficult for yourself?" Dilys asked. "If you co-operate with us it could help you avoid going back inside. Would your 'woman' want that to happen?"

There was a flicker of alarm in his eyes. That had hit the spot. Well done Dilys, Matt thought. But still he said nothing.

Matt took out his iPad, tapped away at it, found what he wanted then turned it towards Hughes.

"This was recorded on the dash cam of the person who came up in the opposite direction. He was driving a red Jaguar. You probably remember it because you only just avoided hitting him as well when you bolted. It's obvious from this evidence that you were attempting to run a red Skoda off the road on the A466, going east towards Tintern. As you can see your Land Rover is easily identified, the colour matches, mud obscures most of the number plate, except for the letter B. It's clear that the passenger side mirror is hanging by its wires. The repair job on your bumper is clear, and will probably be worse now, and we can enhance the image well enough to identify you as the driver. What's more, the two police officers who arrested you last night have viewed this and confirmed that it is the same vehicle. Now, I ask again, where were you between two and three yesterday afternoon?"

Stubborn silence greeted this.

"We have two witnesses as well as this evidence," Matt told him.

"So, you might as well co-operate, Mr Hughes," Dilys said, "make it easy on yourself."

Hughes crossed his arms and dropped his chin on his chest, as he glared at them under frowning brows. The seconds ticked by, then he seemed to sag.

"Okay. If I tell, help you out, like, what about my suspended sentence? I want to do a deal."

"That depends on what you tell us," Matt said. "Come on. Let's have it."

* * *

An hour later Cledwyn Hughes was back in the cells, arrested on a charge of dangerous driving and failing to report an accident. "And I feel like adding a few more to that list," Matt told Dilys grimly as they got back to his office.

Dilys grinned at him. "But fair play, he's given us some really useful information, particularly those two descriptions. I'd say we're a damn sight closer to home now than we were yesterday, that's providing we can believe everything he told us."

"True, on both counts. I must get through to Luke and tell him what we got from our tattooed friend."

"At least we know now that the two investigations overlap." Dilys shook her head. "Who'd have thought that an organisation like that could be based in rural South Wales, but what a marvellous cover."

"I know. It does all sound a bit far-fetched, doesn't it? We're used to these activities going on in Cardiff, London, other big cities, but not in little old Pontygwyn. Now we have to work out which one of them killed Gladwin and Cadogan and exactly why."

* * *

Fabia glanced at her watch and saw that it was only half past ten. She wondered how Matt was getting on with questioning the driver of the Land Rover, and whether they'd got the right man. It would be a relief if they had. She hadn't been able to settle to anything that morning and put this down to reaction. She felt stiff and achy and thought maybe a short walk down to Gwyddon Park might help. It was a cold but sunny day and she was sure a bit of fresh air would do her good. Taking care not to jar her bruises, she put on her puffa jacket and wrapped a scarf round the foam collar. But as she turned to close her gate someone cannoned into her. "Ouch!" Fabia said, as the bruises reacted to the contact.

"Oh, Fabia, I'm so sorry." It was Eve Kemble. "I wasn't looking where I was going."

Fabia looked at Eve and was disturbed by what she saw. Her eyes were reddened behind her elaborately framed glasses and her usually neat hair was untidy. Shoulders hunched and hands deep in the pockets of her coat, she gave the impression she was only just in control of her emotions.

"Eve, what on earth is wrong?" Fabia asked.

Tears began to creep down Eve's cheeks and she said, "Oh Fabia, I'm so worried. I just don't know which way to turn."

Fabia had been determined to have a quiet morning, but she could never resist investigating unusual behaviour, and the way Eve was behaving was totally out of character. She found herself taking Eve's arm and saying, "Why don't you come in and tell me all about it."

"Could I? It would be such a relief to talk to someone."

"Come on then, I'll make us some coffee and we can sit and talk."

As Fabia unwound her scarf, Eve noticed the foam collar. "What have you done to yourself?" she asked.

"I was in a bit of a car accident yesterday, nothing serious," Fabia said, not wanting to go into lengthy explanations.

"I'm so sorry, are you sure it's alright for me to bother you?"

There was no way Fabia felt she could put Eve off now, so she assured her it was fine and said, "Come through to the kitchen."

Eve followed her down the passageway, saying as they went, "I'm so sorry to disturb you, but I can't think of anyone else I'd rather talk to. With your, well, background, and you might be able to speak to Matt for me…"

Fabia didn't react to this, just switched the kettle on and said, "Sit down, Eve, and get your breath." She made the coffee and then sat down opposite her agitated visitor. "Now, tell me what's up?"

But Eve didn't get directly to the point. "It's so kind of you to see me. It's not as if we know each other that well, and I do feel as if I'm imposing, but you're the best person to talk to. I didn't want to speak to Cath because she has enough on her hands looking after poor Sally, and I suppose I could have contacted the police, but I'm too scared to do that. It's so awful."

"If it's something to do with the current investigation, then you really should speak to Matt."

"I know, but I thought, perhaps…"

Fabia sighed. Why did everyone seem to think they could leave it to her to pass information on to Matt? But she was curious now, so she didn't want to put Eve off.

"Eve, I can't help if you don't tell me what's up."

"Sorry, yes, I know." There was silence for a while, then Eve said, "It's Trevor, I'm so worried that he's mixed up in something, well, illegal."

"What makes you think that?" asked Fabia.

"He keeps getting these weird phone calls. Usually it's a man and he just demands to speak to Trevor. When I ask who's speaking – I like to know who's phoning my husband – he won't tell me. He actually said it was none of my business. I'm afraid I've taken to listening to Trevor's side of the conversations, and he's been talking about consignments and passports and stuff, oh, and he mentioned the border force."

"I would have thought that was unsurprising since he runs a freight business."

"Yes, but he doesn't usually get these calls at home if it's to do with work."

"Have you asked Trevor who this man is?"

"I have, and he said it was just work, but he looked angry that I'd asked and told me to stop going on at him. That it was all to do with some freight that he had to pick up from Bristol docks." Eve paused and took a gulp of her coffee. "I think maybe it's not to do with his business – at least, not the legitimate one. The thing is, years ago, when he first started up, I discovered that he was smuggling. Nothing big, cigarettes, other stuff that attracts a duty. I begged him to stop and he said he would, and we've not mentioned it since, but maybe he's started up again. And" – she put up a hand to her mouth – "and maybe Ivor found out." The words were muffled by her fingers, her eyes enormous behind her glasses and the tears very near the surface.

"Are you suggesting Trevor was responsible for Ivor's death?"

"No, no! At least– no he would never, but…" She stumbled to a halt, rummaged in her bag for a tissue and blew her nose.

"Have you told him what you suspect, how worried you are?"

"Oh no, I couldn't. He'd be so angry."

Fabia leant her crossed arms on the table and frowned across at Eve. "But what do you expect me to do about it?"

"The thing is, I really don't feel I can go to the police and... and drop Trevor in it, so to speak, but I'm so worried about what he's doing and what effect it will have on us. If there is something going on, I just want it stopped. Could you speak to Matt?"

"If I do that, Eve, it will simply mean that he comes round to speak to you both."

Eve took her glasses off and rubbed a hand across her eyes. "I hadn't thought of that. Oh dear. What am I to do?"

"And now you've told me, that puts me in a rather awkward position. I really should pass what you've told me on to Matt in case it's relevant to the investigation into two deaths." Fabia didn't bother to keep the resentment out of her voice.

"Yes, I do see that. I'm sorry. I wasn't really thinking straight."

"You're going to have to talk to Matt, I'm afraid."

"Oh dear, oh dear, yes, I suppose I must."

"Why don't you persuade Trevor to talk to him, tell him if he doesn't, you'll do so. That might work. And you never know, it might all be perfectly innocent."

"But that's not all. There are the other calls."

"From the same man?"

"No, I'm sure these are a woman. First of all, I was getting calls and, when I picked up the phone, there was silence on the other end and then the call was cut off. But a couple of times I've caught him talking quietly to someone and he, well, sounds as if he's talking to someone he's" – she took a shuddering breath – "he's having an affair with."

"Did you tackle him about those calls as well?" Fabia asked, deciding not to tell Eve about the fact that Carmen had been meeting Trevor Kemble in Hywel's Cafe the day before.

"No." Eve chewed at her bottom lip. "I sort of didn't want to know. Do you understand what I mean?"

"Yes, I do. I'm so sorry, Eve, this is all very upsetting for you. Obviously, Matt wouldn't need to know about your suspicions that Trevor's having an affair, but if he has gone back to smuggling, Matt should be told. I don't think you have any choice now that you've told me all about it."

Eve's shoulders sagged, but then she looked up, her eyes a little brighter. "I know you're right, and if he is having an affair, I don't think I mind so much, the bastard. I'm going to leave him and go to my sister in Usk."

"You have a sister close by?" Fabia said, instinctively wanting to know more.

"Yes, Daphne Sheldon, she's a GP." She straightened, looked across at Fabia and gave her a shaky smile. "In fact, I think I'll do that anyway. I'll go home and pack some stuff now and Trevor can bloody look after himself."

Fabia didn't quite know how to respond to this, so she smiled and said nothing.

CHAPTER 24

Morgan sat on the edge of the bed in the dingy hotel room at a services on the outskirts of Cardiff and opened another can of lager. Eleven o'clock on Wednesday morning and it was his fourth. Unable to keep still, he began to pace up and down in the small space between the bed and the window. He took out his mobile and switched it on. Immediately several missed calls and texts came up. The calls he ignored, the texts he read. There were two from his sister, 'Morgan, where the hell are you? Phone me', and then another, 'I've had the police round, where are you? Phone me now', and a third that had just arrived, 'Morgan. If you don't phone me I'm going to report you as a missing person.'

His thumb hovered over the keys, but in the end he put the phone back in his pocket. What the hell was he going to do? He resumed his pacing. He'd only just missed bumping into that sharp-faced police sergeant when she'd come in to speak to Carmen yesterday. Hiding behind the door at the back of the salon, he'd heard her speak to his sister and realised that Carmen had given her the keys to the garage. How dare she do that? As fast as he could, he'd gone around to the Spar car park where he'd left the car and driven to the garage. He must get that stuff out of the cupboard before any of them found it, but he was delayed by a lorry unloading boxes in the high street. It took him far longer than he'd anticipated. He'd finally parked the car down the road and hurried to the back of the flats but, as he came around the corner, he'd seen that bloody copper opening the garage door. Too late.

He'd got back in the car and driven like a mad man down the motorway, lucky not to be stopped at the speed he was going, and had only slowed down when he came to the outskirts of Cardiff. The gauge had told him he was down to twenty-five miles' worth of petrol left, so he'd turned into the services. After filling up the car, looking round as he did so in case someone recognised him, he'd considered sitting in the cafe, but was too afraid of being seen, so he'd booked a room, thinking that would give him time to work out what to do. He'd gone and bought a bottle of cheap whisky and some sandwiches in the shop and, having drunk half the bottle, had slept it off and woken with a headache and a mouth like the bottom of a bird cage. His breakfast had been sausage rolls from the shop downstairs and this lager, a hair of the dog.

He considered phoning Tony Vaughan again, but couldn't trust him not to tell Matt he'd made contact. He thought about replying to Carmen's texts, but he knew what she'd say, particularly if the police had told her they'd searched his garage. In the end he knew he'd have to tell her everything, maybe that way they could work things out together. Would they have found the box in the cupboard? Of course they would. What a fool he'd been! But he'd only put it in there a couple of days ago. He'd been planning to transfer it to a safer place as soon as he could get it past Carmen. Would she really report him as missing? He doubted it, but you could never be sure with his sister.

What if he went to the police and told them what he knew? But, no, he couldn't do that. Or could he? Maybe he could make some kind of a bargain with them. That Matt Lambert, he was a decent bloke, he might play ball. He turned this over and over in his mind but came up against the same obstacles every time. Feeling sick, stupid and a little drunk, he continued his pacing.

* * *

On their way back to the incident room Matt decided to pop in and check on Fabia. "Just for a couple of minutes, Dilys," he said, slightly apologetic. "I told her to rest and I want to make sure she's doing as she's told."

Dilys laughed. "A fond hope, I'd call that."

He smiled across at her. "You're probably right."

Fabia was delighted to see them. "I've had an interesting morning," she said.

"That doesn't sound very restful." Matt frowned at her and Dilys supressed a grin.

"Don't start nagging, Matt. Come into the kitchen and I'll tell you all about it."

As they were settling themselves round the table, Matt's phone rang. He glanced at the screen. "It's

Luke," he said, and answered the call. "Hi, Luke, I was wanting to speak to you. Dilys and I interviewed the low life that drove Fabia off the road … This was yesterday … No, she's fine, but we've got some very useful information to pass on … What's that? … Ah, better and better. Look, where are you? … Okay, we're at the house, it'd only take you ten minutes to get here, we can bring each other up to date." He cut off the call. "He's got some useful information, he says, so it finally looks as if we're getting somewhere."

Fabia, who had been making coffee for them, brought the mugs back to the table and said, "Can I tell you about this morning?"

"Fire away," Matt said.

As briefly as she could, Fabia told them everything that Eve had told her, about the strange phone calls, her fears that Trevor had gone back to smuggling and that she also thought he was having an affair. "I don't think the affair is relevant really, but the rest is noteworthy. Although I wouldn't have thought smuggling cigarettes and a few bottles of booze to avoid the duty would lead to people trafficking, but he does run a freight business and that rings alarm bells for me."

"I wonder if Luke has picked up on that," Matt said.

"He should have, surely?" Dilys said, frowning.

"I hope so." But Matt didn't sound too sure.

The doorbell rang at that moment and Matt got up to let Luke in. When he was provided with a steaming mug of coffee, and he'd commiserated with Fabia about her injuries, Matt asked Fabia to repeat what she'd told them for Luke's benefit. Luke admitted that he had been aware of Trevor's business but hadn't had enough evidence to get a warrant to search his depot in Cwmbran. "But I think this might just do the trick," he said. "And how about the info from your hit and run driver?"

"Ah, the delightful Cledwyn Hughes," Matt said, with a grimace.

"More like Clodwyn, I'd say," Dilys said.

"Very good, Dilys." Matt grinned at her. "Well, to begin with he was ordered by someone he calls 'The Boss' to put the frighteners, as he described it, on Fabia. He wasn't told why but he said you don't refuse when 'The Boss' tells you to do something. He absolutely refused to give us a name, said it was more than his life's worth to do so. We've thrown the book at him, dangerous driving, failing to report an accident, and we're hoping that he'll come up with a name when he's had time to think things over."

"We've indicated that, if he gives us names, we might not be so hard on him," Dilys said. "That might work, but I got the impression he was shit scared of this boss person, wouldn't even tell us if it was a man or a woman, although he did slip up once and refer to them as she, but insisted we heard wrong. We'll have to check the recording."

"A woman involved," Fabia said, "that sort of follows, doesn't it, Matt?"

"What do you mean?"

"Remember all those bits and pieces I told you yesterday."

"Ah yes. I'll come to that," Matt said. "Anyway, Hughes has given us a pile of information about being hired to drive trucks full of what he calls 'migrants' from Cardiff docks to Bristol, Chepstow, Swansea and various other places in and around

South and Mid Wales. He says he's simply the driver and just follows orders, so long as he gets paid plenty and in cash he doesn't care. He drops them off at various locations, crappy motels or warehouses, and doesn't ask any questions."

"I find that hard to believe," Luke said. "Surely he must hear stuff even if he doesn't actually ask for any information."

"You'd have thought so, wouldn't you?" said Matt. "Either he does and isn't telling, or he doesn't care so long as he's paid well. I don't think we're dealing with the brightest penny in the bunch here." He turned to Luke. "You said on the phone that you'd had a breakthrough. Let's have it."

Luke put his mug down on the table. "I had a call from someone in the Cardiff force yesterday, an officer called James Brent. He's been seconded to the NCA, but he's still based at Cardiff Central. A woman, her name's Irina Melnik, was brought in having been arrested for shoplifting. She's from Ukraine and hasn't much English, but once they brought in an interpreter, they managed to get plenty of information from her."

"She'd been trafficked?" Fabia asked, unable to contain herself.

"Yes. She arrived with a group three months ago, was taken to a hotel, like those two Romanian girls I told you about, and the usual happened, passport taken away, etc. She was then taken to a house in Cardiff which she shares with ten other women and was put to work in a nail bar. There is a person, a woman called Galina Petrovka who she says is in charge of them, and she answers to another woman, but they've only seen her once."

"Did she describe either of them?" asked Matt.

"Oh yes, very clearly. This Galina — at least that's what she calls herself, we've no idea if it's her real name — speaks Russian, which Irina can understand."

Dilys was frowning across at Luke. "These people are carefully watched. Is she there all the time?"

"It seems so."

"So how come, the other woman, Irina is it? How did she manage to go out shoplifting?" Dilys asked.

"She had quite an incentive. A few days ago, Galina told her the boss had a friend that Irina should 'be nice to'. She knew exactly what she was asking and refused, but Galina got nasty and started threatening her, said if she didn't do as she was told, she'd be dealt with. She's heard about a girl whose face was cut when she refused to give in to similar requests, so she was very near to agreeing, but she had a bit of luck. Usually, when they're escorted — her words not mine — back to the house they're all locked in, but yesterday she discovered the front door had been left unlocked, she thinks because Galina had had an urgent call from her boss."

"She legged it?" Fabia asked, admiration in her voice.

"She did just that, and the shoplifting was deliberate, she wanted to be arrested."

"Bright girl," Fabia said.

"I suppose, except for believing the spiel they were given to persuade them to travel to the UK," said Luke, "but then, so many have been taken in, and who am I to criticise? I've never been dirt poor and desperately needed to make money, however I did it."

There were murmurs of agreement round the table, then Matt asked, "So, what have you got? She was able to tell your friend where this house is?"

"Yes, and it was raided at crack of dawn this morning. They've handed the girls over to the social services, and Galina is in the cells refusing to say a word. James is going to have another go at her later today and I'm going to be there."

"Good," Matt said, then looked up at Luke. "And the description of the other woman involved, did he tell you about that?"

"He did," Luke said, with a satisfied smile. He repeated it word for word, and Fabia and Matt looked at each other.

"I have my uses," she said.

"You certainly do," Matt said, grinning at her. "But we still have to work out who killed Ivor Gladwin and Ellis Cadogan, and whether it was the same person, and that's going to take some doing."

* * *

When Matt and Dilys got back to the incident room, Tom bounced up to them full of news. "The CCTV has come up trumps. We've got that bloody taxi!"

"Brilliant. Where is it?"

"Parked at the Moto Services at Pontyclun. Sharon and Dave went to have a look. They did a trawl through the cafes and shops, but there was no sign of Conway, not yet anyway. They're keeping an eye on the car."

"Isn't there a Travelodge at that services?" Dilys asked.

"There is. Perhaps he's holed up there," Tom suggested.

"Well, if he hasn't been seen anywhere in the cafes or shops," Matt said, "it's always a possibility."

"Do you want them to check the hotel?" Tom asked.

"Yes. Get them to speak to reception, they should know which room he's in. If he's given a false name, or they won't co-operate, if necessary, go from room to room."

"Will do."

"You and I, Dilys, must go and have a word with Eve Kemble. Have you got her address?"

"Right here, sir."

But they were out of luck. No-one was at home at the Kembles' house. Matt and Dilys were making their way back when Tom came back to them with news of Morgan Conway.

"They've found him, sir," Tom told them. "He came quietly. Sharon says he's obviously been on the booze and wasn't in a fit state to resist. They're taking him back to the station to sleep it off."

Matt glanced at Dilys and she wondered what he was going to say. He looked slightly self-conscious. "What's up, sir?" she asked.

"I'm going to involve Fabia again."

"In what way?"

"It's occurred to me that she may be able to find out where Eve Kemble is. I'm going to ask her to try contacting her."

"Good idea," said Dilys briskly. "Didn't the chief suggest, right at the beginning, that you bring Fabia in on this?"

"I suppose, but after that accident I'm not so sure."

"She's been involved right from the beginning, and she's dug up plenty of useful information, so there isn't really any point in worrying about asking her to help now, particularly if it's just to phone someone."

"True," Matt said, and gave Fabia a quick call. She told him about Eve saying she would go to her sister in Usk, and Matt put Sara on to checking which surgery she worked for and getting her address.

CHAPTER 25

Activity had increased in the incident room. Matt had gathered everyone together and given them all precise instructions. Sharon, who seemed to be more enthusiastic the busier they got, and Dave were sent off to speak to Eve Kemble who had been tracked down to her sister's house in Usk. Sara and Tom had been set to collating every bit of evidence they had, however trivial, and feeding it on to a spread sheet.

Just as Matt and Dilys were about to leave for the station to interview Morgan Conway, a call came through to Dilys from Claire Gooding.

"The two SOCOs going through the rubbish bags by the garages that the boss wanted collected, they've come up trumps."

"Oh yes? What have they found?"

"A pair of lacy black flats, blood stained, and the blood group is the same as Ellis Cadogan's."

"That's great, Claire, thanks for letting us know." Dilys turned to tell Matt what Claire had said.

When they got to the interview room, Conway was a sorry sight. His eyes were bloodshot, his cheeks were covered in dark stubble, and his clothes looked as if he'd slept in them.

Once they'd set the recording equipment up and gone through the usual preliminaries, asked if Conway wanted a solicitor present and been told, defiantly, that he didn't need one, Matt sat back in his chair. "Can you explain to me why you didn't turn up for the interview we'd arranged yesterday afternoon?"

Morgan cleared his throat. "I... er... had trouble with my car."

"And you didn't think to make contact and let us know?" Matt demanded.

"I tried, but I couldn't get through."

"You expect me to believe that when you were found hiding in a hotel room with no luggage, not even a toothbrush, and definitely the worse for wear."

Morgan wouldn't look Matt in the eye, just sat in the chair staring blearily at the opposite wall.

"I haven't got time to waste," Matt told him. "Show him the contents of the bags, Sergeant."

Dilys leant down and put three transparent, sealed bags on the table. One contained the scales, one the block of cannabis resin and one the roll of small plastic bags. Morgan looked at them and a flash of panic showed in his face before he got himself under control.

"These were all found in a cupboard at the back of the garage where you keep your taxi," Dilys said. "Would you like to explain why they were there?"

After a pause in which he shifted in his chair then dragged his hand down over his face, he finally said, "They don't belong to me."

"Come on, Morgan," Matt said, "your fingerprints are all over the bags" – he flicked a finger at one of the evidence bags – "and on the scales. They're yours, that's obvious."

"No, they're not, I– I was looking after them for a friend."

"Who?" Matt snapped back.

"I'm not going to tell you that."

"I'd advise you to do so," Dilys said. "Of course, we can always ask your sister, she may know."

"No!" There was real fear in the word. "Okay, okay, I've– they're for my own use, I haven't been dealing. Been inside once for that, never again."

"Then why the scales and bags?" Matt asked.

Morgan didn't answer this.

"Come on, we know a lot about drug dealing. Own use doesn't match up with this little haul," Matt told him. "You might as well tell us why they were there and who you were supplying. The more co-operative you are, the better it's going to be for you."

"It occurs to me, sir," said Dilys with a glance at Matt. "I wonder whether Ivor Gladwin found out about these activities." She turned back to Morgan. "Was he threatening to tell the police? Is that why you killed him?"

Morgan leant his hands on the table and pushed himself up from his chair, his face sheet-white behind the dark stubble. "What the fuck?"

Standing up too, Matt ordered, "Sit down."

There was a moment of confrontation, then Morgan subsided back into his chair.

"We are not just investigating your drug dealing," Matt said, "we're investigating two murders and we know how Ivor used to snoop around and dig up people's secrets. We have a great deal of information about his activities which has been downloaded from his phone and other devices, and we have several possible suspects in our sights, you included."

"What about Ellis? He was my friend, we were mates."

"Maybe you were supplying him, and he refused to pay up," Dilys said. "We know he was in financial difficulties."

He slumped back in his chair, his eyes flickering from Matt to Dilys and back.

"I swear I had nothing to do with their deaths, either of them."

"Then have you any idea who did?" Matt asked quietly.

"No, no, no, of course I don't. Why would I?"

Is he protesting too much? Matt wondered. "We all speculate in these circumstances. Are you sure you have no idea?"

Morgan leant forward with his crossed arms on the table, gave a slightly sickly smile and said, "Well, you've said yourself that Ivor liked to snoop around people's private lives, pick up this and that so he could wind them up, so I'd say the field is wide open. And I got the impression, I think we all did, that Ellis abused his poor wife. I do feel awful sorry for her, poor girl. It'd be hardly surprising if she snapped and went for him."

"But why on earth would she kill Ivor?"

"For the reasons you just mentioned." He looked a little smug. "Found on his phone and that."

"Sorry, I don't buy that, and the evidence doesn't point her way, whereas you, that's another matter."

A smug triumphant look came into his eyes. "You can't bloody pin Ivor's death on me, and I'll tell you why. I was rehearsing with Ellis and Eryn when he was killed – thought you'd have known that."

"We've researched the times and you could have got to the theatre on time, so that theory doesn't hold water," Matt said.

This wiped the smugness off his face. He protested vociferously, but Matt ignored it.

"Now let's get back to these drugs. Who's your supplier?"

"No comment."

They went on trying to get information out of him for an hour, but he'd retreated into a sulky shell, replying 'no comment' to virtually everything that was said. It wasn't until Dilys mentioned his sister again that they got more of a reaction.

"I think, sir, that it would be best to get Mr Conway's sister in and question her. Maybe she'll be able to help us get to the bottom of this drugs business."

"You fucking leave Carmen out of this. She knows nothing about it."

"I'm not so sure," said Matt. "I think my sergeant is right, it would be worth bringing her in for an interview. You aren't co-operating, maybe she will."

"I tell you she knows nothing!" He was shouting now.

"Why are you so afraid of her?" asked Dilys softly.

"I'm not, it's just that I promised her…" He didn't complete the sentence.

"Promised her what?" Dilys asked.

At that moment there was an interruption. A young police constable, Claire Gooding, knocked and came into the room. "Could I have a moment, sir," she asked.

Matt frowned but got up and went into the corridor as Dilys recorded his departure.

"Sorry to disturb you, sir, but Dave Parry just phoned, and he said it was urgent."

"What's up?"

"I gather he and Sharon Pugh went to interview a Mrs Kemble, at her sister's?"

"Yes."

"Not only does she suspect her husband of being involved in the people trafficking, she also thinks he could be involved in the first murder, Ivor Gladwin is it? What's more, she says he's done a bunk."

"Bugger!" Matt said. "Has she agreed to sign her statement?"

"Dave says she has."

"Right. We'll have to stop now with Conway and get going. It may be a good idea to leave him to kick his heels in the cells for a bit, we're not getting very far with him. Thank you, Claire."

Claire was about to go back upstairs when Matt thought of something else. "Do you know if Dave and Sharon are back at the incident room?"

"He said they were on their way."

"Good. Dilys and I will get going once we've got rid of Conway."

On the way back to Pontygwyn, Matt remembered that he'd planned to go and speak to Sally and find out what was worrying her. He glanced at Dilys and said tentatively, "We should be talking to Sally again, but there's no time at the moment. Do you think it might be okay if I asked Fabia to go and have an informal word?"

"I don't see why not, sir. She can let us know if we're needed once she's worked out if it's something important."

"At least going to the vicarage won't put her in danger."

"Absolutely."

Matt laughed. "The longer I know that woman, the more I'm inclined to stretch the rules. I'm going to get caught out one day."

"I won't tell on you," promised Dilys.

Matt took out his phone and tapped in Fabia's number.

* * *

Cath opened the door at Fabia's knock. "It is so good to see you, Fabia, come in," she said, giving her friend a hug. "We're in the kitchen."

"How's Sally?" Fabia asked quietly.

"Not good. She's definitely got something on her mind, quite apart from everything that's going on, but she won't tell me what it is. I hope she'll open up to you."

"I'll do my best," Fabia said.

Sally was curled up in an armchair in a corner of Cath's untidy but homely kitchen. She was holding a book in her hands, but Fabia got the impression she wasn't really reading it. She looked up as they came into the room and, from her expression, Fabia couldn't tell whether she was pleased to see her or rather wary of her.

Fabia went up and took Sally's hand in both her own. "How are you? I do hope you're feeling a little better, although I can imagine it must be very difficult."

Sally uncurled her legs and sat up straighter. "I'm fine," she said, then gave a wan smile. "Silly saying that, because I'm not really, but Cath is being an absolute gem and looking after me so well."

Fabia thought it best to get straight to the point.

"You told Cath you had something you wanted to tell Matt," Fabia said as she pulled a kitchen chair forward and sat down. "She said it was something you've remembered, and it's been worrying you. Matt thought it'd be easier for you to talk to me first, then we can decide what to do about it. Does that sound like a good plan?"

Sally nodded but said nothing.

"I'll leave you two to talk," Cath said, but at that Sally looked up, a flash of panic in her eyes.

"No, don't go," she said.

Cath looked from her to Fabia and back. "Okay. Would you like a gin and tonic, Fabia? And I can get you your usual juice, Sally, then we can be comfortable."

"Juice will do for me too, Cath," Fabia said, not wanting to have Sally tempted by alcohol.

Cath bustled around and Fabia turned back to Sally.

"The thing is, Fabia, it's not just one thing, it's several incidents that have been going round and round in my head that mean something different – more now than they did before… before…"

"Before Ellis was killed," Fabia said gently.

"Yes, before that."

For a few minutes there was silence. Fabia waited. Cath handed out glasses. Then Sally went on.

"Often, when Ellis was talking on his phone and didn't realise I could hear, he sounded frightened. He had a gambling habit, used to lose so much of our money."

What would we do without these women eavesdropping on their husbands? Fabia wondered ruefully.

"Once I remember him protesting that Sebastian was getting suspicious and he couldn't do it any more, that was definitely something to do with money. Whoever it was, and I think it was a woman, insisted and Ellis said, 'Okay, but this is the last time.' Then he added, 'It has to be, you can't force me.' There were several calls like that." Sally took a sip of her juice then licked her lips as if they were dry. "Then another time, and I'm sure it was the same person, I could just about hear the voice."

"Were you actually in the room with him?" asked Fabia.

"N-no." Sally's cheeks became a little pink. "I was standing behind the hall door and he was in the sitting room. He must have been very close. When I look back, I wonder how I dared, but I was so desperate to know what was going on."

"You said 'then another time', what happened that other time?"

"Ellis was really agitated. He said something about drugs being one thing, but people were different, and he wasn't going to have any more to do with it. And then he almost shouted, 'you can't do that', and then, a moment later, 'I'll go to the police and take what's coming' and that they, the police, already knew about the money."

"Do you remember exactly when you overheard that last conversation?" Fabia asked.

"I think it was Wednesday evening," Sally told her.

"You say you think the person was a woman," Fabia said. "Have you any idea who?"

"Yes, I think I do." Sally's voice had dropped to a whisper. "Because once I answered Ellis's phone and that's who it was, and her voice is distinctive, it carries a lot."

"Can you tell me who it was?" Fabia asked, almost holding her breath.

Sally told her and Fabia heard Cath give a little gasp, but Fabia wasn't really surprised. It fitted.

"Is there anything else that you've remembered?"

"There was one other thing. Once when Morgan came round, which he did often, this was about a month ago, I got back from shopping and they were in the kitchen. I was very quiet when I let myself in, probably because Ellis hadn't given me permission to go out. When I opened the kitchen door there was this brown stuff in packets on the kitchen table and some little bags with pills in, and a large carrier bag. Morgan scooped it all up and threw it into the carrier bag then left. When I asked Ellis what was going on, he told me to shut up and that I was to keep my effing mouth shut. He was so angry! I was far too scared to push it."

"Did you tell anyone about it?" Fabia asked.

"No! How could I? Ellis would have killed me." Her eyes widened suddenly and filled with tears. "Oh God! And instead of that he was killed. Maybe if I'd told someone, he'd still be alive."

Cath came over and sat on the arm of the chair, put a comforting hand on Sally's shoulder and gave Fabia a pleading look as Sally covered her face with her hands and began to sob.

CHAPTER 26

Once Fabia had given Matt a detailed account of what Sally had told her, Matt decided to clear the incident room and bring the team back to the station. He was confident that they'd be able to move within the next couple of days and wanted the whole team in one place before they did so. But things took off a little faster than he expected.

Early on Thursday morning, just after Matt had finished bringing Dilys up to date and they were about to go on with interrogating Morgan Conway, Claire Gooding came into his office.

"Galina Petrovka is asking to speak to 'someone in authority' as she puts it." She gave Matt a slightly cheeky smile. "I'm not important enough, she wants the boss. I think she may be ready to co-operate, sir."

"Now that would be useful. Come on, Dilys, let's go and see what she has to say."

An hour later they came back upstairs.

"Right," Matt said decisively. "Let's go and have another word with Morgan Conway and, depending on what he tells us, I think we can go for it. We'd better bring Luke in on this."

"I'll get on to him," Dilys said, taking out her mobile.

"He says he'll come into the station immediately," Dilys told Matt a few minutes later. "Are we going to wait for him before we tackle Morgan again?"

"No. Let's get down there and have a go. With all the information we have now, I don't think it's going to be long before he coughs up."

It took them about half an hour to persuade Conway to admit that he knew about the people trafficking ring and that the money had been laundered through the Little Theatre account. It took another half hour to persuade him to name names, after which they charged him with possession with intent to supply and sent him back to the cells.

By the time Matt and Dilys got back upstairs, Luke had arrived. Matt then arranged two warrants in record time, and they gathered the team together for a briefing.

"We want a two-pronged attack," Matt told everybody, "both arrests to be made at exactly the same time. That's essential. We can't wait to do this early tomorrow so we're going to have to sacrifice the surprise element. We have to go now. They must not be given any chance to communicate with each other. You know the system. Let's go."

They all went quickly down to the parking lot and piled into cars. Two made their way to Cwmbran, the other to Pontygwyn. But they were too late. When Matt, Dilys, Tom and Sara got to the Cut & Curl salon the place was closed, the lights were off and there was no sign of Carmen Lloyd either there or at her flat. When the rest of the team got to the freight depot, they were told Trevor Kemble had not been seen since the day before and no-one knew where he was; a check at his home got no response. There was no sign of his red Passat car or of Carmen's BMW.

Everything stepped up a gear. When they got back to the office Matt and Luke went straight up to see Chief Superintendent Rees-Jones. He was sitting in his office looking like thunder.

"I gather it's a no-show on both suspects. Why did you leave it so late, Chief Inspector?"

"We only just got the last few essential pieces of information this morning, sir." Matt didn't wait for Rees-Jones to continue. "We've got the make and registration of both their cars, that's gone out to the CCTV chaps. What we need now are warrants to contact the airlines, we need to check their passenger manifestos. We've also contacted the airport police at all the major airports and they're on alert."

"And I've spoken to my boss," Luke told him, "she's working on it from that end, so I think, between us, the chief inspector's team and my lot, have got things covered."

"I should bloody hope so. Get those warrants sorted and keep me informed. Now, get going."

Luke and Matt clattered their way down the stairs in too much of a hurry to wait for the lift, and joined the hive of activity in the main office.

* * *

Matt fell into bed beside Fabia at three in the morning, muttered an apology for disturbing her and slept for three hours. At half past six, after a quick shower, he gave her a kiss and drove back to the station.

Fabia dragged herself out of bed two hours later, still feeling sick and achy, and decided to go and speak to the pharmacist at the chemist in the high street. It was probably just a reaction to the accident, but she wanted some reassurance and speaking to the pharmacist was quicker than trying to get a doctor's appointment.

She heard nothing from Matt all day, although Dilys did send her a text saying, 'Bloody madhouse here, looks as if we're finally going to be able to make those arrests, xx Dilys'. Fabia smiled, bless Dilys, she was so thoughtful. She still wished the text had been from Matt, but knew she was being unreasonable.

Several times through the day she'd nearly given in and phoned Matt, but she managed to resist the temptation as she knew from experience that this stage of an investigation took all the concentration a person could muster. Having wasted the whole day, unable to settle to anything, and unable to stop the thoughts whirring around in her head, she sat down and tried to take in the local news. Maybe there'd be something about the case. But she couldn't really concentrate.

At last, at half past six in the evening, Matt phoned. "I'm so sorry to have neglected you, darling," Matt said, "but it's been manic here. How are you feeling?"

"Fine, fine," Fabia lied. "What's happening?"

"Good news, we've got them both. Carmen Lloyd at Birmingham Airport en route for Spain and Trevor Kemble at Heathrow, also on his way to Spain. Your info about her grandparents living in Seville was very

291

useful. They're both under escort back to Newport and we'll be interrogating them tomorrow. I'll be home about ten, sorry it can't be earlier."

"No problem, I might be in bed."

"Are you sure you're okay?" Matt said, concerned at this unusual lack of curiosity on Fabia's part.

"I'm fine, Matt," Fabia insisted, trying to put as much conviction into her voice as possible. "It's just a bit of reaction from being battered about by that low life. I've got a casserole out of the freezer. I'll leave it keeping warm for you in the oven."

"You are a treasure beyond price. I'll see you later."

* * *

At ten o'clock on Sunday morning Fabia opened the door to Luke and Dilys who'd arrived at the same time. "Thank goodness you're here. Matt's been refusing to put me out of my misery until the two of you arrive. He's got some strange idea that I must rest all the time because of the accident, but I'm not even wearing the collar any more. I think it's just that he likes keeping me in suspense."

All day on Saturday the team had been working on the two suspects. It had taken intensive interrogation of both Carmen and Trevor and a lot of playing the one against the other before they'd managed to break through their silence, but around eight o'clock on Saturday evening they'd finally managed to persuade them to talk. Each blamed the other. Carmen insisted she would never dream of dealing in drugs, and this they decided was probably true. But she also insisted she had nothing to do with the people trafficking, and Trevor was adamant that he had killed neither victim.

At last a clear pattern had emerged and Matt had been able to charge them both and return them to the cells 'to contemplate their future' as Dilys put it.

They settled in the kitchen where Matt was busy making a pile of toast and scrambled eggs. "I have a packet of smoked salmon in the fridge, shall we add that?"

"Sounds like a good idea," Luke said. "I wasn't expecting to be fed."

"I was," said Dilys, grinning, "and smoked salmon would be lush."

"Not for me," said Fabia, "don't fancy it somehow. Just scrambled eggs, please."

"But smoked salmon is one of your favourites," Matt protested.

Fabia shook her head. "Not today. Now, please, please tell me everything, all the gory details, or I'm just going to die of curiosity."

They all settled round the table and, once Matt had dished up their brunch and Fabia had provided plenty of coffee and orange juice, Matt began.

"There's been so much information coming in from so many different people on this case, that it's difficult to work out where to start. Because of the way Ivor Gladwin used to behave, all that snooping and winding people up, the list of suspects was long. There was always the chance he'd turned up something really serious, which it turned out he had. But at first, we couldn't work out what would just be embarrassing or hurtful and what was worth killing for. Some we crossed off quite early, and it wasn't until Ellis Cadogan was murdered that we began to narrow it down a little. One problem was the nature of the two killings. In Gladwin's case it seemed like an opportunist crime, whereas in Cadogan's we felt it was more carefully planned. The different nature of the two crimes made us begin to think that there may have been two different people involved."

"Stupid. I can't believe that hadn't occurred to me," Fabia said.

"Don't worry, it took Dilys and I a while as well," Matt said, smiling across at her.

"Once we knew about the people trafficking from Luke, it opened the whole thing up."

Luke gave an apologetic grimace. "I still feel guilty about having kept you in the dark all those months."

"I have to admit, I was angry at the time, but your input in the last few days has been invaluable."

"Thanks," said Luke.

"We crossed the Aubreys off the list quite early on. His activities as a broker were iffy but not illegal, and we decided they're so obsessed with the theatre that they wouldn't do anything to damage it. Sally Cadogan we did wonder about in Gladwin's case." Matt glanced at Luke, who made no comment. "But character-wise we thought it unlikely, and in her husband's case the fact she's right-handed cut her out."

He reached out a hand to take Fabia's. "I'm sorry, Fabia, but we did think it might have been Geraldine. She's tall, she's left-handed, and she was in the theatre at the time Gladwin was killed, and we thought his winding her up about her son could push her over the edge, but we couldn't think of any reason for her to kill Ellis. It was about this point that we began to wonder if there were two murderers involved."

"I thought at one point," Dilys said, "that Morgan Conway was bang to rights. The way he was behaving indicated that he was a very frightened and worried man but, in the end, it was the drugs he was angsting about, not the murders. Apparently, his sister had no idea he'd gone back to dealing and he was terrified she'd find out as she'd told him she'd chuck him out and give him no more financial help if she found out he was dealing again. He was useful to her in one way, though."

"How was that?" asked Fabia.

"He has a photographic memory, particularly for numbers. He was probably the one who told her what your car was and its registration number."

"I was wondering about that," said Fabia as she got up and poured herself a glass of water, then filled the cafetière again and brought it back to the table. "So, when exactly did you start suspecting Carmen Lloyd?" she asked Matt.

"Before Trevor Kemble, to be honest, but we found out that she couldn't have killed Gladwin as she was in the salon at the time and half a dozen people saw her there."

"What about Eryn Jackson and all that business about knowing me when we were teenagers?" asked Luke.

Matt grinned at him. "That really got you going, didn't it?"

"Well," Luke said, a little embarrassed, "it's a bit awkward when someone swears you've had a relationship with them, and you can't remember a thing about it."

"We did wonder whether she was responsible for Ellis's murder. Being a dancer, she's very strong, and she's left-handed, but we couldn't think of a motive. And as to your 'affair' with her–"

"I didn't have one!" Luke protested.

"—we think," Matt went on, ignoring his protest, "that was a straightforward bit of spite. She realised that you had an interest in Sally and was just plain jealous. Like I've said before, if you'd been on my team—"

"I know, I know," Luke said wearily. "I think I'll apply to be taken off undercover work, I don't think I'm cut out for it. Anyway, I've got to get a job where I can concentrate on Sally rather than work and not the other way around."

"But you still haven't told us how you put it all together, Matt," protested Fabia.

"It was all a bit like gathering grains of sand to make a castle," Matt said. "We had so many little bits and pieces that didn't mean much on their own but, when we added them all together, there it was. There was the fact that the two murders were so very different, there was Luke's information about the people trafficking, there was Eve Kemble's information about her husband's past activities and the fact that he runs the freight business."

"And there was the information you got from that bastard that drove me off the road," said Fabia.

"Yes, he identified both Trevor Kemble and Carmen Lloyd. I suspect it was her that Morgan was most scared of. Once we got the information from the minder, Galina Petrovka, where that group of girls were kept. Then Morgan told us about all the nail bars his sister owns, the majority not in her own name, and he told us most of the girls who work in them are either Ukrainian or Romanian, so we were on to the final straight. Having Irina Melnik identify them as well was a bonus."

"Were Ellis's anonymous donors Kemble and Lloyd?" asked Fabia.

"We think so, a bit more delving will have to be done on that."

"Neither of them has actually confessed yet," Dilys said, "but they've each of them started to accuse the other, so we don't think we'll have long to wait. We'll check on the DNA on those shoes that were found in the rubbish and we're pretty sure it'll match up with Carmen's. She must have pushed her feet into the boots once she realised there was blood on her shoes, stupid thing to do really, but I think she must have panicked."

"I've just thought," said Fabia. "That kickboxing I heard her talking about in the cafe, that must mean she's pretty strong."

"Absolutely, that was a great tip," Matt said, smiling at her. "And you know when you made an appointment at the salon—"

"As you requested."

"As I requested... what you didn't realise was that the excuse you gave, about your own hairdresser in Usk having closed, didn't hold water. There's been no closure of a salon in Usk in the last two years, and she probably knew that."

"Oops," said Fabia. "Of course, I realised when I was there that she was left-handed. And when she complained that someone had taken her special scissors, that made me double-check."

"I know. That titbit was useful too."

"And when I was in the salon a woman called Paula came in and I recognised her as someone who's taken drugs in the past, that's why I thought that

Carmen might be her supplier, but I'm not so sure now."

"Like I said, we don't think she was involved in the drugs," Matt said, "but we're certain she's the main mover in the people trafficking."

"So it was her that put that shit on to me on the way to Tintern."

"Yes, he was told to 'put the frighteners' on you."

"Bastard!"

"He also told us they hired the vans they used to transport the girls from Ivor Gladwin's garage, which is one of the reasons Ivor clocked what was happening and did some further research."

"You look tired, Fabia," said Dilys. "I think we should leave you in peace now."

Matt gave Fabia a concerned look but didn't comment.

Luke and Dilys got up, said their goodbyes, and Matt told them, "I'll see you both in the office first thing," Matt told them. "I think we'll be able to wrap this up tomorrow."

* * *

Once Luke and Dilys had gone, Fabia and Matt settled together in front of the sitting room fire. Matt put his arm round her and pulled her to him. "How're you feeling? Dilys is right, you do look very tired, and you haven't been your usual self for days now, even before the accident."

Fabia didn't respond immediately, and Matt gave her a worried look.

"Darling, what's up?" he asked.

"I've been trying to pluck up the courage to tell you something."

"Now you're really worrying me, what is it?"

She didn't give him a direct answer. "Can I ask you something, Matt?"

"Of course, you can."

"Have you ever thought of having children?"

He frowned at her. "I suppose, sometimes." His eyes widened. "Bloody hell! You're not…?"

She looked at him, her eyes full of tears. "I'm pregnant. I went and got a test from the chemist yesterday. I think I'm about five weeks gone."

"I– when– how?"

"The usual way, I think, my love."

"Then why are you crying?"

"Because I'm not sure you'll want it. We've never discussed children, and I'm so bloody old," she wailed.

Matt burst out laughing. "Forty-two is not old, you idiot. Oh wow, me a dad!"

"So, you don't mind?"

"Mind! I'm a bit shocked, but no, absolutely not." He leant over and gave her a long, gentle kiss. "My darling Fabia, I couldn't be more pleased, and I shall definitely have to stop involving you in my work now. No more being beaten up or run off the road by lunatics."

Fabia gave him a watery smile. "We'll see," she said.

Character list

Fabia Havard – Artist and ex-police superintendent.
Cath Temple – Vicar of St Cybi's church and close friend of Fabia.
Ivor Gladwin – Local garage owner, plays the dame in the pantomime.
Hywel Shaw – Ivor Gladwin's business partner.
Luke Melville – Recently returned to Pontygwyn.
Tony Vaughan – Fabia's neighbour.
Sally Cadogan – Plays Princess Jasmine in the pantomime.
Ellis Cadogan – Sally's husband, treasurer to the Little Theatre committee.
Eryn Jackson – Local ballet teacher, choreographer for the pantomime.
Sebastian Aubrey – Chair of Little Theatre committee, writer of the pantomime.
Jean Aubrey – Sebastian's wife and collaborator.
Eve Kemble – Wardrobe mistress for the pantomime.
Trevor Kemble – Eve's husband, looks after maintenance at the theatre.

Carmen Lloyd – Owns a local hairdressing salon.

Morgan Conway – Brother of Carmen, plays Wishee Washee in the pantomime.

Geraldine Humphries – Friend of Fabia's, plays Empress of China in the pantomime.

Oliver Talbot – Plays the Grand Vizier in the pantomime.

Peony Smith – Youngest member of the pantomime cast, plays Lotus Flower.

Lewys Bennion – Genie of the Lamp in the pantomime.

Jason Phillips – Aladdin in the pantomime.

Cledwyn Hughes – Local driver and petty criminal.

Irina Melnik – A trafficked woman from Ukraine.

Police personnel:

Detective Chief Inspector Matt Lambert of Newport Police – Fabia's partner.

Detective Inspector Jess Foyle

Detective Sergeant Dilys Owen

Detective Sergeant Sharon Pugh

Detective Sergeant Dave Parry

Detective Constable Tom Watkins

Detective Constable Sara Gupta

Chief Superintendent Charlie Rees-Jones – Matt's boss.

Police Constable Aidan Rogers – IT expert.

Police Inspector Alun Richards – Head of Traffic Division.

Police Constable Glyn Evans – Drugs squad.

Dr Pat Curtis – Police surgeon.

Acknowledgements

Thanks to my writing guru, Jeannie, to Dallas for setting me on this path, and to Ros and Caroline for their excellent proofreading. To all in the Guernsey Writers' Group for their support and encouragement, I shall miss them so much now we've moved but will definitely keep in touch. To all at The Book Folks who've travelled with Fabia, Matt and me. And most of all, thank you to Niall for listening and contributing, for his unfailing encouragement, and for concentrating on the logistics of our move to the UK while I wrote the fourth book in the Havard and Lambert series.

If you enjoyed this book, please let others know by leaving a quick review on Amazon. Also, if you spot anything untoward in the paperback, get in touch. We strive for the best quality and appreciate reader feedback.

editor@thebookfolks.com

www.thebookfolks.com

Also by Pippa McCathie:

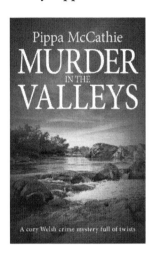

MURDER IN THE VALLEYS

The first book to feature Fabia Havard and Matt Lambert

Having left the police following a corruption investigation, ex-superintendent Fabia Havard is struggling with civilian life. When a girl is murdered in her town, she can't help trying to find the killer. Will her former colleague Matt Lambert stop her, or realize the value of his former boss to the floundering inquiry?

Available in paperback, audio and FREE with Kindle Unlimited.

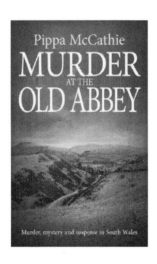

MURDER AT THE OLD ABBEY

The second book to feature Fabia Havard and Matt Lambert

When an overbearing patriarch and much begrudged ex-army officer is found dead in his home, there is no shortage of suspects. DCI Matt Lambert investigates, but struggles with a lack of evidence. He'll have to rely on his former boss, ex-detective Fabia Havard, to help him. But will their fractious relationship get in the way of solving the case?

Available in paperback, audio, and FREE with Kindle Unlimited.

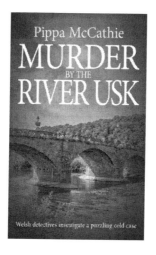

MURDER BY THE RIVER USK

The third book to feature Fabia Havard and Matt Lambert

Almost ten years after he went missing, a student's body is found. Forensics show that he was murdered and a cold case is reopened. But when detectives begin to investigate his background, many people he knew are found to be keeping a secret of sorts. Faced with subterfuge and deceit, rooting out the true killer will take all their detective skills.

Available in paperback, audio, and FREE with Kindle Unlimited.

LIBERATION DAY

A standalone romantic thriller

Having become stranded in the English Channel after commandeering her cheating boyfriend's boat, Caro is rescued by a handsome stranger. But when the boat is impounded on suspicion of smuggling, she once again finds herself in deep water.

Available in paperback and FREE with Kindle Unlimited.

Printed in Great Britain
by Amazon